The BLANE GAME

PHILIP GAUNT

The BLANE GAME

TATE PUBLISHING
AND ENTERPRISES, LLC

The Blane Game
Copyright © 2012 by Philip Gaunt. All rights reserved.

No part of this publication may be reproduced, stored in a retrieval system or transmitted in any way by any means, electronic, mechanical, photocopy, recording or otherwise without the prior permission of the author except as provided by USA copyright law.

This novel is a work of fiction. Names, descriptions, entities, and incidents included in the story are products of the author's imagination. Any resemblance to actual persons, events, and entities is entirely coincidental.

The opinions expressed by the author are not necessarily those of Tate Publishing, LLC.

Published by Tate Publishing & Enterprises, LLC
127 E. Trade Center Terrace | Mustang, Oklahoma 73064 USA
1.888.361.9473 | www.tatepublishing.com

Tate Publishing is committed to excellence in the publishing industry. The company reflects the philosophy established by the founders, based on Psalm 68:11,
"The Lord gave the word and great was the company of those who published it."

Book design copyright © 2012 by Tate Publishing, LLC. All rights reserved.
Cover design by Matias Alasagas
Interior design by Mary Jean Archival

Published in the United States of America

ISBN: 978-1-62147-498-2
Fiction / Action & Adventure
Fiction / Suspense
12.10.12

Dedication

Dedicated to Jean.

Chapter 1

Washington, DC, December 21, 2006. 9:30 a.m.

"The vice president apologizes, but he may be ten to fifteen minutes late. Please help yourself to coffee and donuts."

The five men sitting around a long conference table in Room 203 of the Executive Office Building nodded and smiled.

"Thank you, Madeleine," one of the men said as Madeleine left.

"I hope this is not going to take all morning," another said as he stood to refill his coffee cup. He then pulled out a Blackberry "Jennifer, I think I'll be late for my eleven o'clock meeting. Please reschedule. Thanks. See you later."

"Anyone know what this is all about?" Harrison said, pushing away a black leather folder with a Shell logo on it."

"Well," Carter said, "I was told that the vice president had an announcement, a very positive announcement, to make to us, and considering who we are and what we represent, it must have to do with oil."

The five men, representing the five largest oil companies in the world, nodded again. "And, if it's very positive, as you say, then it must have to do with the Caspian Sea pipeline. When you think about it, it's been five years since we went into Afghanistan, and we still can't get that pipeline built. I mean the whole reason behind 'Operation Enduring Freedom,' as they called it, was to make sure we could get a pipeline from Turkmenistan south through Western Afghanistan and Pakistan to the Indian Ocean."

"That's right," Kelner said, and the Caspian Sea reserves are so huge, they could replace the Middle East reserves."

"And that's why we have signed contracts for up to seventy-five percent of them," Koehner said.

"Well, someone thought Kazikhstan was the answer, but that's too far north in the Caspian."

"And, of course, Thompson said, there's no way we can go west through the Russian pipeline."

"No way!" the men echoed.

"No, Afghanistan is the only way to go, but the Taliban are still playing hard to get. It's such a total mess" Carter echoed.

"Talking of which, what about Iraq?" Kelner kicked in. The whole Middle East catastrophe is going to compromise what we can get out of Iraq, or Iran, or Saudi Arabia, or anywhere else. If we cannot get the Caspian Sea situation sorted out—and soon—we're going to be ruined. People are complaining about the price of gas now. Just wait!"

"There's always Central Africa," Harrison said.

"Yeah, right! That's still a long way off, and I can already hear the media: 'Oil moguls cause the death of millions of innocent, starving AIDS-infected peasants!"

At this point, the door opened, and in walked four people: three men and a woman.

"Well hi, Skip," said the Shell executive, Jack Koehner.

"Hi, Jack. Hi, everyone. I'm afraid the vice president cannot make it. The new Secretary of Defense has called an urgent meeting."

"Uh-oh. Something bad?" Koehner said.

"Yeah. But that's not what we're here for. Let's sit down and get on with the job at hand."

The four newcomers settled around the conference table, and Skip said, "I'm not sure if everyone knows everyone, so let's go round the table and introduce ourselves. My name is Skip McDonald, and I'm senior advisor to the vice president. On my right is Sandy Marler from the Department of Energy."

The tall woman who had come in with McDonald nodded.

"Then on my left is Larry Smith from the CIA. And last but not least—" he gestured at the fourth newcomer, a grizzled-looking, clean-cut man with close-cropped graying hair "—Colonel Henry Packham of the US Army. You'll see why he's here in a minute. Okay, Jack, let's start with you."

"Jack Koehner, Shell Oil."

"Paul Harrison, Conoco Phillips."

"Rick Kelner, Chevron."

"Harry Thompson, BP."

"Frank Carter, Exxon Mobil."

"Okay," McDonald said, "let's get started."

"Well, before you came in, Skip, we were all thinking that if you have a positive announcement to make, it must have to do with the Caspian pipelines." He smiled encouragingly.

"I'm afraid not," McDonald said. "That's still up in the air and may take a while to resolve, but—" he paused rather dramatically "—but we have some news that's really going to make your day. I'm going to let Sandy tell you what this is about. Sandy."

Sandy Marler pulled a folder from her briefcase and began, "Gentlemen. There's been a huge, huge, gigantic new find in the North Sea."

The oil executives looked a little puzzled, not to say skeptical. "You mean another Groningen?" Koehner said, referring to another "huge" find going back to the late 50s and early 60s.

"Hold on a minute," Sandy Marler said. "I know a lot of the North Sea finds have petered out or shown themselves to be too expensive to exploit. But this is different. Very different."

"Cut to the chase, Sandy," McDonald said, but Firth Oil, a relatively small and newer company, has some kind of arrangement with Talisman. Anyway, they sank a deep, deep hole in Southeast Blane and found this monster that looks like it will be bigger than the Caspian and Middle East reserves combined."

"What?" three of the executives almost shouted.

"Has this been authenticated?" Kelner said.

"Definitely," Sandy said. "As you can imagine, we've been all over this, and Firth Oil, being a British company, is very much in our favor. If it had been a Norwegian or Dutch company, we'd have been in trouble. As you know, the United Kingdom Continental Shelf run by The Deep Trench Location is very supportive of US oil."

"But how in the world did they find this? How did they know where to drill?"

"This is where things get very strange. Please bear with us. You're going to find this rather hard to believe. I'm going to turn this over to Colonel Packham. He knows more about this than anyone. Colonel."

"Yep. It's hard to believe, but here goes. You've heard of UFOs, unidentified flying objects, right?"

"Well," Kelner said, "heard of 'em. Sure. But do they exist?"

"Sure do. This is something I've been working on for years. Anyway, Firth Oil spotted a couple of them zooming over Southeast Blane time and time again. One of their young engineers figured out they were somehow narrowing down their trajectory and took some cross bearings that produced a very precise location. That's where they put down an exploratory hole and, using what I've heard referred to as 4D seismic probes, concluded that there was something very big, and very deep, and went for it, and bingo!"

"Now, wait a minute," Kelner said. "I'm not sure I'd go for this UFO crap. Forgive me, Colonel, but does this mean we can get into this new find and not worry about the Caspian or Middle East situation?"

"That's right," interjected Sandy, "but there are some problems."

"I knew it!" Carter said, throwing himself back into his chair. "Let's have it."

"Larry," Sandy Marler said, "you're on."

"All right," said Larry Smith, "as you know, there are five countries granting licenses in the North Sea, UK, Netherlands,

Germany, Norway, and Denmark, and you all have received licenses from some of them. But Russia, which has its hands on a lot of the Caspian oil, would like to get its hands on the North Sea. And, believe it or not, they have been systematically monitoring UFOs for decades."

"You're really serious about this UFO stuff, aren't you?" Kelner said.

"Oh, yes! You may be skeptical, but look at it this way. If they knew somehow where that new field is, just think what they could do for the oil industry if they could locate other major deposits."

"So, who's going to ask them?" Koehner said.

"Ah! That is the question."

Chapter 2

New York, May 6, 2007. 4:00 p.m.

A few months later, Colonel Henry S. Packham of the US Army sat fidgeting with impatience in a meeting of the United Nations Committee on the Peaceful Uses of Outer Space (Subcommittee Three) at United Nations Headquarters in New York. He was fidgeting because he had a plane to catch, and the subcommittee's chairman, a tired-looking Indian by the name of Romesh Bhongar, was being more long-winded than usual in summing up the proceedings of the meeting.

The official title of Subcommittee Three of the UN Committee on the Peaceful Uses of Outer Space was "Subcommittee on Hypothetical Situations." This subcommittee was initially created to handle nonfactual or speculative issues that always threatened to impede the work of the main committee and, as such, became the depository of dozens of crackpot ideas from a large and surprisingly distinguished body of international cranks. However, under the inspired chairmanship of a British astronomer called Gerald Craig, the subcommittee had become a place where the most advanced thinking on what could only be called extraterrestrial affairs was discussed. Craig had been killed in a road accident in Wales, and since then, the committee had lost some of its brilliance, although it was still observed with great interest by a number of eminent scientists, thinkers, and writers.

The subcommittee had also become a place within the main committee for "pretense" issues. In other words, this was where countries liked to fly kites, usually of a political nature. To take an extreme example, a delegation could introduce a resolution setting forth procedures to be followed in case of attack from extraterrestrial powers. The preamble to the resolution might well contain clauses which, if adopted, could be interpreted in a number of different ways. The country introducing the resolution could then interpret them in such a way as to find justification for invading a neighbor, initiating a purge, arresting dissidents, muzzling critics, or nationalizing foreign interests. So a lot of very devious thinking went into the work of this UN body, and everything which came out of it was scrutinized with a great deal of attention.

The particular series of meetings from which Henry Packham was so anxious to escape was devoted to the eventuality of some form of extraterrestrial intelligence seeking to make contact with the inhabitants of earth.

"And this brings me to a final point," the chairman said, placing his hands on front of the table in front of him and staring impressively round the room.

Good! thought Packham. He would just have time to pick up his bags from his hotel and make for Kennedy Airport. He leaned sideways toward the other members of the US delegation.

"As soon as our Indian friend has finished," Packham whispered, "I'm going to run. Okay? He would never forgive me if I left in the middle of his summing up."

Around the room, other delegates were beginning to show signs of wanting to leave, with some surreptitiously sliding their papers into piles and others unashamedly and noisily packing their briefcases. Behind the soundproofed windows of the interpreters' booths, shadowy figures could be seen moving. The interpreters always worked in pairs, and since the end was now in sight, this meant that those not actually interpreting could get out a few minutes early.

On the other side of the horseshoe table, the Russian delegation sat in stolid immobility, occasionally glaring at the Chinese delegation. One member of the delegation, a thickset man with the long upper lip of the Georgian peasant, sat taking copious notes and, from time to time, casting a curious glance at Packham.

Packham himself, a large man in his early fifties, was what many people outside North America might have thought of as a typical American male, although they would have been hard put to say why. He was not in uniform, but his short hair, lean features, muscular frame, and slight tan suggested something of the military or perhaps outdoor life.

"And so," continued Bhongar, the chairman, "We cannot guess what kind of contact might come from an extraterrestrial intelligence source. It could be direct, or it could be mechanical or electromagnetic. We just don't know. We should be prepared for any of these forms and others we have not even thought of yet. The difficult problem is how are we going to recognize that a message or signal is actually from an extraterrestrial source?"

He looked round the room triumphantly, as though this were an entirely novel idea, whereas in reality it had been one of the few underlying assumptions shared by a majority of the delegations present.

"How are we to be certain, for example," he continued, and here he shot a baleful glance at the delegate of Pakistan, a lone, thin figure in oversized glasses resting on pointed, oversized ears, "How can we be sure it is not a trick from a violent and dangerous neighboring country intent on wreaking havoc and chaos on a peaceful and peace-loving nation?"

Packham stirred restlessly. So that was what this was all about? A piece of personal axe grinding? Some countries, not very many, fortunately, were always ready to seize any opportunity to snipe at their avowed enemies.

"The distinguished delegate from the Russia," Bhongar went on, "raised the whole problem of controls, and I think this is a very good example of why controls should exist. So I am suggesting that this question be included on the agenda of our next meeting. Mr. Lopukhin, perhaps you might wish to propose this formally."

The note-taking Georgian peasant on the Russian delegation stopped writing and leaned across the table in front of him to switch on his microphone.

"Thank you, Mr. Chairman. Yes, I would like to propose that item four on the agenda of our next meeting, following the standing items, should read as follows: 'The necessity for verification of authenticity of signals presupposed to emanate from extraterrestrial sources and the desirability of rapidly creating an organism to monitor and evaluate such signals.' I thank you, Mr. Chairman."

"I thank the distinguished delegate of Russia. Would anyone like to second that proposal? Yes, Byelorussia. Thank you. I think we can take a show of hands on this. Yes?" He glanced round the room. "Good. Those in favor?"

Most of the delegates raised their hands.

"Those against?" Here the United States, Canada, Australia, Britain, France, Germany, and the Scandinavian group raised their name boards.

"Abstentions?" There were none. "Good. Well, that means the proposal is adopted, and this item will appear on the agenda of our next meeting. If there are no further comments—" he raised his gavel and looked inquiringly round the room again "—then I declare this meeting closed." He let the gavel fall. "I thank you all for your cooperation, and I look forward to seeing you all at our next session."

Packham grabbed his briefcase and ran for the door. It was six p.m. Provided he could find a taxi, he would make his flight easily, even with the usual security hang-ups at JFK. He was in luck. A yellow cab had just dropped someone at the main entrance to the UN building, and he was able to stop it before it headed for the street. He picked up his bags from his hotel on Lexington Avenue and then settled back into the taxi for the boring ride to JFK. It had been a tiring trip—first a series of consultations with his superiors in Washington and then these meetings in New York. *What a waste of time*, he thought. *What a lot of hot air for nothing!*

Not many of the people attending the UN meetings had the technical background to really know what was going on. Ever since the death of Gerald Craig, the caliber of the delegates sitting on the subcommittee had steadily dropped. Now most of the delegates were mid-level government officials, some very competent, a few political officers, and of course the usual contingent of hangers-on who were always eager to sit on any delegation, provided it involved travel to exotic places.

Packham was none of these. He was, in fact, a very odd combination as a professional soldier with a master's degree in psychology. Officially, he still belonged to the US Army but was currently assigned to the Special Projects branch of an agency based in the Washington area and not very well-known to the public. He took an interest in this subcommittee because it was the only truly international body in the world that dealt with extraterrestrial matters unconnected with space flight, which was where all the money and research had been going over the last few decades.

The new Russian proposal introduced right at the end of the meeting was typical of some of the time-wasting that went on in the committee. Packham and his colleagues on the delegation knew perfectly well that it had nothing, or very little, to do with the monitoring of signals from space. It was, in fact, yet another attempt by the Soviets to create a mechanism that could control, curtail, or otherwise hinder US shortwave broadcasting toward former Iron Curtain countries. But this was part of the political reality of such a body. Much of the real work of the committee went on behind the scenes and in the bars and lobbies and at private dinner parties. The real problems were rarely debated in open meetings until they had been thoroughly worked over in private. The only drawback to this system was that it took time, and that was a luxury Packham could not afford. He was, in more ways than one, a man in a hurry.

He was all right for time now, as far as his flight was concerned. It was just seven-thirty when the taxi dropped him at Kennedy.

His flight, British Airways 190 to London, was scheduled for nine, so he even had time to buy a few things at the duty-free shop—things he would not be able to buy where he was going.

The flight was very full, as are most transatlantic flights during the summer months, but he pulled his government pass and persuaded the purser to give him a seat in the upstairs section of the 747. That way he could sleep perhaps, and he had no intention of seeing the film. He chatted briefly with one of the stewardesses who was both attractive and forthcoming. In other circumstances, he might have had the time and inclination to do something about it. Instead, he had a couple of cocktails and some wine with dinner, which made him suitably drowsy. The flight was uneventful, and he slept until the stewardess woke him with hot towels and orange juice. After a wash and a cup of coffee, he was feeling almost human.

There was a little congestion at Heathrow Airport, and the plane had to circle for a quarter of an hour before being given permission to land. Packham drank another cup of coffee and looked out over the green fields of Kent. Southern England looked very lush, not much like the landscape he would be seeing tomorrow. Despite the delay, the plane landed only five minutes late, but, as always with these big aircrafts, he had to wait a long time for his baggage.

He was met by a driver from the embassy, and as they drove into town, Packham's thoughts returned to the meeting in New York. He guessed that in a few hours' time, his colleagues on the US delegation would be meeting in Washington to discuss the political ramifications of the Russian proposal. But that did not really concern him. That was a political problem. What did concern him was the main substance of the meeting, the business of monitoring signals, either from space or toward space, and of seeing how all this fit with the oil initiative.

A number of countries had been monitoring for signals from space for decades, ever since the first signals had been accidentally detected by such people as Marconi, and even earlier. But these had been simple radio signals or rather radio waves. There were far more sophisticated forms of communication known now, such as high frequency color spectra, laser beams, and ultra high-speed transmission. And others were being developed all the time. So monitoring had become a very complex affair. Also, the possibility of responding to such signals had been and still was the subject of much research.

The driver cursed softly. The car was beginning to meet the tail end of the rush hour traffic snarled up along Cromwell Road. As the traffic crept jerkily forward toward Knightsbridge, Packham looked distastefully at the rows of derelict-looking terrace houses on the right. He longed for another cup of coffee and a hot bath. His eyes felt as though they had sand in then. A hot bath and a stretch out in a real bed! His mind went back to the problem of monitoring, which had become even more complex when various countries decided that they ought to know what other countries were receiving or sending in the way of messages to and from space. And so, further operations had been set in motion to monitor the monitors. Packham knew very well that any US message beamed from earth to space would be routinely picked up and processed by the Soviets, and vice versa. Once again, as in the arms race, a stalemate had been reached.

The car turned into the forecourt of the Royal Lancaster Hotel. Packham told the driver to pick him up again at two o'clock. He checked into the hotel, went to his room, and began to run a bath. While the bath was running, he stood at the window and stared out over Hyde Park. A stalemate is always an uncomfortable position to be in. It is neither one thing nor another. It was a long-standing problem already—one to which an entirely new answer would have to be found.

Henry Packham, along with a handful of people in the United States, knew such an answer existed.

Chapter 3

London, May 6, 2007. 8:55 p.m.

The green landscape behind his eyes sharpened into focus. The clouds parted, and as his body tensed, his mind flew like a silver dart into the blue of space, bursting into a thousand fragments of light, sparkling splinters of citrus yellow and carmine red.

She lay beneath him, throbbing and glistening slightly, with her dark hair across the pillow. Like spent fireworks, the fragments of light dulled and began to fall, sinking back into the gray ordinariness of life from which they had been fired.

His heartbeat slowed, and a wave of depression contracted his solar plexus. Where had she been while he was making love to her? A million miles away, he knew, thinking, as she went through the motions, of another man, a man she had known many years before. And yet, as he moved to turn on his back, she tried to stop him, holding him briefly and then abruptly letting him go. A gesture of affection? No. He knew this was no affection, not for him at least. Perhaps for the other man.

He groaned inwardly. He couldn't be himself, even in this most intimate of functions. How he wished other people's thoughts would not invade his head, particularly at times like these. There was nothing he could do about it. It had become part of his everyday existence, ever since that crash in Afghanistan, that sickening, grinding crash as his helicopter tore through the trees and thudded into the desert close to Kabul. He had been unconscious for days, and then he remembered waking up in the field hospital with his leg in a cast, a splitting headache, and an instant awareness of what the nurse by his bed was thinking. Since then, these moments of insight, these glimpses of other people's minds, had returned frequently but at irregular intervals.

And now he was lying beside a girl he had only just met but knowing her innermost thoughts—knowing that even as she had held him and moved in response to his own movements, her whole being was yearning for someone else. He turned and looked at the small dark head beside him. How could he blame her for thoughts that were perhaps even unconscious?

Apart from that, making love to her had been pleasant enough. She was certainly pretty. In fact, she was very good-looking. He had noticed her as soon as he had walked into the crowded bar of the Fox and Hounds, a pub he often used in the West End of London. She was perched on a stool at the end of the bar, looking a little lost.

He exchanged a few pleasantries with Reg, the landlord, before buying himself a drink and moving down the bar.

"Hi," he said. "I don't think I've seen you in here before."

She looked a little startled but recovered herself quickly and even managed a smile.

"I'm not surprised," she said. "This is the first time I've been in here. You wouldn't have the time, would you?"

"Sure. It's a quarter of seven."

"Damn!" She frowned and made a little snorting sound. She shook her head ruefully, bouncing her dark curls around, and then she looked up at him, smiling again.

"You're American, aren't you? Or Canadian perhaps?"

"American. I suppose it's my accent."

"Yes, and the way you said 'a quarter of seven.' We say 'a quarter to,' you know."

He hesitated then said, "Why did you say 'damn' just now? Are you late or something?"

"No-oo." She drawled this on an ascending scale. "But I have a feeling my friend is not going to turn up now."

"Heavy date?" he inquired lightly.

"Could have been." She looked at him coolly. "You're mighty curious, aren't you?"

"Sorry." He laughed. "You're right. Let me get you another drink."

"Look, I don't know whether I want to accept—"

"Come on," he interrupted, "just to make up for my curiosity."

She pursed her lips and held her head on one side, looking at him through narrowed eyes, judging him.

"All right," she said finally. "You look honest, although I don't know whether your intentions are. I'll have a gin and tonic."

"Coming up! Reg!" he called. "Let's have a gin and tonic and another bourbon."

Reg poured the drinks and came waddling down the bar.

"There you are, Mike. One G and T and your bourbon with ice."

"Well, thank you…Mike," the girl said.

"Sorry again! I'd better introduce myself. Mike Marshall."

"I'm Maggie Reynolds. How do you do?"

They shook hands rather formally. He pulled up a stool and sat down. He sipped his drink, studying her over the top of his glass. She was pretty. Small, slim, dark. Well dressed. Very London. Pity she had a date. She smiled at him.

"So, you must be a regular."

"Here? Sort of, when I'm in London, that is."

"You don't live in London?"

"Uh-huh, pretty much. But I'm away a lot."

"Now *I'm* going to be curious. What do you do to live 'pretty much' in London, but be away a lot? No, let me guess. Traveling salesman? No, you don't look the part. Diplomat? No, hardly! Engineer? Ah, maybe. No, I've got it. You're a CIA agent! You know we think all Americans work for the CIA." She laughed then went on. "I give up. Tell me."

"Well, I'm none of those things, not even the CIA. Sorry! No, I'm a helicopter pilot."

"Oh, really? How exciting!" she said it as if she meant it.

"It can be fun, I guess," he said, "but it can be a huge bore too, you know. There's a lot of hanging around and getting up early and odd hours. Well, it's a living anyway."

"Who do you work for?"

"Myself. By that I mean I'm freelance, which is kind of nice. I work for anybody who needs a helicopter pilot—executives, oil companies, film crews, surveyors, engineers, all kinds of people. You'd be surprised. I've just finished a job over in Rotterdam, flying surveillance over a new oil rig jacket being delivered."

"It certainly sounds good. How did you get into it?"

"Flew a chopper in Afghanistan. Learned to fly at the expense of Uncle Sam. But that was a very different kind of flying."

It certainly was. He preferred this kind, without the heat, the snakes, the fire, the shells, the dark, hostile hills, and that junketing, arm-juddering ride down into them, with teeth clenched and gut turned to water. That was all over now, thank God. There was not much flak over Rotterdam.

"At least you got out of it unharmed," said Maggie.

"You mean Afghanistan? Oh, sure."

Unharmed! True, his leg had mended beautifully, without even a scar. He'd been lucky compared to some of those walking vegetables he had seen come out of Kabul. But his mind carried a scar somewhere. He sometimes thought this ability he had acquired to see inside other people's minds was as much a handicap as a missing leg or a permanent limp. Nobody could ever appreciate how disturbing it could be to get a sudden insight into someone's private thoughts and emotions, to realize that the person you were talking to was lying or hiding something. He had learned to handle it pretty well now, but at first, right after the crash, while he was still recovering, he thought he would lose his mind. He usually did not talk about it, and he saw no reason to discuss it with this total stranger, however attractive or interested.

"Oh, sure," he said again. "I guess I was pretty lucky. But tell me, what do you do? Or am I being too curious again?"

She pulled a face, and they both laughed. She told him about her job as a copywriter with a large advertising agency in central London. She described how difficult it was to satisfy some of the clients.

"The problem is that everyone thinks he can write. You know, if you're a doctor, or a plumber, or a helicopter pilot, for example, no one is going to question your abilities or try to tell you how to do your job. They trust you, because you have a job they don't know how to do. But writing! Ah, now that's a different matter. Everyone knows how to write or thinks he does. So that makes everyone qualified to judge and criticize and generally tear your work to bits."

It was a nice, relaxed conversation, and Mike enjoyed it. Maggie was entertaining and intelligent, and Mike was feeling expansive, perhaps because of his third bourbon but also because he had been working long, hard hours in Holland and felt like unwinding. So when Maggie finally said she ought to be going since her friend would not be coming now, Mike suggested dinner round the corner at a little Indian restaurant he had been planning to go to anyway. She accepted at once, and they continued their conversation over a curry.

As they ate, she described her home in Surrey and the pleasures of English rural life. Mike talked about his life before the army and how he had gone to law school in Chicago but had never been able to settle down again after his experiences in Afghanistan. He had come to London in search of something different, and he was happy in the easygoing life he led. He did not tell her that his "insights," as he called them, had made him feel very restless.

It was a nice meal, and they drank some wine which did not really go with the food, but they felt good and warm and comfortable. So when they left the restaurant, it seemed natural for Mike to offer to drive her home. His car was just round the corner. And it seemed equally natural for Maggie to ask him up for a nightcap. After all, it was still early. She lived in a top floor flat in Lower Islington; it was not the choicest of areas but one that was expected to improve, and it had been a cheap and good investment, everyone said.

They made love almost immediately, with no sense of shame. They were both a little lonely; both were in need of affection. It was comforting to hold someone and to be held, to feel at least an animal warmth and to share a function which involved them both but which stayed beyond the fringes of commitment. And Mike had seen into Maggie's head and grasped the difference that really separated them. At that moment, he felt very much alone. How could people be so far apart? Uncommitted, yes. But so distant? So lonely? Could two individuals ever really relate? Or was that too an illusion?

He rolled over and sat up. Maggie sighed. Was that supposed to be a sigh of contentment, he wondered, or was Maggie as lonely as he felt himself?

"Mind if I take a shower?" he said.

"No, of course not. There are some clean towels in the bathroom cupboard."

He looked tired in the bathroom mirror. When he raised his eyebrows, there were white lines in the sunburn between his blue eyes. There was some white too over his ears, but it did not show much in his blondish hair. A nondescript face. A full, drooping mouth, a slightly hunted look. A good chest. Strong legs.

He showered quickly, dried himself off, and came back into the bedroom where Maggie was sitting up in bed with a newly opened bottle of wine and two glasses. She filled one and handed it to him. He drained it, put it on the bedside table, and began to hunt for his clothes.

"What are you doing?"

"Getting dressed."

"You're not going, are you?"

"Yes, Maggie." He looked at his watch as he strapped it on. It was almost ten. "I have to meet someone."

"Oh, come off it! At this hour? I don't believe you. Why don't you stay? You don't have to go, do you?"

Maggie was right, of course. He did not have anyone to meet, but he wanted to be alone and to get away from someone who could make demands on him. She had made love to him emptily, meaninglessly, deliberately, and now she wanted something more in return. Everybody did. Everybody wanted something more—company, affection, talk, warmth. Everybody wanted something, some form of contact, reassurance, comfort, because deep down inside Mike knew this only too well, they were all frightened children, frightened, cold, and alone.

"No, I must go. Really. Thanks…for the drink. Ciao!"

She shrugged and raised her glass in mock salute, pulling a wry mouth. "Sure, Mike. You must go. Ciao!"

He ran down the stairs and out into the street, despising himself. He could at least have left her his phone number, he thought. What a cynical fool he was becoming. He walked down the street toward his car and toward sounds of revelry coming from the corner pub. Perhaps that's what he needed: an anonymous crowd in which no demands would be made upon him. He walked into the noise. It was quite a scene. Heavy workingmen jostled for pints of beer at the bar. A woman screamed with amusement. Four drunken sailors were arguing halfheartedly with the barkeeper. Bright lights glinted on the piles of upturned glasses and miniature bottles at the back of the bar. Mike smiled despite himself and felt better. A good noisy pub. He pushed over to the bar, wedged himself between two large men, and finally succeeded in ordering a drink. Scotch, of course. They did not have bourbon in a place like this.

This was one of the things he liked most about London. You could mingle with a crowd in a pub and become part of it, sharing its noisy bonhomie and raucous good humor without having to relinquish your anonymity. Also, he knew from experience that in a crowd he was rarely bothered by his "insights," perhaps because there were too many thoughts around.

He looked round the room. The noise level really was incredible. The woman with the scream continued to shriek with amusement over in the far corner as a thin man with a long nose and large red ears regaled her with a constant stream of what could only be dirty stories.

The four sailors had stopped talking to the landlord and were now arguing loudly and drunkenly among themselves about the relative merits of their favorite soccer teams.

Mike began to feel much better. He lifted his glass to drink, and one of the sailors next to him knocked against his elbow, making him spill the entire contents down the front of his jacket.

"Hey," Mike shouted. "Watch what you're doing!" He dabbed at his clothes. When he looked up, he found himself confronted with a sweating red face and two bloodshot eyes.

"Wassat, mate?" said the face. "You say somefink?"

"Yeah. You spilled my drink!"

"Oy, Jack, Fred. Darn Yank 'ere. You accusing me of spilling your drink, mate?"

The landlord leaned across the bar and put a large hand on the sailor's shoulder.

"Now wait a minute, lads," he said placatingly, "there's no harm done. I'll give the gentleman another drink."

"Oh no you won't! Wassis bleeder doing insulting the British navy, eh? Who does 'e bleeding well think he is? Darn Yank!"

With this, the sailor threw a punch at Mike, hitting him high on the side of the face and cutting his cheek with a heavy signet ring. Mike reeled back, slamming into a tight pack of men at the bar, spilling their beer. Within seconds, the place was in an uproar. The indignant beer drinkers, correctly assessing the situation, thrust Mike to one side and waded into the group of sailors who, by this time, were backed up against the wall and ready for battle. Nobody got hurt much. There wasn't enough room to swing any really damaging punches, but glasses were broken, a table collapsed under the sudden weight of one of the sailors, and there was a general jostle to get away from the fighting. The landlord must have phoned the police, for within minutes, a van came screeching down the street siren blaring. The crowd, trying to get out of the door, parted, and a burly police sergeant thrust his way in, blowing a whistle.

"All right now," he shouted and blew his whistle again. "Now then, let's have some quiet!"

A group of policemen pushed their way over to the corner, where the sailors were still flailing around and spitting and swearing, with their uniforms out of place.

"All right now," the sergeant repeated. "Break it up. Break it up!"

One of the sailors aimed a fist at a constable and was promptly seized and frog-marched out. The others stopped fighting and stood swaying slightly, sheepishly straightening their clothes.

"All right," the sergeant said, "we're running you in."

"He started it," said one of the sailors, jerking his head at Mike who was dabbing blood from his cheek.

"You two, outside!" the sergeant said to Mike.

"But," Mike protested, "I was just standing here—"

"Out!" barked the sergeant. "Out! Or we'll take you out. Suit yourself."

Mike allowed himself to be hustled out of the pub and helped into the black police van. He was told to sit on the greasy bench which ran around the interior of the, van. In the far corner, one of the sailors felt his teeth to see if any had been loosened in the fray. Another sat holding his head in his hands and groaning, "Oh my gawd, oh my gawd!" As soon as the van started, this one turned his head and threw up down the length of the van, splashing Mike's trousers with beer-sour vomit.

A few minutes later, Mike was standing in front of the duty sergeant at Islington Police Station.

"Very well, then," said the sergeant, "we're taking you into custody on a charge of drunk and disorderly behavior. Case will be heard tomorrow morning."

He took Mike's wallet, keys, and other possessions and handed him over to a young constable who conducted him to the overnight detention cells.

"Cor," said the young policeman good-naturedly, sniffing the air, "how much did you have to drink anyway? You smell like a flipping brewery. I wouldn't like to have your head in the morning!"

Chapter 4

Moscow, May 7, 2007. 10:30 a.m.

Katrina Klimenkova was very happy. At about the same time that Colonel Henry S. Packham was stepping out of the British Airways Boeing 747 in London, Katrina Klimenkova was entering the GUM department store on Red Square in Moscow. She was happy and elated. This could be the most important day in her twenty-six-year-old life. In less than two hours, she had an appointment with Professor Leonid Kamikov! Her friend Tanya had told her that GUM had just received a consignment of the sheerest nylon stockings and if she wanted some, she had better rush down there as soon as possible before they were all sold. If there were any left, they would add a touch of perfection to her new pastel blue suit. She had to look her best for Professor Kamikov.

She pushed her way through the long glass-covered gallery where crowded shoppers were trying to buy tea, cheese, sausage, and Armenian brandy, and she turned right into the women's clothes department. There was already a long line of women waiting for stockings, but at least there still seemed to be plenty left. She was glad she had given herself ample time. It would not do to be late for Professor Kamikov. She had been up since six that morning to wash and set her long blonde hair before getting her father's breakfast ready.

She lived alone with her father in a nice suburb to the southeast of the city, only seven metro stops from the center. Her father was a railway clerk who was now close to retirement age. She had moved back with him when her mother had died. This had coincided with the breakup of her marriage to a young engineer called Yuri who had wanted to go out east to work on a new development project. Katrina refused to move away from the university, and they had both decided that it was better to end their marriage then and there, after only a year, before adding further complications like children. They still wrote to each other occasionally, and neither of them regretted either their marriage or their divorce.

Her father was greatly affected by the death of his wife, and Katrina was quite glad to move back home to look after him. She did not feel particularly attached to the small apartment she and Yuri had rented close to the university, and living with her father was a way of saving money until she finished her research. She had always done well at school and romped through all her examinations, including a first degree in languages. Pushed by her teachers, she had begun doctoral work in applied linguistics with enthusiasm but some misgivings. Firstly, her parents were by no means wealthy, and although she received a very good state grant, she did not want to be a financial burden for them. Also, she was already involved with Yuri, who was a few years older than her and who wanted to get married as soon as possible and have children.

So when her mother died and she and Yuri decided to split up, it suited her very well to go home and live with her father, and get on with her doctoral research. She felt secure in the knowledge that she was being useful, and she threw herself into her work with renewed vigor. Her father doted on her, and although he had only the haziest notion of what her work consisted, he was very proud of her, and when he heard about her meeting with Professor Kamikov, he was almost as excited as she was.

Katrina's dissertation was a success, and one part of it, a section on the relationship between certain language patterns and thought processes, was even acclaimed by the Soviet Academy as a breakthrough in applied linguistics. While she was still writing up her dissertation, she had applied routinely to a number of universities and institutes around the country for possible positions, and some of them had shown interest, saying they would like to interview her after her work was completed. This was most encouraging. And then, to her very great surprise, after defending her dissertation, she had received a letter from Professor Kamikov himself, saying that he would like to meet her and discuss the possibility of employing her at the Moscow Institute of Parapsychology. This was far better than the highest acclaim from the Academy for Leonid. Kamikov was an extremely well-known figure not only in the Soviet Union but even in the West, and to be noticed by him was a distraction in itself.

He was a controversial figure. As a first-class physiologist, he had earned the respect and admiration of his colleagues, but later, as a student and disciple of the great Leonid Vasiliev, he had gone on to do remarkable work in the field of parapsychology that loosely defined area which includes telepathy, extrasensory perception, and other phenomena of the mind often referred to as "psi capacities." When Vasiliev died, Kamikov became the recognized leader of Soviet research in this field, a field sometimes sneered at by other serious scientists.

Partly because of the hostile attitude toward his work and partly because of his own enormous energy and enthusiasm, he had become a tireless champion of his cause, popping up all over the world at international roundtables, delivering lectures, holding seminars, accepting academic distinctions, giving interviews, and taking part in conferences and appearing on television. He was a very popular figure, particularly in Russia where his outbursts against the central establishment had earned him more than one official reprimand as well as the admiration of the public. He also had all the makings of a popular hero. He was a huge man, almost six-foot-five and big to match, with a great thatch of white hair and an animal magnetism that seemed to bear out all the stories about his appetite for women. The fact that he survived his anti-establishment outbursts and was allowed to travel so extensively throughout the world fed rumors that he had friends in very high places.

And this was the man that Katrina Klimenkova was about to see. So it was not surprising that she felt a little apprehensive as she continued to stand in line for her stockings. As she gradually moved toward the counter, she wondered what kind of work he might ask her to do, or whether he would even want to employ her! She had read some of his most recent publications. They were all brilliant, but they covered such a wide field that she had difficulty in imagining how her own qualifications in applied linguistics might be useful. She knew that ever since Kamikov had taken over the Institute of Parapsychology, it had grown considerably. Somehow he had succeeded in obtaining major state funding, and by now, there were several departments running literally dozens of projects. Most of these were too specialized to appeal to popular imagination, but now and again Kamikov would go on television and delight audiences with some of his more spectacular findings.

She bought three pairs of stockings, the maximum allowed, and went to the ladies' room to put on a pair immediately. They were expensive, but they were certainly worth it. She straightened her hair, pushing a curl into place, retied the velvet ribbon at the neck of her pleated blouse, and applied a touch of lipstick. She did not want to look flighty, but after all, she was a good-looking woman, and if all the rumors were true—and she was prepared to believe them—Professor Kamikov was not insensible to feminine charms. She might as well put all the chances on her side.

She fought her way out of GUM and walked down Red Square and around the corner to the Metro in front of the Russia Hotel. It was only a short ride to Leninsky Prospekt. There she got out and climbed up Leninsky to Universitetsky Prospekt, which bordered the large plateau on which one part of the old university was built. It was warm walking in the sun, and when she reached the top, she stopped to breathe and enjoy the view of Moscow.

Like all Muscovites born and bred, she loved her city, and this was a view of which she never tired. She leaned against the stone parapet and looked down at the river curving through the old quarters of the city in a tight loop. Directly beneath her were the Lenin Stadium and the ski jump which looked frail and abandoned without snow. In winter, Moscow was a drab city often shrouded in a mantle of snow and gray skies, but in summer there were trees and flowers everywhere, and today the towers and minarets of the Kremlin shone with color in the bright sunlight. She looked at her watch. It was almost time for her appointment. She turned her back on the view and walked across the sandy gardens to the institute, which was just behind the University Museum of Geography.

The Institute of Parapsychology was housed in a newish building but had apparently inherited some of the university's oldest and shabbiest furniture, or so it seemed to Katrina as she waited in Professor Kamikov's outer office while his secretary went in to announce her.

The secretary reappeared and smiled. "You may go in now," she said.

Kamikov rose to greet Katrina as she entered. He really was a big man, and Katrina felt small and fragile as he shook her hand and pulled her toward a chair.

"So you are Katrina Klimenkova. You are very lovely, my dear."

The stories must be true, Katrina thought.

"I am honored to meet you, Professor."

"Oh, are you now?" he said, his eyes twinkling at her.

"Well, you know, I am happy to meet you too. Since I wrote to you, I have had time to read parts of your dissertation. Most of it's beyond me, of course. You linguists! You use more jargon than any other people I know. And I think a lot of your ideas are utter nonsense. Not yours personally, you understand, but you linguists as a race! However, there is one bit in particular I found very interesting because it may have some bearing on some of the work we're doing here, and I wanted to talk to you about it."

Katrina was thrilled. Professor Kamikov had actually read some of her work! She felt very flattered but a little uncomfortable at the same time. The man's magnetism was almost overwhelming.

"Which bit are you referring to, Professor?" she tried to say calmly.

"Where you go into this business of how some forms of language are better understood or at least might be more easily perceived by certain types of mental patterns since, if I understand you correctly, language too is based on mental configurations. Now, you suggest—although you do not develop this—that certain new forms of language could perhaps be invented to match mental patterns perfectly. Is that correct?"

"Well, Professor, to be perfectly frank with you, this is something I believe but cannot prove. Or rather, should I say I have had neither the time nor the resources to be able to prove it. I am convinced that it could be proved, but it would take months of research with a powerful computer just to make a start on the language aspects of the problem. And then I'm afraid I just don't know well enough about the physiology of brain structures. I suspect one would need all kinds of EEG equipment and stimulators and recording apparatus, and I don't know what else!"

Kamikov had begun to smile broadly during this. He held up his hand.

"Ever heard of the Sergeyev Detector?"

Katrina shook her head.

"Never mind. Listen, Katrina—do you mind if I call you Katrina? Let me tell you what I want. I want you to work on a new form of artificial language that is both easy to project and easy to receive, and then—"

"Excuse me, Professor," Katrina interrupted, "did you say 'project and receive'?"

"Don't bother about that now. Just let's say I'd like you to develop this new language. Don't worry about the physiological part. We know all about brain structures here. We can give you all the specialized support you need. And you said you would need a computer. Well we have two very high-capacity computers here. So that's not a problem either. What do you say?"

"Well, Professor, I hardly know what to say. You're going so fast!"

"We're short of time. Look, we're running some very important projects here. I can't tell you about them now, but I want you to know that they are of great importance for the future of our country."

"Professor Kamikov. Obviously, I'm flattered. I'm flattered and pleased that you are asking me to work for you, but I'm not quite certain even what you do here. Parapsychology is a big word."

"Yes, it is," Kamikov agreed. "I can hardly spell it!" They both laughed. "It is a big word," he went on, "and it covers many different fields, from suggestology to poltergeists. We have projects in all of these areas incidentally, and if you agree to work here, I want you to spend some time on all of them, just to get an overall idea. However, our two key areas are ESP, extrasensory perception, in particular long-distance thought transfer, and secondly, psychokinesis, or PK, as we often call it. These are areas in which scientific tests and controls can be applied, and they are also areas which may produce some very practical applications. You'll get an inkling of this when you visit our laboratory."

"Forgive me, Professor, but do you study ghosts and things like that?"

"Why, of course!" Kamikov chuckled.

"Would you like to see one? I'm joking, of course. Please excuse me, but that's the first question everyone asks. Of course, we do have people working on such phenomena, but believe me, parapsychology is much more than that. It is a science which, under a variety of different names, goes back to the very origins of man, back to when man was very close to nature, much closer than he is now to all the mysteries and secrets of the cosmos."

Kamikov rose from his chair and began to pace up and down his office as he spoke.

"At that time, man could communicate with nature and through nature with his fellow beings, both human and animal. Today, with all our ultra-rapid communications, radio, television, and telephones, we have lost the art, the instinct, of communication, except via external means. Our great Soviet psychiatrist, Lazar Soukharebsky, suggests in his book *Spontaneous Telepathy and its Biological Significance* that our ancestors were probably highly telepathic. And of course, with the development of sophisticated language, we have gradually lost both the need and ability for telepathic communication. So, what is normal, what is natural, what is supernatural? Here, at the institute, we think they are all part of the same phenomenon. Let me give you a little lecture, Katrina, if I may."

Katrina nodded with enthusiasm. This was exactly how she had imagined Kamikov: brilliant, controversial, inspired! As if conforming to this image, he took a deep breath, pushed back his hair, and resumed his pacing.

"Let us forget our modern distinctions between ghosts and witchcraft and telepathy and mysticism and what have you. These are all part of a vast field outside our immediate perception which today we tend to call 'parapsychology.' Now, I expect you know your classics, so I won't talk about all the great names from John Dee and Roger Bacon to Swedenborg. Just let me tell you that the first scientific research on this subject here in the Soviet Union was begun even before the revolution by Vladimir Bekhterev in 1916! In the twenties, his work was continued by two academicians, Alexander Leontovich and Pavel Lazarev, and of course later by the great Leonid Vasiliev. All these scientists were concerned with what was then called 'suggestion at distance.'

"As you know, and if you don't, you should, this kind of subject became very unpopular, forbidden even, during the thirties and forties, and so it is remarkable that Vasiliev, under whom I had the privilege and honor to study, kept on most of his experiments throughout this troubled period. Following this, there was a bad patch when nothing much happened, or at least when nothing much could be published, and then things started to pick up again in the early sixties. This was when I met Vasiliev and of course Bernard Kazhinsky, whose work, *Biological Radio Communications*, published in 1963, probably led to the now-famous symposium in Moscow on 'The Scientific Problem of Telepathy,' organized by the Bio-Information section of the Scientific and Technical Association for Telecommunication and Electrotechnology."

"But were all these people working exclusively on telepathy?" Katrina asked.

"Well, yes and no," Kamikov replied. "They were working on what they could get hold of. For example, Naumov, Edward Naumov, only really achieved fame because of Nelya Mikhailova."

Ah, yes, thought Katrina. She was beginning to find her feet again. "Yes, I've heard of her."

"I'm glad to see you do know some of your classics! Now, Nelya was not a telepathist, but she did have this extraordinary mind over matter ability to make objects move by willpower alone. That was how Naumov began pioneering work on psychokinesis and, as a matter of fact, how he resigned as vice president of the Bioinformation Section."

"I'm afraid I don't follow," said Katrina.

"I'm not surprised. This must be all ancient history to you. It's a long story, but briefly what happened was that Naumov, who incidentally had met both Vasiliev and Kazhinsky and was very taken by their ideas, was convinced that it was necessary to consider all aspects of parapsychology: telepathy, of course, telekinesis, levitation, eyeless sight, hypnosis, and so on. But the president of the Bioinformation Section, a man called Kogan, wanted to confine experiments to telepathy. So when Naumov decided he wanted to work with Nelya Mikhailova, who was no telepathist, remember, he was virtually obliged to resign and, of course, went on to do the great work we all know."

"What were these experiments with Nelya Mikhailova?" Katrina asked.

"Oh, there were lots of them. Many of them were carried out in strictly controlled laboratory conditions. For example, she could make matches move until they fell off a table. She could move cigarettes too. But the most famous experiment of all, and certainly the most difficult for her, was the egg experiment. This was actually set up by a neurophysiologist from the Utomskii Institute in Leningrad, a man called Genady Sergeyev, who kept Nelya connected to an electroencephalograph and an electrocardiograph throughout the experiment, which went like this: a raw egg was broken into a container of salt water some six feet from where Nelya sat. After a tremendous effort which lasted for half an hour, she succeeded in separating the yolk from the white, moving them apart!"

"That sounds unbelievable," Katrina said.

"It sounds unbelievable, I know, but she did it, and there was no way it could be faked. One interesting fact was that during the test, her pulse raced to 240 beats a minute while the electroencephalograph showed intense activity."

"Amazing!" Katrina added.

"Oh, yes. It was a truly amazing performance and one that proved beyond all doubt that psychokinesis was possible. But as far as we are concerned, there is something even more interesting about this experiment. While it was taking place, Sergeyev had another instrument in use, an instrument now known as the Sergeyev Detector, a complex affair of capacitors and amplifiers connected to an ordinary cardiograph and designed to detect any change in the life field. As Nelya concentrated on separating the egg, the detector showed significant changes in her electrostatic and magnetic field, and gradually, the electrostatic field began to pulse at four cycles per second. This was exactly in phase with a heart rate of two hundred and forty or four beats a second and a low Theta wave beat, also at four pulses per second. So, in fact, at the very moment of psychokinesis, her mind and body were totally in phase, pulsating at four beats per second."

Katrina sat back in her chair, wide-eyed.

"And, needless to say," Kamikov went on, "we now use a Sergeyev Detector in many of our own experiments."

"Would I be working on experiments like these?" Katrina asked.

"I don't think so, no. But ESP can be just as fascinating, you know, even if there is a lot of very routine work involved."

"Have there ever been people like Nelya Mikhailova in ESP?"

"Several. There have even been animals, like Durov's dog, Mars. But the most conclusive experiments, in my opinion, were those performed by the Popov Group with two men called Karl Nikolaiev and Yuri Kamensky. Ever heard of them?"

Katrina shook her head. "I don't think so."

"Don't worry. Not many people have. Anyway, these two men were close friends who had successfully sent telepathic messages over great distances, with Nikolaiev in Novosibirsk and Kamensky in Moscow, a distance of more than eighteen hundred miles. The Popov Group heard about them, took them in hand, and began a series of experiments to see if they could find out what happens in the brain when telepathy occurs. With Nikolaiev in Leningrad this time and Kamensky in Moscow, they soon discovered that the production of Alpha waves in Nikolaiev's brain was suddenly interrupted as soon as Kamensky started to send a telepathic signal. They also discovered that different telepathic images were received in different parts of the brain—for example visual images in the occipital region and sounds in the temporal region.

"However, the most impressive evidence of telepathy produced by this team was an experiment involving flashing lights. Let me explain. It was found that the telepathic process worked best when the receiver and the transmitter, Nikolaiev and Kamensky respectively, had the same rhythms, when they were on the same frequency, as it were, in the Alpha wave range, between eight and twelve cycles per second. In one experiment, a strobe light was flashed at a given frequency at Kamensky, the sender, producing a regular brain rhythm. This rhythm was picked up and matched by Nikolaiev, and if the frequency of the strobe flashed at Kamensky was varied, then Nikolaiev's brain rhythms changed to match it. The clincher came when they fitted a binocular strobe to Kamensky, flashing a different frequency in each eye. Kamensky was beset by conflicting brain patterns which rapidly produced nausea, and Nikolaiev, who was some distance away, was immediately 'seasick.' What do you think of that, Katrina?"

"I find it absolutely fascinating, Professor, but I also find it a little difficult to believe. I don't doubt your word, of course. It's just that the facts are so amazing. I have never heard of anything like it before."

"You'll get used to it. Of course, these are classic experiments. A lot of the experiments we are doing are much duller than this, but some are very interesting. Since the Popov Group, we have done a lot of work on signals. What I want to know now is how far ideas, not just shapes or objects, can be transmitted telepathically and whether or not the kind of language used is important and whether or not we can develop an artificial language particularly suited to telepathic transmission. And that, as I said earlier, is where you come in."

He leaned back in his chair and looked expectantly at Katrina.

"Well, what do you say?" he prompted.

"What can I say?" said Katrina. "When do I start?"

"Excellent, excellent! That's what I like. A bit of decision. It may take a few days to get the papers processed, but you can start as soon as you are ready. The pay's the same as anywhere else in the state university. You'd better talk to my office on the way out and give them all your details."

He stood up, and Katrina followed his example.

"I have to go now," said Kamikov. "I have a meeting over at the ministry. I expect my office will call you when everything is in order. I'll want to talk to you again before you start. I'll look forward to it. Until then, good-bye."

With this, he strode from the room, and Katrina heard him rattling off instructions to his secretary. She was a little dazed, and her mind felt bruised. What had she accepted? What would it be like to work in such a field, with such a man as Leonid Kamikov?

Chapter 5

London, May 7, 2007. 12:30 p.m.

After a bath and a brief nap at his hotel, Henry Packham felt considerably better. His eyes had stopped hurting, and the kink in his back from the night in the plane had almost disappeared. He ate a belated brunch at the downstairs grill and went outside to meet his driver. His appointment with John Stanton over at the embassy was for 2:30, and when he arrived, Stanton was waiting for him in his office.

"Good flight?" he inquired.

"Uh-huh. Pretty good."

"Sit down. Like some coffee?"

"Thanks, I would."

John Stanton, chief political adviser at the US Embassy in London, was a tall, stringy man in his early forties with rimless spectacles and a dark business suit, which made him look a little like an accountant or a business attorney. He poured himself some coffee and joined Packham at a table by the window.

"Well, Hal. Good news from Washington?"

"Yes, we're going ahead full speed. Any noises here?"

"No. Of course, we've got ears out everywhere, and we're monitoring the press, both here and up there too. As far as I can tell, the British government does not have the slightest idea of what is going on. Not any more than I do! Jesus, Hal, don't you think it would make things easier if I knew what this was all about? Hell, I don't even know what it is we're supposed to be hearing rumors about. You can imagine what it's like briefing my people here. They must think I'm crazy. 'Keep your ears open,' I tell them. 'What for?' they ask. 'Well, I really don't know!' I have to tell them. 'Just anything you hear about the Shetland Islands, Sullom Voe, Distant Early Warning.' They're beginning to look at me a little strangely, Hal, and I can't say I blame them."

"I know. I'm sorry, John. But I've got my orders. You can understand that. Nobody, not even you, is to be fully informed. But obviously, we have to know if there are any rumors going around, particularly in British defense circles."

"Okay." Stanton sighed. "I know. Well, as I said, there are no noises anywhere. Whatever it is you're doing, you certainly had a brilliant idea doing it up there in that Distant Early Warning station. The locals accepted it years ago, and now any unusual comings and goings are likely to be lost in the oil boom."

The conference phone on the end of the table rang. Stanton leaned across and picked it up. As he listened, he motioned Packham to get himself some more coffee.

"Oh very well," Stanton said, after listening for some time. "If no one else can see him, I guess I will. But get him over here as soon as you can. I have an outside appointment later."

He looked up at Packham who was sitting down again with a fresh cup of coffee.

"You don't know how lucky you operational people are, Hal. The things we get stuck with here!"

"What's wrong?"

"Oh, nothing much. Just a time-wasting chore. Some flyboy of ours, ex-Afghanistan, had too much to drink last night and got himself into a fight in a pub. The British police don't know what to do with him, so they called the embassy. They've checked his police record and he's clear, so they don't really want to bring charges. Could we please take care of it? And, of course, at this time of year, the Consular Section is so busy with visas, there's no one to see him. Anyway, I said to bring him over, and I'd tear a strip off him and tell him not to do it again. Jesus, the things we waste our time on!

"Anyway, where were we? Yes, I was going to say, whatever it is you're doing up there in Sullom Voe, you've certainly got the big boys on your side. I had a confidential message from Washington yesterday, giving me your new priority rating. Hal, I've never seen a rating that high before. I had to look it up to see what it entitles you to. Looks like you can order just about any damn thing you please, from a cavalry regiment to a nuclear sub. Perhaps I should be calling you 'sir'!"

"Oh, cut it out, John! Let's be thankful nothing's leaked out yet! We'd be the ones getting our butts kicked around if it had. So just keep your boys on their toes and let me know if they hear anything. I'm going up to Scotland tonight, so you'll know where to reach me."

"Sure. Are the supplies arriving all right now?"

"Yes, I meant to thank you. Since we got the chopper, things have been much better. We feel a little less cut off from civilization. But that reminds me, there is something you can do for me perhaps. You know nobody is allowed to leave the station when I'm not there. Well, understandably the personnel get a bit bored and stale. What could we do to liven things up a little? Could you find us some DVDs or something?"

"Sure, I'll see what I can organize."

They continued to discuss practical matters until the phone rang again. Stanton picked it up.

"Already? Okay, send him up." He put the phone down. "Our drunken pilot's here. They're sending him up. They didn't waste any time getting him round here! Say, Hal, why don't you sit in on this? After all, you're military. Perhaps you'll know better than I will how to talk to him."

There was a knock at the door, and an usher appeared, holding a manila file.

"The, er, gentleman's outside, sir." He handed the file to Stanton. "All his papers are in there, sir, and Mr. Johnson's office has put in a memo for you too."

"Thank you. Bring him in."

Stanton sat down behind his desk and opened the file. The door opened again, and Mike Marshall appeared, looking unshaven and very untidy with a gauzedressing across his lower cheek. He still smelled of stale alcohol.

"Come in," Stanton said and pointed to a chair in front of his desk. "Sit down."

"Look," began Mike, "I don't know who you are or—"

"Just sit down, Marshall," Stanton interrupted. "You look terrible. I don't think this is any fun either. If you're interested, my name is John Stanton, and this is Colonel Packham. It's not my fault if you got yourself into a mess. If you will get drunk and start fighting in pubs, then you can expect to get into trouble. Now, sit down!"

Mike obeyed, and Stanton continued. "All right. Now I see from this memo that you were something of a war hero." He looked up at Mike.

"So, what am I supposed to say?" Mike asked coldly. "Sure, I was in Afghanistan, if that's what you mean. So what? So were a lot of other guys. Look, Stanton. I didn't start any fight. Okay, I'd had a few drinks, but I wasn't anywhere near drunk. It was this bunch of British sailors. They really *were* drunk. They got a bit rowdy and spilled whisky all over me. That's why I stink like this. The whole thing is ridiculous!"

"It may seem ridiculous to you," Stanton said sternly, "but when the British police come to us with a US citizen arrested in a pub brawl, we have to do something about it. The only reason they did not book you was because of your war record. That's why I mentioned it. And you must have been drinking if you were in a pub."

"Okay, okay! So what do you want me to do?" Mike snapped, rubbing his temples with both hands.

Packham observed him from across the room. He really did look a pitiful sight. His eyes were bloodshot, and then there were dark bags under them. *Very sad,* he thought. *Another victim of the*

Afghan war. He had seen others with their personality warped, ambition destroyed, and nerves shot to pieces. Poor chap!

"Just tell me what I have to do," Mike said to Stanton, but now he suddenly turned to Packham. "And I don't need any of your pity either. You can shove it!"

"I didn't say a word," said Packham. "What do you mean?"

"I know what you were thinking: 'Personality warped. Another victim of the Afghan war. Poor bastard!'"

Packham stared at Mike. "How did you know what I was thinking?"

"Never mind," Mike said, turning to Stanton again. "Just tell me what I have to do. I don't want to have to spend all day here. I'm tired. I'm dirty. I need to take a shower and change my clothes."

"Wait a minute," said Packham. He continued to stare at Mike. "Now just wait a minute! Excuse me, John. Do you mind if I have a word in private with Marshall? It could be very important. It has something to do with my project."

Stanton looked at Packham curiously. Then, after a hesitation, he rose and said, "All right, Hal. Go ahead. I have to go and have this release note stamped anyway." He picked up the file and left.

"Now, Marshall," Packham began, "I want to ask you some questions, and I want some straight answers. I don't have time to fool around. Tell me, how did you know what I was thinking just now?"

"I don't know. I just did."

"Is this usual, this ability to know what other people are thinking?"

"Well, yes and no."

"What kind of answer is that?" Packham said.

"Sometimes I do and sometimes I don't. Look, it's not that simple. Sometimes I can read people's minds. Sometimes I can't. It comes and goes, and sometimes it's clearer, and sometimes it's not so clear. I don't like to think about it. It's more of a nuisance than anything else, believe me."

"Have you always been like this?"

"No, I haven't. What is this anyway? I don't see what business it is of yours."

"I have to know about this, Marshall. It may be very important. When did you first notice this ability?"

"Right after I got shot up in Afghanistan."

"What happened?" Packham asked.

"Jesus." Mike sighed noisily, rubbing his temples again. "I was flying this helicopter on a reconnaissance mission. I was looking for some Talibani who ambushed a fuel convoy. Anyway, they'd taken to the hills, so I was flying very low, looking…and I found them! They shot off the tail of my helicopter, and I came down in the desert. I was lucky—lucky I only broke a leg and lucky they didn't get to me. I was picked up unconscious by a patrol. And when I woke up in a hospital, I didn't know where I was or what had happened to me or anything, but I knew exactly what this nurse was thinking."

"Go on," Packham prompted after a pause.

"I know it sounds crazy, but there was this nurse standing next to my bed, putting a drip in my arm, and I knew exactly what her thoughts were. At first I thought I was delirious or something and that they were my own thoughts. But then I realized they couldn't be mine. You see, she was thinking about this guy in the bed next to me. It was incredible! She was thinking about taking her clothes off and getting into bed with him. She was all steamed up. People got like that in Afghanistan sometimes. Anyway, I knew in every detail just what she would have liked to do to that guy. Some things I never would have dreamed of! So I knew then, even though I was in pretty bad shape, I knew that somehow I was reading her thoughts. It was really weird—and frightening. I never told her."

"Were you suffering from a concussion?" asked Packham, who was taking notes. "Were you badly shaken? How fast did you come down when you crashed? Was your head injured?"

"Well, I guess I was pretty shaken. I sure came down fast enough. I must have had a concussion, I was unconscious for days. Like I said, I was lucky to get away with a broken leg."

"And increased perception," Packham added. "Not the first time. And do these periods of mind reading occur very often?"

"It all depends. I try not to think about it. They happen more often than I want."

"Can you control them?"

"Not really. Well, sometimes. Now, would you mind telling me what all this is about?"

"You'll find out soon enough. Have you ever had an EEG? An electroencephalogram?"

"No."

"Ever had any trouble with your heart?"

"No. Look, this has gone far enough!"

"What am I thinking about now?" Packham insisted.

"Oh for God's sake!"

"Concentrate," Packham snarled.

"A red triangle."

"Good. And now?"

"A blue circle."

"Excellent! And now?"

There was a pause. Mike looked puzzled. "Wait a minute," he said. There was another long pause.

"Well?" Packham prompted.

"It's extraordinary. I can't see anything now. It's blank."

"Good," said Packham. "That's how it should be. Now, tell me more about yourself. Where do you live?"

"In London."

"Alone?"

"Yes, if you must know. But I don't see what all this has to do with you!"

"You will. Just be patient. Any family in England?"

"No, I don't have any family left at all."

"I see. Any girlfriends?"

"Some, but nothing regular. I'm away too much to have any kind of permanent relationship."

"Better and better. And what exactly do you do now?"

"You mean my profession? I'm a helicopter pilot. I work freelance."

"And what are you working on right now?"

"Nothing. I've just finished a job in Holland."

Packham nodded in a satisfied way. "All right. Now listen, Marshall. I need you for a project I'm working on, and I need you right away. From what you tell me, no one would notice particularly if you disappeared for a few weeks. So I want you to take a trip with me. First, we are going to go round to your place and pick up some clothes and, on the way, I want you to write down the names of all those persons who might try to contact you in the next few days."

"Now wait a minute!" Mike exploded angrily, jumping to his feet. "I've had about enough of this. What the hell do you think you're trying to do? I'm not going to have anything to do with your project, whatever it is. For your information, I have just finished an assignment, and I have every intention of taking a vacation. You really are incredible. First, you ask me all those stupid questions, and now you want me to drop everything and take a trip with you! You must be out of your mind! Now if you'd get Stanton back in here, I'd like to get my papers and go."

"I'm sorry, Marshall, but I need you, and you're going to come with me, whether you like it or not. I can make you if necessary. I can't tell you any more for the moment, but this project is of vital importance. You'll want to cooperate once you know what it's about. Just trust me."

"The hell I will!" Mike said, striding to the door. He flung it open, and there was Stanton, waiting in the corridor.

"Ah, there you are, Stanton," he said. "Will you come back in here and explain what's going on? This maniac here wants me to work for him. He says he can make me. Would you please tell him that I'm an American citizen, that I have certain rights, and that I have no intention of working for him or his lousy project?"

Stanton walked back into the room and raised a quizzical eyebrow at Packham.

"Tell him," Packham ordered.

"I don't know what Colonel Packham wants you to do for him, Marshall, but believe me, he can make you do it if he wants. He has absolute priority from Washington for his project. And don't ask me what the project is either. I don't know any more than you. All I know is that it is top secret and that it has the full support of the government."

"But," Mike protested, "you can't exploit a private individual like that. I'm not in the army anymore, you know."

"Listen, Marshall, don't tell me what the colonel can or cannot do. If he wants, he can put you through a grinder and sell you for dog food, and no one would say a word, except maybe a few dogs. So, why don't you just cooperate? I'm telling you, it's a top-priority government project, secret maybe, but very official. I thought you were freelance. What's wrong with working for the government? I take it it's paid, Hal?"

"Well of course. You can name your own salary, within reason," Packham told Mike. "And you'll have the satisfaction of working for a good cause."

"Oh, rats!" Mike retorted. "Don't give me that." He turned to Stanton. "Do I have a choice?"

Stanton shrugged.

"Yes, you have a choice," Packham answered. "You can come and work for me, or I can confiscate your passport, ship you back to the United States, and clap you in jail forever. What's it going to be?"

Mike stood between the two men, looking from one to the other. Finally, he shrugged. "Where are we going?"

"Sullom Voe. Come on, we've got a lot to do!"

Chapter 6

Military Airport, London, May 8, 2007. 5:45 p.m.

"Fasten your seat belt," said Packham.

Mike obeyed, with his mind still in a whirl. The last few hours had been hectic. Before leaving the embassy, Packham had made a number of phone calls. They had then driven across town to Mike's apartment, with two large men who appeared to belong to the embassy. On the way Mike asked to stop at his bank. While Packham and the driver stood outside to make sure he did not run for it, Mike went in and withdrew a fairly substantial amount of cash from his account. Back at the apartment, Mike packed a few clothes and took a quick shower. Packham gave the men detailed instructions about stopping newspaper and milk deliveries, picking up the mail, settling bills, and generally keeping the apartment under surveillance.

They had then driven back to the embassy, where Packham had made more phone calls while Mike was photographed, fingerprinted, and medically examined. The doctor who examined him clucked sympathetically as he looked at the bruise on his cheek and gave him a pain reliever. He was questioned thoroughly by a polite but unsmiling young man who wanted to know everything about his childhood, schooling, further education, military career, and recent life.

After another brief meeting with Stanton, who returned his papers, he was rejoined by Packham, and they were driven to a small airport south of London where a military aircraft was awaiting them.

As the plane taxied down to the end of the runway, Packham yawned and rubbed his eyes. It had been a long day. He turned to Mike who was staring in front of him, scowling.

"Relax, Marshall," he said. "I said I would explain and I will, just as soon as we are in the air."

The plane took off, climbed steeply, and banked to set a course north across the Thames Estuary.

As soon as they leveled out, Packham unfastened his seat belt, stood up, and stretched. Except for the crew, they were alone in the aircraft, a fast troop carrier partially converted to transport freight. Packham leaned over the back of the seat in front of Mike.

"Okay, Mike. I'm sorry I had to get rough with you, but you'll understand when you know what this is all about. I must have seemed very unfriendly back there." Mike looked at him stonily, so he went on. "Do you believe in extraterrestrial life?"

"As a matter of fact, I do," said Mike, looking a little startled, "but there's never been any solid proof that I know of."

"What about UFOs, unidentified flying objects?"

"What about them? No one's ever photographed one."

"Don't you be so sure," said Packham. "The US Air Force has analyzed literally thousands of reports about UFOs, many of them by trained observers such as pilots, radar operators, scientists, and air traffic controllers. And the air force is now convinced they exist, even if many of the sightings reported can be attributed to meteorological balloons, clouds, reflections, aircraft, or optical illusions of some kind. Publicly, official circles tend to ridicule the whole idea of 'visitors from outer space' and 'flying saucers,' but I know for a fact that, privately, they are not only convinced that we are being visited by some form of extraterrestrial life, but they are also very concerned about it for a number of reasons which I don't need to go into now."

"Have you ever seen a UFO?" Mike asked.

"No. But I have seen some official reports that leave no doubt in my mind. I'm not talking about the kind of sensational story you read in the papers. I'm talking about hard, factual observations made by respectable and reliable people, confirmed and corroborated by other qualified observers. Do you know, for example, that on several occasions, air force pilots have been given orders to try to capture a UFO? They have never succeeded in catching one, but they've tried."

"Okay, Packham," said Mike. "So flying saucers exist. I believe you."

"Call me Hal," said Packham. "Anyway, we're less interested in UFOs as a phenomenon than the fact that they prove the existence of some form of extraterrestrial life or 'galactic society,' as someone once put it. But, of course, you don't need that kind of proof when you know that extraterrestrial sources have attempted to communicate with us, and when—"

Mike sat up in his seat. "Wait a minute. Say that again."

"I said that we're less interested in UFOs as a phenomenon than—"

"No, no." Mike interrupted again. "The other bit about extraterrestrial sources trying to communicate with us. Is that what you said?"

"Ah, so you're beginning to be interested. Yes, that is what I said. And it is perfectly true. Extraterrestrial sources have attempted to communicate with us."

"How? When?" said Mike.

"Well, I think they must have been trying for a long, long time, for centuries or perhaps even thousands of years. You know that there are descriptions in ancient literature, even in the Bible, that could be interpreted as referring to extraterrestrial visitors."

"Yes," said Mike. "I've read something somewhere about Ezekiel's wheel being a spacecraft. Is that the kind of thing you're talking about?"

"Precisely," Packham continued. "And then there are all those fantastic carvings and drawings from South America and Africa representing what could be space vessels and figures that look like astronauts. There's the cosmogony of the Dogons in Mali, the whole Cuzco story, and countless unexplained and inexplicable events throughout history. So I think they've been around for a long time."

"You said they'd tried to communicate with us," Mike said.

"That's right," said Packham, "but if they have been trying to contact us all this time, say by radio transmission or some other form of signal, our technology just has not been sufficiently advanced to receive their messages. Or rather it wasn't. Not until the beginning of this century. The first known message of this kind was picked up in 1899 by an inventor, an electrical wizard called Nikola Tesla who claimed to have received intelligent signals from space at his laboratory in Colorado. He was convinced they were some form of message, or an attempt to establish contact. And Tesla was no crank. He was a respected scientist at the time. As a matter of interest, it was he who built the power system at Niagara Falls."

"But," Mike asked eagerly, "what did the messages say?"

"They were unintelligible. Or at least Tesla was unable to understand them, which of course does not mean to say they did not have any meaning. And as far as we know, he never received any more, unless he kept them secret so as not to invite ridicule. He refused to talk about them."

"I suppose that's understandable. People must have thought he was crazy. I mean radio didn't even exist then, did it?"

"Only just, I think. But since you mention radio, you might be interested to learn then that another reputable scientist, none other than Marconi himself, picked up signals from space in 1921. And then, a few years later, in 1924, when the planet Mars was close to Earth, an astronomer at Amherst College in Massachusetts, a man called David Todd, succeeded in making a photographic record of signals received."

"Wow," said Mike, "that must have been a first!"

"And there have been other instances recorded at various times, but I am convinced that there must have been hundreds, perhaps thousands, of such instances around the world in laboratories, radio stations, ships, planes, military vehicles, even with amateur radio operators, which have not been reported because people are frightened of being held up to ridicule. And as you just said, that's very understandable. Anyone who mentions visitors from outer space these days is automatically labelled a crank. Just think what you would be called if you started to talk about receiving messages from them!"

Mike nodded. "Go on," he said. "I'm listening."

"I thought you would," Packham observed. "Then there's the weight of official disapproval. Many governments publicly deny all such phenomena. And that's understandable too. Can you imagine what would happen to a government's authority, to its position in world politics, to the credibility of its long-term planning, if it were to acknowledge the existence of extraterrestrial visitors? It doesn't bear thinking about!"

"Are you suggesting that some governments actually believe in all this stuff but will not admit it?" Mike asked.

"Oh yes, most definitely. They cannot afford not to believe in it, even if they deny it publicly. The truth is just too strong. Look what happened in the United States. You may not know this, but back in 1959, NASA picked up some signals from a source believed to be a satellite, origin unknown, circling the earth. That same year, 1959, at the National Radio Astronomy Observatory at Green Bank, in West Virginia, a program was started to listen for messages from space—an official program sponsored by the National Science Foundation under the control of Otto Struve, the distinguished astronomer, who had just been appointed director of the observatory. Struve told the press that there were at least a million inhabited planets in our galaxy and that some of them were probably trying to communicate with us. It was important, he said, to try to capture their messages and, at some later stage perhaps, respond."

"I never heard about this," said Mike. "Surely it must have created quite a stir."

"Not so much as you might think. Despite Struve's credentials, the press played the story down for some reason. As we were saying a moment ago, people are very skeptical about this whole subject.

"Anyway, the best was yet to come. A year later, after an initial build-up period, the project started its first major listening operation, a scan of a close-by solar system, and to their amazement, the scientists immediately picked up a strong, unmistakably intelligent signal. What it was, nobody knew, and it faded after a few minutes, but it was a more than encouraging start. Unfortunately, the project was closed shortly after this—officially, that is, although I know that it is still being pursued secretly elsewhere."

"How do you know all this?" said Mike.

"It's part of my job," Packham replied.

"Why are you telling me all this? Has this anything to do with the work you're doing?"

"Yes," said Packham, "and you're going to be part of it too." He held up a hand as Mike started to say something. "No, just let me explain. Since it became established that there is extraterrestrial life, that there are literally millions of inhabited planets out there in space, there has been a tremendous battle going on, in secret, over whether or not we should try to communicate with our neighbors in space. Some people say we should and that we have everything to gain from contact with what is probably a superior form of life. We could perhaps learn how to cure disease and prolong life, how to live together in peace, how to solve our energy problems. Other people, including a number of eminent scientists, believe that we should not attempt contact. They say this would be a foolhardy and dangerous move. These aliens, they say, may be waiting to invade us. They may wish to destroy us.

They may even think of us as food! Well, who knows? What do you think, Mike?"

"I think if there are extraterrestrials, if we know they exist, we should try to make contact with them. It's probably the most important thing we'll ever do. I think we stand to gain far more than we can lose. But hasn't there been any contact? What about all these secret projects you keep talking about?"

"Well, some of them have recorded signals," Packham said. "But so far, no one has ever been able to decipher them. So we don't know how to respond. Of course, we've tried transmitting all kinds of codes and sequences corresponding to mathematical formulae, molecular structures, and so on. But we've never received any specific response. And then, quite apart from any language difficulties, I suspect we just don't have the necessary transmitting power to reach out into space."

"This is all very interesting," Mike said with some annoyance, "but would you mind telling me how I fit into all this?"

"All right," Packham said, sitting down next to him, "we have tried every communication technique known to man: radio, television, radar, ultrasonics, laser, square waves, round waves, short waves, long waves, all to no avail—that is, if we are to judge by response, which has been nonexistent! But there is one technique we have not tried yet which I am certain will work." He paused and looked at Mike.

"And that, I imagine," Mike said "is telepathy."

"I see you're with me. Yes, this project of ours up in Scotland is going to use telepathy to try to reach extraterrestrial intelligence. The project is all ready to roll. I have been working on it for months, and now I have just had the official go-ahead from Washington. Do you understand now why I need you?"

"Yes, but you're not going to tell me that telepathy is powerful enough to reach across millions of miles!"

"Why not? It's the only communication method ever used successfully from a submerged submarine, and that's more than the most sophisticated radio equipment can achieve. If it can be used to penetrate water, which no radio wave can, surely it can penetrate space. In any case, we may not be working with such huge distances."

"What do you mean?"

"It may be sufficient to contact UFOs."

Mike looked at Packham to make sure he was being serious. He did not know what to believe. Packham certainly looked in deadly earnest, and the fact and figures he had quoted had a ring of truth about them. Also Stanton at the embassy had told him that Packham was running a bona fide project with the blessings of officialdom. There was a lot he did not understand, and there was something at the back of his mind that was worrying him, but he couldn't put his finger on it.

"Look, let me get this straight," he said. "Are you telling me that you want me to sit around and read the minds of little green men in flying saucers?"

"Come on now," said Packham reproachfully, "now you're talking like all those people who pour ridicule on the whole idea. But you of all people, you should know that it is possible to communicate by telepathy."

"'Communicate' is a big word. I can occasionally read people's minds, but that does not mean I can read the minds of extraterrestrials."

"Okay, okay. I don't expect you to do that, or at least not right away. What I want you to do is take part in a planned program of mind projection and mental signal scanning, along with some other people chosen for their special abilities. You won't be alone, and you will be working to a set pattern with properly organized procedures. You'll see. It's not as crazy as you seem to think. You're going to need training, but you have natural abilities far superior to anyone else working on the project. That's why I had to have you."

Mike nodded thoughtfully. Packham's explanations made some kind of sense. But there was still something bothering him. What was it? Something Packham had said earlier.

"How many people do you have working on this project?" he asked.

"At the moment, about thirty-five. That's including scientists, research people, technicians, support staff, and so on, but apart from you, there are only two other telepathists. You'll meet them tomorrow. I'm sure you'll like them."

"How do you propose to contact these extraterrestrials? What messages are we supposed to transmit? What are we supposed to be listening for, if 'listening' is the right word?"

"All in good time," Packham said with obvious relief. Mike seemed to be beginning to accept the idea. "Just be a little patient. You'll get answers to all these questions tomorrow when we have our first briefing session in Sullom Voe."

"And where the hell is Sullom Voe anyway? What kind of a name is that?"

"That I can tell you. Sullom Voe is a natural inlet harbor on the west coast of Mainland in the Shetland Isles, about one hundred and twenty miles northeast of the northernmost tip of Scotland."

"And why are we going there? It sounds like a pretty godforsaken spot."

"Because there's an American station up there—a Distant Early Warning station built years ago in the first stages of the Cold War. It's perfect cover for our operation."

"Surely you could have found something a little closer to civilization. Why bother to go all the way out into the middle of the North Sea, for God's sake?"

"Ah," said Packham mysteriously, "there is a very good reason for that, and I'll explain that tomorrow too. It's not that I'm trying to be mysterious, Mike. It's just that I prefer not to have to go over all this several times. I'll explain at the briefing session tomorrow when everyone is present."

"Okay," said Mike reasonably, "I can understand that. But why all the secrecy?"

"Well, partly because the British might not have taken kindly to our conducting experiments of this nature on their territory. If the experiments are successful, then logically there is at least the possibility of a UFO landing. And that would be enough to make any government fidgety."

"You can say that again," Mike retorted. "If they ever found out, they'd have us out of the country in about five seconds flat. If they didn't shoot us, that is!"

"Also," Packham went on calmly, "another reason to keep the whole thing quiet is the press. They'd have reporters here in no time. And remember what I said about ridicule. This administration's in enough trouble as it is. Can you imagine the White House trying to explain this away? Congress would have a field day. There would be blood all over Washington. And then," Packham continued after a pause, during which he looked oddly at Mike, "we have reason to believe that the Russians may be thinking along the same lines. They may even be running similar projects. So there's a question of international security too. Anyway, there are plenty of good reasons to keep the project as quiet as possible."

He broke off and looked out of the window. "We're just crossing the Wash, so it'll be about another hour to Aberdeen. I think I'm going to try to get a little sleep, if you don't mind."

Packham got up and went to sprawl out across three seats. Mike moved over next to the window. It was about eight in the evening, but the sun was still shining brightly. He guessed that even farther north, in the Shetlands, there would be almost perpetual daylight at this time of the year. It was not quite the land of the midnight sun, but the sun would probably only set for a couple of hours or so, at the most. He sat back in his seat and thought about his conversation with Packham. He was still somewhat angry at the way he had been treated, but he was intrigued by what Packham had told him. Little green men in flying saucers! He smiled to himself. Could it be possible? He had never really doubted the idea that there could be life on other planets, even if he had not thought about it much.

As for contacting extraterrestrial beings by telepathy, that was another matter. Since his crash in Afghanistan, he knew that telepathy was possible—more than possible, an everyday reality. But there were still a lot of questions in his mind about how contact could be established. What would they be listening for? What messages would they themselves project? What language would they use? Would they achieve contact, and what would happen if they did?

He looked out of the window. The visibility was excellent. Far below him, to the left, the flat green fields of Lincolnshire stretched away into the distance. His mind returned to Packham, who was snoring gently a few feet away. What kind of man was he? There was something about him he did not understand; there was some secret core he could not sense. Perhaps he would learn more about him later. He also wondered about the men he would be working with. What would they be like, and how would he relate to them? What would their telepathic abilities be? Would they be like him? Would they suffer from the same insights and the same exposure to often unwanted truth? Would they help him come to terms with this special ability, or would they themselves be in need of help?

He felt drowsy. He had spent a very uncomfortable night in the police station. He must have dozed off because the next thing he knew, Packham was shaking his arm and telling him to fasten his seat belt again. They were about to land. As they came in low over Aberdeen, the light gray stone houses gleamed almost white in the late evening sun. Approaching the airport, Mike was surprised to see how busy the place looked. There were dozens of small aircraft and helicopters parked in rows off the main runway, and what were obviously new office buildings and car parks fanned out from the terminal. Even at this late hour, there were plenty of cars and vans bustling around the airport approach roads. He guessed this was the result of the North Sea oil boom. Many of the new fields were only a hundred miles offshore, and Aberdeen had become something of a boomtown. The Aberdonians, renowned for their Scots dourness and tight-fistedness, had not yet become fully accustomed to the jeans and boots image of the tool pushers, many of them American, who worked the rigs and who occasionally came into town on spending sprees, although most of them preferred to fly straight down to London in search of pleasure.

The plane landed smoothly, and as it taxied to a halt on an empty corner of the field, it was joined by a small van with no windows in the back. When they stepped out of the plane, Packham held Mike tightly by the arm and guided him firmly toward the van. He was not taking any chances, Mike thought. The van sped across the airfield to a large, dirty-looking helicopter, and within minutes they were in the air again, wheeling out over the North Sea.

Mike knew the helicopter. It was a Huey, one of the old Bell 204s he had seen in Afghanistan, now obsolete for combat but still used for reconnaissance and hospital duties. He watched the pilot for a few minutes out of professional interest. It was a cinch to fly and much more stable than some of the small choppers they were building now. As they flew noisily north, Packham pointed out the Orkneys and Fair Isle, and then, suddenly, there was Shetland. Mike made out a small town. It was Lerwick, Packham told him, the main town and the only commercial harbor in the islands. They skimmed over the sound between Lerwick and a small island guarding the entrance to the harbor and turned inland. Apart from a few patches of fertile land, the island seemed to be entirely covered by rough heath, and Mike guessed the soil was probably unable to support much more than the lean sheep grazing beneath them. The ground rose sharply toward the middle of the island, and as they cleared the crest, he had his first view of Sullom Voe, set at the head of a huge natural bay, now silvered by the setting sun. As they sped down the hill, they flew over a line of derelict buildings or abandoned army huts, Packham told him, and he added that Sullom Voe had been a strong military outpost during the last war, a key bunkering point for submarines and other naval vessels protecting the North Atlantic convoys.

Now down by the shore, there were newer buildings, and way over to the left was a gigantic concrete structure, which Mike learned was a new oil tanker port. They banked steeply to the right, and there, surrounded by a tall steel mesh fence, was the DEW station, a collection of differently shaped aerials, a group of huts, some of them quite large, a tall white flagpole, and a grass-invaded concrete runway sloping down the hill toward the water. Some of the huts were freshly painted, and the aerials certainly looked cared for, but the place had a general air of neglect that was reinforced no doubt by the sparse gorse bushes growing round the edges of the compound and buffeted by a rising wind.

The helicopter landed some thirty yards from the largest hut, and Packham took Mike inside where he introduced him to the station commander installed in one of a series of glass-partitioned offices.

"This is Captain Dickinson. Mike Marshall."

"Glad to meet you, Mike," Dickinson said. He turned and beckoned to a young sergeant.

"This is Sergeant Baker," he said. "He is going to be your personal assistant. He will see to your needs at all times. He has been assigned quarters next to yours. You may feel free to call upon him for anything."

Baker smiled, and Mike forced himself to smile back. They were certainly not taking any chances. Baker would no doubt have instructions to keep a careful eye on him—a tame watchdog.

"All right then," Packham said, "I'll show you to your quarters, and Baker can get you something to eat if you want."

They walked across the compound to one of the freshly painted huts, and Mike found to his surprise that his quarters were little short of luxurious. There was a pleasant L-shaped living room looking out over the bay and a large bedroom with a bathroom and dressing room en suite, all furnished with excellent taste.

"Well, sir," Baker said, "perhaps you'd like something to eat. I can arrange an omelette and cheese and salad if that will do. And," he paused, looking at Mike, "you might like to fix yourself a drink at the bar over there."

"Baker, you're a mind reader!" Mike said with an amused glance at Packham. "That sounds great!"

Baker went out, and Packham said he too would be leaving. It was then that Mike remembered what it was that had been nagging at his mind all afternoon. It was something Packham had said—something that had made him feel very uncomfortable.

"Packham, er, Hal," he said. "Remember in London when you were asking me to tell you what you were thinking? You know, red triangle, blue circle, and then suddenly I couldn't see anything more? How did you do that?

"Simple," Packham replied. "I put up a mental shield. We are trained to do that. At first, you caught me out, which probably means that you are very good, or perhaps I was suffering from jet lag and my defenses were down, or both. But believe me, Mike, you won't ever catch me out again. Good night. See you in the morning."

As the door closed, Mike suddenly felt very uncomfortable again.

Chapter 7

Sullom Voe, May 9, 2007. 8:00 a.m.

Marshall was woken by the phone next to his bed. He rolled over with a groan and picked it up.

"Good morning, sir," a voice said, "this is Sergeant Baker. Hope I didn't wake you. You have a meeting at nine-thirty, and I thought you might want to get some breakfast first."

"Thanks," Marshall said. "Yes. Where do I get it? What time is it anyway?"

"Eight o'clock, sir. And either I can fix you something, or you can walk over to the canteen in hut six."

"Okay, I'll do that. I could do with some air. Where's the meeting?"

"I'll pick you up at the canteen, sir, just before nine-thirty and take you over."

Marshall sat up. He felt rested but a little thickheaded. After an uncomfortable night in prison, a very exhausting day, and a couple of late-night whiskeys as he sat and tried to understand what was happening to him, he had slept like a man drugged. He showered, shaved, threw on some casual clothes and, feeling brighter, he stepped out into the thin sunshine.

The station looked deserted apart from a guard sitting in a glass booth at the entrance gate and a soldier sweeping the concrete square around which most of the huts were arranged. It was pleasantly cool, and the air tasted of sea and heather. There was still a light breeze, and the water in the bay sparkled busily as a pair of fishing boats steamed slowly out of sight behind a spur of land. Everything looked peaceful and innocent, and Marshall's spirits lifted.

There were eight main huts around the square, one end of which gave onto the concrete runway on which the helicopter had landed the night before. This hut looked big enough to accommodate a good-sized aircraft. The other end of the square was filled by two large huts, and one of which housed Marshall's quarters. On the other sides of the square were the office block, another very large hut, and several smaller ones, all neatly numbered. He headed for number six, which proved to be filled with a cheery crowd of breakfasters including Captain Dickinson, who hailed him as he came in and explained how to get what he wanted.

Marshall went through the serving line, filled his tray, and sat down at Dickinson's table.

"How far are we from the nearest town?" Marshall asked.

"Well," Dickinson said, "there's nothing really very close. In any case, no one's allowed off the base, and we're completely independent. We have everything flown in. There's a chopper that flies in every day at four. So we get fresh food, mail, newspapers, and so on, probably much quicker than through normal channels. And like that we stay away from the locals, keep a low profile, you know. This is a top-secret project," he added rather pompously after a pause, and then he stood up to leave. "I have to get over to my office now."

By the time Marshall had finished his breakfast and glanced at one of the newspapers piled on a table by the wall, he was the only person left in the canteen. Baker appeared and asked him if there was anything he needed before going into the briefing. There wasn't, so they walked over to hut three where, according to Baker, all the project activities were concentrated.

From the outside, the hut looked identical to the others, but when they stepped inside, there was an armed guard behind the door, and the door itself was lined with steel. Also, Marshall noticed the hum of air conditioning, which was a totally unnecessary luxury in this climate, he reflected. The walls were painted in pleasant pastel colors, and the floor of the corridor in which they stood was thickly carpeted. Baker motioned him to follow, and they walked down the corridor toward an open door and the sound of voices. The room from which the voices were coming held a small group of men, Colonel Packham and six others, standing or sitting around a large cloth-covered table.

"Ah, Mike, come in," Packham said. "That means we are all here now. Come in and sit down." He motioned to the others. "Let's be seated, gentlemen. Thank you, Baker. You may go." Baker went out, closing the door behind him.

"Very well, gentlemen," Packham continued, "this is our first full meeting. Some of you don't know each other yet, so I would like to go round the table to introduce you and maybe ask you to say a few words if you feel like it."

Marshall glanced round the group. No special characteristics. Some young, some not so young. A pretty representative cross section.

"First of all," Packham went on, "my name is Colonel Henry Packham, but I don't want any formality here, so just call me Hal. I am in charge of this project which, as most of you know, is designed to attempt contact with extraterrestrial intelligence through telepathy, or some other form of mind projection technique yet to be developed. I'll come back to that later. Some of us in this room—" here he nodded at two of the men "—have been working on the preliminary stages of the project for several months, but now the time has come to bring together all the people who will be involved in the operational phase. We also have three telepathists who will be the frontline combatants, as it were, and a number of technical specialists whose job it will be to provide them with supplies and logistical support. I suggest we start with our telepathists."

Marshall glanced round the table, trying to guess who the other telepathists were, but there was no way of telling. "Let's start with the youngest." Packham smiled. "Chuck Pierkowski. Would you stand up please, Chuck, and tell us who you are?"

A tall, broad-shouldered young man with a deep tan stood up at the end of the table and looked sheepishly at Packham and then at the others.

"Hi," he said. "Er, I'm a tennis coach at Duke University, and I've been doing experiments with Dr. Gardner over there." He jerked his head in the direction of the oldest man in the room who was sitting at the other end of the table.

"Yes," Packham said, "Chuck's quite a telepathist. Perhaps Jim Gardner will tell you a little more about him in a minute. Next, Jan Andersen. Would you stand up please?"

Andersen was a man of about thirty and no doubt of Scandinavian origin; he was tall and very fair with a thick blond beard and deep-set blue eyes.

"Hello," he began, "I'm happy to meet the people I'm going to be working with at last. I'm a naval officer. I discovered I had a gift for ESP a couple of years ago when I found I could often guess sextant readings during navigational fixes. So I got interested in random number selection and precognition and other types of ESP phenomena, and Hal found out about this through my commanding officer. I look forward to working with you all."

He sat down and looked intently round the table. *Now he's another breed of cat altogether,* thought Marshall. *Very cool and sure of himself. Sounds as if he knows what he's talking about, but he could be a pain.*

"And finally," Packham was saying, "our third telepathist and a very recent addition to our team, Mike Marshall, who flew in with me last night. Mike."

Marshall got to his feet.

"I'm Mike Marshall. I'm a helicopter pilot. I found I could read people's minds—sometimes—after a crash in Afghanistan.

The colonel here dragged me into this. I'm not certain what it's all about, and when I get a chance, I have a whole bunch of questions I want to ask."

"Okay," Packham interrupted, "you'll get your chance later. Let's just get on with the introductions for the moment, if you don't mind, Mike. Now, Chuck mentioned Jim Gardner. Jim's a distinguished scholar, a researcher at Duke, and the author of several books on human relations. I say that because he's probably too modest to say it himself. Jim."

Gardner unwound himself from his chair and stood up. He was a very tall man, probably in his early sixties, with a stoop and thin locks of gray hair falling over his horn-rimmed glasses. He looked precisely what he was—an aging academic, slightly frail, but when he spoke, it was in a deep, confident voice.

"Gentlemen," he began, "I too look forward to working with you. Chuck Pierkowski and I have done some very interesting experiments together already, but I am very anxious to see what we can do with three gifted telepathists. Chuck is a wonderful subject, but so far we've only been able to work on receptivity tests. With a group of telepathists, we'll be able to develop projection abilities. But more of that later. You'll find I'm an incorrigible enthusiast when it comes to ESP. I first started research with J.B. Rhine many years ago, and I'm still as excited about it as when I first began. So I'm really looking forward to working with such talent. Hal has told me about you all, and I'm flattered to be part of such a team."

"Thank you, Jim," said Packham. "Well, we've got another Jim here. Jim Elrich. Jim's a doctor, so maybe we can call you Dr. Jim, if you don't mind, Jim, to distinguish you from our other Jim."

"Sure," said Dr. Jim, rising to his feet, "anything you say."

He was a neat-looking man in his late thirties, with crinkly brown hair receding at the sides and a smooth, almost unlined complexion.

"I gather I'm going to be the project doctor here," he said easily. "Until I was pulled on to this project, and it took some pulling, I might add, I was working at the London University Department of Psychology. I specialize in brain waves. I don't mean ideas but the waves produced by the brain. And I suppose my work on human energy fields has its relevance here too."

"Thank you, Dr. Jim," said Packham. "Maybe we can move on to Sam Goldman. Sam's a mathematician from NASA." He paused and nodded toward a small, dark-haired man with a very high forehead and thick, heavy glasses.

"I guess I'm a mathematician," said Goldman, rising and pushing his glasses up on to the bridge of his nose, a gesture he was to repeat at frequent intervals as he spoke. "But I'm more of a physicist really. You see, I'm a specialist on radio waves and signals. You can see how that fits in here, but I've also been associated with biotechnology and human research at our Office of Advanced Research and Technology, and I've done some work on what we call 'psychophysiological information transfer.'"

As he sat down, Packham added, "Sam, you forgot to mention that you were one of the scientists who worked on the Green Bank Formula. For those of you who don't know what that is, in a nutshell, the Green Bank Formula established scientifically and mathematically that there are between forty and fifty million planets, or heavenly bodies, capable of communicating with us. I think those figures have a certain significance for what we are doing here. Anyway, last but not least, Frank Mambrino. Frank is our resident UFO expert. He's seen several."

"Yeah, that's right," said Mambrino, a large, heavy man with dark jowls and a quick, brilliant smile. "I used to see lots of them when I was a flight engineer. But no one ever believed me. Anyway, now I'm working for a private foundation and compiling statistics on UFO sightings. I bet you we're going to see some more before this project's over!"

"So there we are," said Packham as Mambrino sat down. "Welcome aboard, all of you. I hope we'll be able to get along together. Now we all know each other, I want to give you a few more details about our project." He ran a hand over his close-cropped hair and stared sternly around the table. "I have to warn you, however, that this is a top-secret project and that everything you learn from now on is classified. There will be no communication with anyone outside this station, except—" he paused and allowed himself a smile "—except with extraterrestrials, of course!"

There was a ripple of laughter, and Packham continued, "I have explained to all of you at various times that messages, or, to be more precise, signals from space, are a reality. We don't know where they're coming from, and there's no way of knowing whether they are repeated signals from the same source or separate signals from different sources, but there is no longer any doubt possible that some form of extraterrestrial intelligence has attempted and is probably still attempting to make contact with us. We have never been able to understand any of these signals, and we have never succeeded in receiving any response to signals we ourselves have sent into space. Of course there may be any number or reasons for this: signal strength, beaming direction, frequency, language, and sheer distance, to name but a few. Now I believe, and I am not alone in this, that some of these problems can be solved by using telepathy. This is why we are all here, and this is why this project has the full support and blessing of the US government. Believe me, gentlemen, never has it been more important or more urgent to establish contact with our neighbors in space. The whole point of this is to get our hands on oil. The country that gets its hands on the most oil will rule the world. And that is going to be our country and not Russia."

Packham paused for effect. Young Chuck Pierkowski and Jan Andersen were nodding in approval. Jim Gardner uncrossed his long legs and scratched his chin. Sam Goldman pushed his glasses up on to his nose. Frank Mambrino grinned nervously, and Dr. Jim Elrich looked totally uninterested. Marshall raised a hand.

"Do you mind if I ask a question?" he asked.

"Go ahead," Packham replied.

"I can understand why it's important to establish contact with extraterrestrial intelligence, but why is it so urgent? According to you, and I have no reason to disbelieve you, this has been going on for centuries, perhaps thousands of years. So what's the hurry?"

"A good question and I'm glad you asked it. I think you'll all agree this world is in pretty bad shape. We've managed to avoid a further global conflagration over the past few decades, but it's becoming more and more difficult to maintain this situation in the face of overpopulation and increasing shortages. Conflict lies just beneath the surface of what passes for peace, ready to be set off by the next famine or oil crunch or pseudo-religious revolution. We're all sitting on a powder keg, and there are too many damn matches around for comfort or safety!

"Now, it seems reasonable to suppose that any extraterrestrial intelligence capable of achieving long-distance space travel will have reached a far more advanced state of technology than we have, and many of the problems waiting to spark off our powder barrel could be solved by advanced technology. I mean problems like food, disease, energy, locomotion, communications… If we could get rid of these problems, this world would be a much happier—and safer—place. But the way we're going now, if we don't do something quickly, it may be too late."

"Plus the fact," Marshall cut in, "that we might get beaten to it!"

"What do you mean?" Packham asked.

"Didn't you tell me yesterday that the Russians might be trying to do something similar?"

"Yes, I did," Packham replied. "That's perfectly true." He sat up straight, and his eyes went very still. Marshall sensed his wariness, and he could almost feel the steel shutter dropping down behind that blank gaze. Chuck Pierkowski shifted in his chair, frowned, and shook his head as if to clear it. Marshall wondered if the young coach was getting some signals he wasn't.

"There's very little either we or the Russians do without the other side knowing about it almost immediately," Packham said. "The Russians have been interested in ESP and other psi phenomena for a long time now. In fact, Russia is one of the very few countries in the world to have state-funded institutes working on such phenomena. We know that a few months ago, the Moscow Institute of Parapsychology in particular began recruiting more staff and taking delivery of lots of new equipment. Now the type of equipment being acquired, according to intelligence from specialized sources around the country and other bits of information we've gleaned here and there, all lead us to believe that the Russians have launched a crash program on long-distance telepathy. It is entirely feasible and indeed highly likely therefore that they too are trying to contact extraterrestrial life and that they may have a project similar to ours. How far they have gone, we just can't tell. But believe me, it's vital that we get there before they do. And I'll tell you why, because I think it's important you should realize what is at stake.

"First of all, in any discussion of possible contact with extraterrestrials, we have to consider the impression they are going to receive from such an encounter. The person or persons they come into contact with will be seen as representative of the whole population of the planet, so it is vitally important that they gain the right impression. It is essential to convince them that we are friendly and not hostile. Otherwise, we run the risk of being stamped out as a potential threat. So, we don't want to foul this up. We don't want the Russians crashing around in their usual heavy-handed way, giving off all the wrong vibes. We all know how aggressive they can be. And if the world gets destroyed because of the Russians, we get destroyed too.

"No, we firmly believe that only we can give the right impression and project the correct, friendly, sane, balanced image that will persuade them that we are worth dealing with. As the leaders of the free world, it is the responsibility of the United States of America to make certain our principles and fundamental beliefs are represented and understood."

Marshall groaned audibly and grimaced. "You don't really expect us to believe all this, do you?" he said "You're not trying to tell us the only reason you've brought us up here is to spread the gospel of the American way of life through outer space!"

Packham held up his hand and smiled, but the eyes were still blank.

"Mike, please. Let me finish. No, I won't insult your intelligence by telling you that's the only reason. Obviously, there's a political reason too. Just think what international prestige there would be in being the first country to make contact with life outside the planet! It would be like winning all the gold medals at the Olympics, landing a regiment of marines on the moon, and giving birth to quintuplets on top of Mount Everest, all rolled into one. And there would be all the technological spin-offs as well. We'd be hailed as the benefactors of mankind! But I beg you, gentlemen, don't belittle the other reason I gave you. There may be political realities involved, but I for one would like to think that the task which lies ahead is not devoid of grandeur and nobility."

There was an embarrassing silence and then Jan Andersen rose to his feet, with his blue eyes shining. "I agree, sir," he said. "I think you'll find everyone here behind you one hundred percent. After what you've said, it would be unpatriotic not to give you our fullest support!"

With this, he sat down and scowled at Marshall, who shrugged and glanced round the table again. Dr. Jim Elrich grinned at him and turned to Packham.

"I have no wish to be 'unpatriotic'," he began and raised a quizzical eyebrow at Jan Andersen. "But I too have a question, which is: why here? There must be plenty of more accessible and civilized places with better facilities. I know there are in London. Why not Duke University, for example, which must have some of the best facilities and equipment in the world? Isn't that right, Jim?"

Gardner nodded. "Yes, you're perfectly right of course, and when Hal approached me for this project, that was one of the first things I said to him. Naturally, I would have preferred to work in my own lab, but Hal convinced me otherwise." He stopped and looked expectantly at Packham.

"Okay," said Packham, "let me explain. As I said, this is a top-secret project, and this DEW station gives perfect cover. We might have found good cover elsewhere, but there's another reason. The largest distance covered by telepathy to date is several thousand miles. We used to be limited to the earth's surface, of course, but it may interest you to know that several telepathic experiments were run during the Apollo missions, and the results were pretty good. However, if we're talking about establishing contact with extraterrestrial life, we're talking about millions of miles, at the very least. We've no good reason to believe that telepathy cannot reach that far, but we don't know. We just don't know enough yet to be able to measure the intensity of telepathic signals or even if they are capable of being measured. Dr. Jim, I'm sure you'll agree with that."

Eirich nodded, and Packham continued. "So, since we know telepathic communication is possible between an Apollo spacecraft and earth, why not between earth and a UFO? There have been dozens of reports of UFO sightings over the North Sea in recent months, and Shetland is about the closest we can get to the middle of the North Sea without using an oil rig or a ship. Frank, perhaps you'd give us a few details."

"Sure," said Mambrino, and he flashed a smile around the group. "I'm glad you mentioned oil rigs, because that's where most of the sightings have been made. I feel pretty certain too that if we're getting so many reports, it's because the UFOs are interested in all the new activity on the North Sea. Oil rigs are pretty big things and highly visible from the air, particularly at night when they look like huge Christmas trees. You could hardly help noticing them, and then, who knows? Perhaps oil drilling is something extraterrestrials don't know anything about. Perhaps there is no oil where they come from! Anyway, I think that's why they're appearing so often. I've got a whole bunch of reports in my room, and most of them are cigars."

Chuck Pierkowski looked a little bewildered and glanced from left to right and back again to see if anyone else was having trouble.

Sam Goldman pushed his glasses up, cleared his throat with a dry cough, and looked at Mambrino.

"Frank, maybe you'd better explain what you mean and why cigars are significant."

"Oh, yes, of course," said Mambrino. "Sorry, everyone! You see, there are different kinds of UFOs. From all the reports I've studied, I've been able to identify seven."

"Really?" Sam said.

"We don't need to go into detail though," continued Mambrino. " Just let's say they fall into three main groups, which I call saucers, light balls, and cigars."

"Saucers!" Chuck said.

Mambrino coughed and cleared his throat.

"I'm just trying to give you a general picture. Light balls are very different. They don't seem to have any shape other than that of a rough sphere. They look literally like a ball of light and zip around in the most erratic manner and at crazy speeds. People often describe them as 'a ball of fire' or say they look like a flash of sun reflected by a mirror. For some reason, they seem to be sighted more often over the sea and in the tropics, although there was a spate of them once over Rome.

"Now cigars are a different thing altogether. They are long cigar-shaped objects, often huge, frequently sighted from flying aircraft. I've seen several myself. The interesting thing is that they appear to have rows of portholes, and this suggests strongly that they may be manned. As I say, they are usually very large and could perhaps be parent ships for light balls and other smaller reconnaissance craft. We don't know. Anyway, the recent observations over the North Sea concern cigars, and for our purposes, that's good, because it means they're probably manned. I mean you might have a hard time trying to contact a light ball. Everybody okay now?"

There were a few nods and "uh-huhs," and Pierkowski murmured, "Jeez, that's wild."

"Hal," said Sam Goldman, "could I make a comment here?" He continued. "Frank, your explanation was excellent, so I'm not directing my remarks at you, but I wouldn't like anyone to get the impression that we'll be concentrating solely on UFOs or indeed on projection. Hal and I have been discussing this for a long time, and we agreed right from the start that we should also monitor for long-range signals."

"Yes indeed," Packham put in, "and that's one of the reasons why Sam is here. "Perhaps I should try to explain how you all fit into this.

He looked around the room and saw people nodding.

"Our prime objective is to establish contact with extraterrestrial intelligence through telepathic means. All right. We know that long-distance radio signals have been received from outer space. Why shouldn't there be telepathic signals from the same sources? If there are, we want to try to pick them up and respond. At the same time, we know there are UFOs in this area, and we want to try to establish telepathic contact with them too. So, in both cases, we have a 'receiver' function, to use a radio term, and a 'transmit' function.

"Oh," Mike said, "so that is what we are supposed to be doing."

"Yes, in both cases, our receivers and transmitters, to go on using radio terms, will be our telepathists, Mike, Chuck, and Jan. We don't know yet which of you is best at transmitting or receiving. That is something we have to determine, and this is where Jim Gardner is going to help. He's going to be your trainer and coach. He's going to help you develop your natural abilities and show you how to concentrate and how to eliminate outside interference. Jim will teach you techniques he's been working on for years.

"At the same time, Dr. Jim will be almost constantly present to monitor your brain functions and check your bodily reactions. We already know there is a close relationship between certain types of cerebral waves and telepathic activity. At the same time, we'll be experimenting with varying conditions: heat, cold, moisture (that's why this place is fully air-conditioned, if you hadn't noticed), fatigue, hunger, thirst, and so on. We'll work at different times of the day and night, in different sequences, with different combinations. And we expect Dr. Jim to keep you thoroughbreds in tip-top form throughout all this."

"Who's going to keep me in shape?" Dr. Jim said, and everyone smiled. Now that a definite program was beginning to emerge, the group seemed to relax.

"Now the next question," Packham continued, "is what signals are our telepathists going to be looking for? And what messages are they going to transmit? Well, this is where Sam Goldman comes in. From his experience of radio signals and the way waves travel through space, he's going to try to give us some indication of what a possible long-distance telepathic signal or message may look or sound like. At the same time, he'll be working very closely with you guys to see what kind of signal we want to transmit, consistent with strength, direction, distance, and so on.

"And Frank is going to keep us informed on UFO movements, if any are reported locally. Also, his experience in determining the speeds and distances of flying objects will be vital once contact is established. Before, too! There may be directional and tracking problems, and we're going to rely on Frank to help us solve them.

"So you see, we all have a role to play in this project," Packham said "and it's vital that we work together as a team." He glanced at his watch. "At our next session, we'll be discussing schedules and mealtimes and other practical details. For the rest of the morning, I suggest you get to know each other a little better. Right now, though, I want to show you your working quarters. Come with me."

They followed him out of the room and down the corridor to a set of double doors bearing a notice with large red letters, which said: "No Entry."

"This is where you will be working," Packham said. "Behind those doors is the most sophisticated laboratory of its kind in the world. Jim, Sam, and Dr. Jim have spent months getting it ready. Only those directly involved in the project, that is to say those of us present today plus a handful of control technicians, will be allowed to enter. Yes, gentlemen," Packham went on dramatically, "behind those doors, I fully expect that we shall witness yet another step for man, yet another giant leap for mankind!"

Chapter 8

Aberdeen, Scotland. May 22, 2007. 4:00 p.m.

"Gentlemen," the president of Firth Oil, James McKinney, said, "I know this meeting was pretty hastily arranged, but I hope you've been well taken care of. This is not the most elegant hotel in the world, but we own it, so we have maximum discretion." He looked around the room, which held about a dozen men. "Everyone get in all right? I know it's a small private airport next to the hotel, but we like it this way. Very discreet. Thanks to all for coming. Jack?" He pointed at Jack Koehner. "Want to get started? By the way, I only met Jack face-to-face last night, but I know he was instrumental in setting up this important meeting."

"Okay. Thanks, James. As you can see, this room has all the major oil players in the Western world. No Organization of Petroleum Exporting Countries. No Russians. No Asians. No Venezuelans. We're clean."

There were some chuckles around the room.

"Further to all our e-mails, teleconferences, and preparatory meetings, we're here to see how we can all deal with—and benefit from—the new Blane field. Jim here tells us that while they own the rights to the field, they don't have enough available resources to exploit it fully, at least not in the near future, which is why we're all here. Firth Oil is an amazing company but small. Together, we can all make this thing work. And…and if we can get to the bottom of this UFO phenomenon, perhaps we can take the world!"

"By the way," said McKinney, "let me introduce the chap who figured this all out, Richard McAlistair."

A heavyset, bespectacled man in his mid-thirties stood up at the end of the table.

"Well, as you know, I'm not sure what I figured out. I just saw the UFOs and tracked 'em, and took some bearings and thought, 'Why this position?' Then, out of the blue, it dawned on me that there's something down there. We looked and there were no wrecks or treasure chests or bodies or ETs, or…nothing. So our chief drilling engineer said that we were going to sink another exploratory hole here soon, so why not use these bearings. And, well, you know the rest of the story."

"And so," said McKinney, "the question is who's going to be tracking UFOs, and where's the next play going to be?"

"Well," said Koehner, "if we're to believe that military guy, Packham, there's stuff going on somewhere. Maybe one day we'll find out."

Chapter 9

Moscow, May 23, 2007. 8:30 a.m.

Katrina Klimenkova hummed as she slipped into her lab coat. This was her third week at the Moscow Institute of Parapsychology, and she was really enjoying it. So far, on the suggestion of Professor Kamikov, she had been dividing her time fairly evenly between getting to know the various projects run by the institute and working over her notes on mental patterns and languages.

She had learned a lot about the history of parapsychology, the importance of statistical evidence, and the difficulties of applying scientific method to phenomena that seemed to defy scientific definition. She found that she was having to grapple with a whole set of new concepts, new to her anyway, and that this required her to reject many of the academic attitudes and prejudices acquired during her formal training. But it was all so fascinating, and as she reexamined her research notes, she was thrilled to see how this different approach was shedding new light on many areas that had remained obscure for her.

Today, she was about to join a team working on random factor selection. She was not quite certain what this was, but she was looking forward to finding out about another new concept, another technique, and another glimpse at the world of psi. She had never felt more curious, more alive, more eager to learn than since she had started at the institute. So this was why she hummed to herself as she hung her street clothes in her locker and turned to arrange her hair in front of the mirror.

There was another reason. Leonid Kamikov had asked her to have a drink with him that evening, to discuss how things were progressing. He had suggested nothing more than a friendly business chat, a quiet drink at a new club just off Gorki, but Katrina was not insensitive to the scientist's charm. She had led a very quiet life ever since her divorce, but she sometimes missed the feel and presence of a man—not that she expected anything to come of her meeting. But she was a young, healthy woman, and Kamikov was a very attractive male, even though he was considerably older than her. She could not help feeling flattered and a little excited.

The door of the cloakroom opened, and Anna Gan walked in, a garrulous redhead who had befriended Katrina on her first day and who had helped her to find her way around. It was good to have a friend, particularly one as unfailingly cheerful and helpful as Anna, who was a research assistant in the PK lab.

"Good morning, Katrina," she said. "You're bright and early!"

"Yes, I'm working today with Vitaly Levkov, and I don't want to be late."

"Oh, old 'Think-of-a-Number Levkov'. He's very nice really, but he's totally obsessed by his work. You'll see. How much do you want to bet the first thing he'll say to you is: 'Think of a number?' He always does. But you'll like him, and he's got a wonderful engineer working with him, a young man called Yuri." Katrina's heart skipped a beat. "Yuri Barchenko." Katrina relaxed. Of course not, her ex-husband was still out East. "They're in lab twenty-four. Do you know where that is? It's on the second floor of the Blue Wing."

Anna burbled on as she dressed for work. Katrina waited, and they walked out of the cloakroom together.

"Go down to the end of the corridor, turn right, right again, then up the second floor. See you at break, perhaps. Have a good morning."

Like most of the institute, the corridor was dingy, paneled in dark oak, and dusty. Even the labs looked old-fashioned, although Katrina knew that much of the equipment was very modern. All the furniture and fittings were massively designed and obviously built to last. Lab 24 proved to be no exception. It was a long, high-ceilinged room with tall windows down one side and the inevitable oak paneling covering the bottom three feet of each wall. There were four dark-brown lab benches, one in front of each window, and in the corners opposite the windows, two large cubicles partitioned off from the rest of the room with what looked like modern soundproofing materials.

The tall fleshy man who rose to greet her introduced himself as Yuri Barchenko.

"Professor Levkov will be here any moment. He had a meeting with Professor Kamikov. He said he wouldn't be long. Ah, here he is now."

The man who entered the lab as he said this advanced upon Katrina with a stern scowl and said, "Think of a number."

"Three hundred and forty-seven," Katrina replied, saying the first thing that came into her head.

Levkov stopped abruptly and said, "Good heavens. Someone told you. No, they couldn't have. No one knows." He peered at Katrina through rimless spectacles.

"Do you know," he said, "you're the first person to get it right? I have asked that question thousands of times, and no one ever guessed the answer. Forgive me, my dear. You must be Katrina Klimenkova. I'm delighted to have you with us. Well, well, well. Most extraordinary. What do you think, Yuri?"

"I am sure it is extraordinary, sir. But I never really knew what it was you were trying to do."

"Just testing a theory of mine—random choice of a random number. The odds against anyone guessing a three-digit number correctly on first meeting are phenomenal. I've been asking people for years! So I'm doubly glad to meet you, young lady. Professor

Kamikov recommends you very highly. I've just been talking to him about you. It seems he wants you to work on some of the linguistic aspects of thought transference."

"That is correct. And I am anxious to learn how your department fits into the whole process."

"Why don't we sit down?" said Yuri. "This may take some time. Professor Levkov is an enthusiast."

They made themselves comfortable around a small table.

"Let me see," said Levkov when they were seated. "Where shall I begin? One of the first major problems facing scientific observers of psi phenomena, whether telepathy, eyeless sight, psychokinesis, or whatever, is that of the reliability of statistical information and, I might add, the standardization of equipment and procedures. Let me try to give you a simple example. One of the earliest experiments done with ESP was card guessing. You design a group of cards with numbers or colors or symbols and get a person to guess which card is turned up by a second person, with the cards remaining out of sight of course. This experiment can be used to test the telepathic powers of (a) the sender or (b) the receiver.

"Let's assume there are five cards. The probability of the first person guessing the correct card is obviously one in five. That is, if chance alone is involved. One in five, that's twenty in a hundred. If the results are consistently over twenty, then there is something other than chance at work, and the more tries are made, the higher the odds against such results being achieved. For example, if the result is two hundred and twenty out of one thousand, which is still the same proportion, i.e., ten percent above average, the odds against this happening are six to one. Are you following?"

Katrina nodded.

"But—" Levkov went on "—if we make five thousand tries and the proportion is still respected, the odds against would then be two thousand to one. The more tries we make, the higher the odds. All right, but if we are trying to assess the telepathic receptivity of the guesser, how can we be certain that the results are not being determined by the excellence of the sender? Or again, how can we be certain that the results are not being distorted by the guesser's capacity for precognition, which would have nothing to do with a telepathic link with the sender? In other words, how can we be sure of a 'pure' message, a 'clean' link?

"One way to achieve this is to build a random factor into any experiment, and our job here is to devise random factor selection mechanisms—for example, ways of selecting cards without any outside interference. The difficulties are enormous, but I'm happy to say we are now achieving some pretty foolproof systems. Yuri here has been wonderful. He has designed some very ingenious mechanisms based on a radioactive quantum process. But we still have a great deal to learn!"

"I see," said Katrina, "so you're building the instruments used by all the other departments of the institute?"

"That's right. But we are also running our own experiments here, if only to test the equipment and find out the best ways of using it. In fact, you're lucky. We have a group of people coming in this morning for some tests. You'll be able to watch them in progress. Yuri, perhaps you'd like to show Katrina round before they arrive. I'm afraid I have a report to finish. So will you excuse me?"

Levkov bounded to his feet and strode quickly to the door. He stopped, shaking his head. "You know, I still can't believe you got it right. Remarkable. Truly remarkable."

"Let me show you round then," said Yuri when Levkov finally went out. "There's not much to see really, except when we're running tests. We work with four main types of apparatus, all based on the random selection principle. This one here throws dice. That one over there selects colored lights. The one down at the end is a random number generator, and in each cubicle, there is a random card selector."

Katrina nodded, looking round the room, and then turned to Yuri.

"Tell me something. Do you think it was so extraordinary guessing Professor Levkov's number? Someone was bound to guess it sooner or later."

"Well, as he said, the odds against anyone guessing a three-digit number the first time are astronomical. But then the chance is always there. I wouldn't worry about it if I were you!" Yuri laughed and was rewarded with a smile from Katrina. "We see some pretty weird things around here!" There was a loud ping from one of the cubicles.

"There's one now!"

Katrina looked startled.

"No," Yuri went on, laughing again, "that's a little invention of mine. I'm not an engineer for nothing. It's an automatic tea-maker, programmed to produce tea exactly half an hour after my arrival. Come on. Come and taste my automatic tea."

An hour later, after an exhaustive tour of the lab, Yuri was telling Katrina about the tests they would be running that morning.

"First of all, the people. They are a random selection of workers from the Department of Agriculture. Men and women. All ages, I expect. I don't know. I haven't met this group before. They usually enjoy it when they come here. Makes a change from routine, I suppose."

"How many are coming?" Katrina asked.

"Twelve. That's about as many as we can handle comfortably."

"Which machines will you be using?"

"The card selector mainly. You remember Professor Levkov talking about telepathy and precognition?"

Katrina nodded.

"Well, we're going to run two parallel tests. First, we are going to get the random card selector to produce a series of cards and ask different subjects to try to guess what those cards are going to be, before they are selected. This is a precognition test. We'll be using standard Zener cards—that is, five cards with different markings: a circle, a square, a cross, a star, and wavy lines. We'll run the test several times with different subjects each time and a number of variables such as a different time lapse between cards, one, two, or three people in the cubicle, and so on. All right. Now, we are obviously going to record the results for statistical analysis. At the same time, we are going to record the sequences produced by the card selector and keep them for another test—a telepathy test this time.

"For this telepathy test, we have pairs, one sender and one receiver, or sometimes two or more senders and a receiver. The sender, sitting in one cubicle, turns over his preselected set of cards, one at a time, presses a buzzer, and concentrates on the star, circle, square, cross, or waves. The receiver who hears the buzzer tries to pick up the correct marking projected by the sender. When he thinks he has it, he notes it down and presses his buzzer to signal he is ready for another card. Apart from the resulting statistical data, this test enables us to gauge telepathic abilities, which we mark from one to ten. It helps us to identify good telepathic subjects, either senders or receivers, since we may wish to use them later."

"So ultimately," Katrina broke in, "you'll be able to somehow correlate the results of the precognition and telepathy tests and come up with a weighted analysis."

Yuri looked at her. "You really listen don't you? It's approximate, of course, but this is the first attempt we know of to get a statistically clean result and to eliminate, partially at least, the precognition factor in telepathy. It's going to be very interesting, when we have enough results, to feed them through a computer. For the time being, though, we have to collect the data, and that is a long, tedious process."

At this moment, the door opened, and a white-coated assistant led in a group of people, as Yuri had predicted, with men and women of all ages.

Yuri walked forward to greet them and explain what was expected of them. Katrina watched as Yuri and his assistants split them into subgroups and pairs and told them where to sit for the first tests. One assistant was dispatched to fetch Professor Levkov, and the tests began.

To begin with, the "subjects," as Katrina was learning to refer to them, were made to sit alone in front of the random card selector in each cubicle and mark down their guesses before the cards were shown. This took quite a long time, as each subject was asked to make a run of one hundred guesses. A second run was made with two people in each cubicle and a third with three.

Levkov's team of assistants was obviously very practiced, for they moved the groups through a very complicated set of combinations without a hitch. Yuri and Levkov walked back and forth between the cubicles, glancing at the growing pile of results, taking notes, and occasionally whispering instructions to one of the assistants. The atmosphere was quiet without being subdued, and Katrina noticed that both Yuri and Levkov seemed to make a point of smiling and chatting in a friendly way with the subjects.

Katrina felt a little useless standing around, but eventually Yuri approached her and told her she could enter a cubicle and watch the next run with a group of four.

Inside the darkened cubicle, four people were seated round a rectangular table placed in front of a blank screen. Each subject had a notepad inside a curved shield, effectively hiding it from the others. There was a soft buzz, which no doubt signaled that a card was about to be produced. The subjects obviously knew what to do, for when the buzzer sounded, they sat up in their chairs, concentrated, made a mark on their pads, and then looked expectantly at the screen. A circle appeared briefly, disappeared, and then the buzzer sounded again. Once again the four subjects noted their guesses and watched the screen. A star. Buzzer. Concentration. A square. Buzzer. Concentration. A star again. And so on.

Katrina watched the subjects. Occasionally, one of them smiled or nodded. Presumably, this meant the guess was correct. As the series continued, the subjects settled into a routine, and Katrina observed them closely for signs of success. Circle, one nod. Square, one smile. Waves, nothing. Cross, two nods. Square, one nod. Circle, two nods. Star, two nods. Were they getting better at it, Katrina wondered, or was she observing a phenomenon of collective precognition? She stiffened. There were three nods on the last card. Could a group develop a capacity in such a short period of time? Were their individual faculties strengthened by the group? She must ask Yuri. The run came to an end. Katrina still could not see a pattern, but there had been a good many twos and, toward the end, even two more threes.

"Interesting?" asked Yuri when she emerged from the cubicle.

"Very," Katrina replied. "I would like to see more."

"Sorry! We're just starting another precognition series, back to single subjects. You know our rules about observers. Unless… why not? Unless you want to do a whole series as a subject. That way, you can take part in every test. Would you like that? It's very tedious, I warn you."

"I'd like that."

"Just let me check with Professor Levkov," said Yuri, and he walked over to where Levkov was glancing through some results. After a brief sotto voce conversation, he came back to Katrina.

"No problem. I'll put you with this group here. We'll be ready to go in about five minutes. I'll talk to you afterward."

A few minutes later, Katrina found herself alone in the cubicle, facing the screen. The buzzer sounded, and she concentrated. She wrote down, "Star." The screen showed a circle. Wrong. Buzzer. She wrote, "Square." The screen showed a cross. Wrong again. Buzzer. She wrote, "Wave." The screen showed the wavy lines. Correct. Buzzer…circle…square…wrong. Buzzer…cross…circle…wrong.

At the end of the run, Katrina totted up her correct guesses. Nineteen. That must be about average. Mathematically under average, she reflected. Perhaps she would improve.

For the next run, another subject—a pleasant-looking woman of about forty—was brought in. They smiled politely at each other as they waited for the buzzer. The buzzer sounded, and Katrina reached for her pencil. She hesitated, started to write, "Circ—" and then hesitated again. The screen showed a cross. Buzzer, hesitation. She wrote, "Wave," but she felt uncertain. The screen showed a square. Buzzer. This time, no hesitation. She firmly wrote, "Star." The screen showed a star. Buzzer. Another hesitation, and then she firmly wrote, "Circle." The screen showed a circle. Buzzer. Hesitation, confusion, total blank. The screen flashed a star before she could write anything. And so it went throughout the run. Hesitations. Clear images and blanks. At the end of the run, she felt a little dazed. She added up her correct guesses. Twenty-one. Some improvement, but she could not begin to explain why she had experienced so much hesitation, even if some of the guesses she had made were very clear and firm.

After a brief rest period, a third subject was introduced, and the next run began. This time, Katrina felt even more perplexed. Sometimes when she concentrated, the image in her mind was crystal clear, but more often it was blurred, as if several images were superimposed. By the end of the run, she was beginning to feel very unsure of herself, although when she added up her correct guesses, she still had twenty.

The fourth run was even worse. This time, there was so much confusion in her mind that she only filled in about half of her guesses, and toward the end, she felt quite nauseous. However, as soon as the screen went dead after the hundredth guess, the nausea disappeared, and her mind cleared. She looked round at her partners who seemed relieved it was all over.

"Does that make you feel sick?" she asked them. They looked at each other in astonishment and shook their heads.

"Perhaps it's just me then," Katrina added.

She was glad to get out of the cubicle and find Yuri.

"That's a very unpleasant experience," she told him.

"Unpleasant?" he said with puzzlement. "Boring, certainly. Tedious, tiring, yes. But no one has ever told me it was unpleasant! What do you mean?"

"It made me feel quite dizzy. It's fine alone, but it gets more confusing, more…mixed up, the more people there are. How can I explain it? It's like looking at a television screen with several pictures on it at once."

"What kind of pictures?"

"In this case, squares, circles, crosses, and so on, all mixed up."

"And you don't feel that when you are alone?"

"No."

"And it gets worse the more people there are?"

"Yes."

"That's very interesting. Tell me, Katrina, have you ever done any telepathy tests?"

"No."

"Would you like to do some this afternoon, along with the other subjects?"

"Of course. Anything to be of help." She looked at him closely. "Is there something else?"

"I don't know. I'm just wondering. Perhaps…" He hesitated and then went on in a rush. "Perhaps you'd better do the telepathy tests first." He smiled reassuringly.

"All right," Katrina agreed reluctantly. "Have we finished for the morning? If so, I'll go and get some lunch."

"Yes. Do that. Take your time. And try to think of something else."

Katrina called Anna Gan, and they had lunch together in the university canteen across the gravel square from the institute. It was a beautiful day again, and after lunch, they strolled for a few minutes in the gardens.

"Don't you miss being married?" Anna asked. She was avidly curious in a very friendly way and had soon learnt all about Katrina's previous life.

"Sometimes," Katrina said. "But you know, Yuri and I did not live together long enough to get really used to each other. And since our separation, I have had my work. That has been very absorbing. Of course, there are some things I miss."

Anna giggled. Katrina joined in and said, "No, I don't mean that."

"Well I would," retorted Anna, who had numerous men friends and who had confessed to Katrina that she was longing to get married.

"What I miss," Katrina went on, "is perhaps something I never had with Yuri, which is why our marriage did not work out maybe. What I want is a relationship. I want to feel close to a man, not just sexually. I want to feel—how can I put it?—merged, interwoven, with him. It's something I've never experienced, but I know it has to exist."

"Katrina Klimenkova!" Anna burst out. "Why, you're a raging romantic! I never would have thought it. Don't worry, you'll find your hero one day. Perhaps tonight," she teased, "I wouldn't say no to Leonid Kamikov!"

"Anna, that's a business meeting, and you know it. Although—"

"Although," Anna mocked, and she made an unladylike gesture. Katrina pummeled her, and they turned into the institute almost helpless with laughter.

Levkov finished his explanation. "Are you sure you've got that? It's simple really. Don't press the buzzer until you've finished writing what you think the sender has been sending. All right. First pair."

Katrina and her partner took up their positions, with one in each cubicle. Katrina was to be the sender. She sat at the table, and an assistant placed a pack of square cards facedown in front of her, next to a bell push set into the tabletop.

"Whatever you do, don't change the order of the cards," the assistant said. "Just turn them over one at a time. And press the buzzer each time before you start sending." She smiled. "And relax! You're not at the dentist's. I'm going to leave you now. Take your time. Whenever you're ready."

Katrina turned over the first card, a star, pressed the buzzer, and concentrated on the card's marking. After about five seconds, her own buzzer sounded, indicating that the receiver had written down what he thought she was sending and was ready for the next card. She turned over the second card, a circle, pressed the buzzer, and concentrated. A longer pause this time, seven or eight seconds, before the buzzer sounded. Third card, a cross. And so on. Katrina felt much more relaxed than with the precognition tests. She wondered whether her partner was receiving the correct images. The whole run of a hundred cards took about twelve minutes.

At the end of the run, the assistant reappeared, collected the cards, and asked her if she was ready to continue as the receiver this time. Katrina said she was.

"So when you hear the buzzer, write down what you think your partner is sending. Then when you've finished, press your buzzer to tell him you're ready for the next. All right? Simple, isn't it?"

The assistant left, and when the first buzzer sounded, Katrina immediately wrote down, "Star." She pressed her buzzer and heard an answering signal from her partner. This time she wrote down, "Circle." This was easy. The run was over very quickly, in less than eight minutes.

The assistant came in, took her pad, and said, "It's all over for you. You can go outside and relax. Thank you."

Katrina strolled out and chatted with a few of the other subjects, asking them what they had experienced and how they were enjoying it. Most of them thought it was fun, or at least a change from their usual work. Some of them were intrigued by the whole operation. Others were less curious. She sought out her partner and asked him how many he had scored.

"I did very well, apparently," he said. "I scored twenty-seven out of a hundred. That's very high, I'm told. I'm sure it's because you were giving me such good signals. Otherwise I would have done miserably, I know!" He laughed, and Katrina joined in.

"I wonder how many I scored," she said.

"Oh, they'll tell you in a minute."

Yuri appeared, looking worried, and he took Katrina to one side.

"Excuse me," he said. "I need to speak to you for a moment."

He smiled at the others and led Katrina toward the door. Once outside, Yuri pulled her round and stared at her, white-faced.

"Listen," he said. "You're sure you've never done these tests before?"

"Yes, of course. Why? What's wrong?"

"Katrina. Your score was ninety-two out of a hundred!"

Chapter 10

Sullom Voe, May 23, 2007. 10:45 a.m.

"Now I want you to try that again," said Jim Gardner. "But this time, I want you to concentrate on consistency. Try to keep the signal even."

"Okay," Mike sighed. "One more time. Then how about a break? We've been at this since five this morning, and this harness is killing me."

"Sure." Jim rumbled and struck a tuning fork on the bench in front of him.

Mike eased the web of wires and electrodes running from the top of his head to the nape of his neck. He hummed the note produced by the tuning fork and then closed his eyes and went silent.

After a few minutes, Jim looked across the room to where Dr. Jim Elrich was scanning a bank of gauges. He shook his head, but Jim motioned toward Mike and raised a finger to his lips. Dr. Jim nodded and folded his arms.

Mike sat on the edge of a large vinyl-covered chair, frowning with concentration. A festoon of wires ran from his neck to a litter of apparatus on a long bench to his left, behind which Dr. Jim sat watching. Opposite, behind another bench, Jim Gardner stared at a stopwatch, occasionally pushing back his long hair. Facing Mike, a third bench completed a rectangular U, and behind this, Sam Goldman stood gazing intently at Mike.

This frozen tableau jerked into movement again when Jim, his eyes still on the stopwatch, raised a hand and said, "Time!" Mike relaxed, opened his eyes, and peeled the harness from his head.

Jim stood up and stretched. Sam sat down and made a note on the pad in front of him. Dr. Jim unfolded his arms and leaned forward to adjust the controls of his apparatus.

"Any good?" asked Mike, rubbing his temples.

"Well...better," Jim replied. "I think you must be getting tired."

"Hardly surprising," Mike retorted, "we've been doing this for six solid hours!"

It was eleven in the morning, two weeks after Mike's arrival at Sullom Voe. Since then, Mike, Chuck, Jan, and the rest of the team had settled into a tough schedule of exercises and experiments designed to develop and strengthen the telepathists' natural abilities.

They had started off with simple awareness exercises, learning how to focus their attention for long periods of time and gradually increase their concentration span. They had been taught how to single out their senses and to understand the basic differences between sight, sound, smell, taste, and touch. And they had played endless games devised to develop their memory. At the same time, Dr. Jim had put them through a series of medical and physical tests and had come up with a complete training program which included jogging, calisthenics, volleyball, yoga, and a special set of exercises to strengthen and loosen up the neck muscles. These proved to be particularly valuable during the long sessions like the one Mike had just completed, when the constant concentration threatened to cause tension headaches and stiffness.

As they developed their powers of concentration, they were also taught to relax and to switch on and off at will. Yoga and breathing exercises were an important part of this, but Dr. Jim had also insisted on giving them lengthy explanations of how the mind and the body interreact and how the mind, which is attached to and yet independent from the body, is able to produce different waves, rhythms, and pulses. At first, much of this had seemed too abstract, too theoretical, but now and again, as they began to put the theories into practice, Mike had glimpsed a brief flash of how the bodily machine was able to generate something as intangible as a thought.

Dr. Jim had spoken at great length about the various waves produced by the brain at different times: the low frequency Delta waves, the Theta waves associated with anger and deception, and the faster Alpha waves generated in a state of rest and peacefulness. It was particularly important to recognize the differences between these waves, Dr. Jim had explained, because in his opinion they were closely linked to telepathic states. Furthermore, Dr. Jim believed that with the help of Jim Gardner, the three telepathists could be taught to produce either Alpha waves or Theta waves at will, thus inducing a state favorable either to reception or projection.

Meanwhile, the team was still experimenting with signal strength and regularity. The purpose of the exercise Mike had just completed was to train the mind to lock on to a certain signal, in this case a musical frequency, and attempt to project it in a steady stream. For some reason, Mike found this exercise difficult even if, in most other areas, he was usually superior to his two fellow telepathists who had just been asked to leave the laboratory to see if that would make any difference. It hadn't. Nor had the very early start that morning.

The whole team obviously spent a lot of time together, but by the very nature of things, the three telepathists were placed in very close contact, both physical and mental. Mike got along very well with Chuck, who had turned out to be a refreshingly open and sincere young man and who threw himself into everything, yoga, memory games, and sit-ups, with the same energy and enthusiasm. Jan had continued to be a little pompous and self-opinionated, but since their first meeting, he had not been openly hostile, and, in fact, Mike found him a better telepathic partner than Chuck.

"All right, let's break for something to eat," Jim said. "Then this afternoon, I have a few ideas I'd like us all to kick around."

After a quick lunch at the canteen, the team reassembled in the lab with this time not only Chuck and Jan but also Frank Mambrino and, to Mike's surprise, Colonel Packham. Packham usually kept well away from these working sessions, although Mike knew that he held regular meetings in the evening with the senior scientists. In fact, this was the first time the whole team had come together since the previous Saturday when they had all attended what had threatened to be a rather dreary beach picnic intended to encourage them to get to know each other better but which, in the event, had turned out to be quite a success, in part, no doubt, because it was a welcome relief from the station compound as well as a rest from the tedium of the laboratory.

Since then, Frank had been occupied elsewhere. Packham had remained aloof while the three telepathists met only sporadically in the lab as and when required. In the evening, there was little social life. Jan played chess with one of the station officers. Sometimes, Dr. Jim and Sam Goldman tried to get a bridge four together. Chuck had discovered a passion for the guitar, and one of the drivers was giving him lessons. Mike usually sat in front of the television or watched the sun try to go down over the bay, nursing a large drink from the well-stocked bar.

In any case, there was never much time to be bored. The hours were long and irregular, and it seemed there was always something to be done. No doubt it had been planned that way. After a long day of mental concentration and regular physical exercise in the strong North Sea air, they were usually only too ready to fall into bed.

Packham rapped on the table for attention. "Hi, everyone," he said. "Nice to see you all. Sorry I can't be with you more often, but I hear you've been doing very well. Just a few words, then I'll let you get on with your work. I'm leaving for Washington in a few hours, and I'm glad I'm going to be able to report that you're making progress. I'm not going to be gone long, but in my absence, Jim Gardner will be running the project from a substantive viewpoint. The station commander will of course be responsible for organizational problems and security. And while I'm on that subject, as you know this is a top-secret project, and during my absence, no one, I repeat no one, is to leave the station for any reason whatsoever. I'm afraid that means no jogging outside the compound, Dr. Jim, and no picnics. Sorry, but it's my neck, and I want to keep it. Okay, Jim. You can take over now. I'll say good-bye to you all, and when I get back, I'll organize another picnic."

With this Packham raised a hand in a gesture of salute and strode out, leaving an embarrassed silence which Jim finally broke with his deep bass.

"All right, everyone. Relax." He nodded at the door. "He had to say it. It's his job. Let's just get on with the job in hand."

He smiled round the group. "Come on. I know he doesn't sound real sometimes, but he doesn't often get on our backs, now does he?"

"We can still jog round the compound, can't we?" said Chuck.

"Chuck, you're something else," Mike snorted. "How can you say something like that? That's not the point."

"Well I think it's a very positive attitude to take," Jan added.

"Come on, fellas, it's only for a few days," Frank said.

"Come on now," Jim intervened, "let's not make a huge thing out of this. You're acting like a bunch of kids. Really. We've got much better things to do. Okay?"

He smiled round the group again, shaking his head, and there were a couple of "okays."

"Very well then. The reason we are here is to discuss signals. So far, you've been in training, rather like raw recruits. We've been trying to get you into some kind of shape. Except maybe you're more like athletes. No, a better comparison would be opera singers. We have shown you how to differentiate between notes, how to breathe correctly, how to develop tone and volume. We've taught you how to relax and build up your stamina. We've worked at strengthening your lungs and vocal cords, as it were. But... but so far, we haven't told you what you're going to sing. In other words, to return to telepathic terms, you are beginning to know how to project a signal, but you don't yet know what that signal is. This is what we're going to try to explain this afternoon. Sam, would you take it from here? You're the signals expert."

"Thanks, Jim," Sam said.

"Let me start off by saying that we don't know how to communicate with extraterrestrials. If we did, I guess we'd have done it already. So in this, as in many other things, we are going to have to proceed by trial and error. We're going to be groping in the dark. However, we have learned enough from existing communications systems to be able to establish some pretty solid principles to work on.

"Let's examine some of them, because I'd like you to really understand what you're going to be involved in. Now, how do we normally communicate?"

They looked at each other, and after a pause, Frank put up his hand. Sam nodded encouragingly, and Frank shone a smile.

"We talk," he said.

"Right," Sam said. "We communicate by talking to each other, although there are other forms of communication, depending on what we're trying to communicate."

Jan nodded intelligently. Mike sat impassive. Chuck looked a little puzzled and cleared his throat.

"Er, how do you mean?" he said.

"Well, Chuck," Sam said with simulated coyness, "I'm sure you'd be able to make it clear to a pretty girl that you're interested in her, without having to talk. Right?"

"Oh yeah," said Chuck. "Yeah, I see. Like the way you look at her."

"That's it. There are all kinds of signals between people which effectively communicate wants or desires or feelings or emotions. But if you want to say something a little complicated, we have to use speech, you know, to explain ideas, events, situations, and so on. Speech is fine as long as people are within talking distance. What happens when they are too far apart? How can they communicate then?"

"I suppose it depends on several factors," Jan said. "If they are out of earshot but within sight, they can use signals, semaphore, or some such method. And if they are out of sight, then they would have to resort to something like a telephone, or a telegraph, or radio or, of course, a messenger or written message."

"Good," said Sam. "You've managed to use a lot of different words which I'd like us to examine—words like signal, message, messenger. They'll help us to understand what the communication process is all about. If we examine all these different situations, speech, telephone, semaphore, letter, or messenger even, we'll find three things in common. I wonder if you can identify them."

Mike sat forward in his chair. Sam was acting like a schoolteacher, and that irritated him a little, but he was posing the kind of questions that Mike had often asked himself about mind reading.

"Well," Mike said, "in all these cases, there is a technical carrier: the voice, the letter, the telephone wire, the radio wave. Am I on the right track?"

"Yes, indeed you are. How about calling that the medium? It's just a word, but we might as well give it a name. Okay. Then what does the medium do? You used a good word just now. You said it was a carrier. What does the medium carry?"

"A message."

"Ultimately yes, but this message is expressed by something else. Let's say you get a phone call. The phone rings, you pick it up, and someone speaks to you in Chinese. What are you getting? A message?"

"Not if I don't understand it," Mike replied.

"Exactly. It may be a message, but you don't know what it means."

Sam looked at Mike, who remained blank.

"Okay, let's try something else. Let's say you're listening to the radio, and you pick up some Morse. If you understand Morse, you can understand the message. But if you don't, what is it you are getting?"

Mike thought for a while. "Just a series of sounds or signals."

"Ah. Right," said Sam. "Now you've got it. First you have the medium. Then a signal. Then, if you can understand the signal, a message. With a telephone, for example, the medium is the phone system itself—the handset, microphone, cable, earphone etc. The signal is the noise coming down it. And the message is what you understand from the noise. With a letter, the paper is the medium, the written word is the signal or symbol, and the message is the meaning. And so on and so forth. Everybody got that? It's a pretty crude way of presenting a very complex problem, but I think it may be understandable."

They all nodded.

"Telepathy may not fit into this pattern," Mike said thoughtfully.

"How do you mean?" Jim said.

"Well, in your sequence, you have three elements—medium, signal, and message, you called them. I think the telepathic process may be more direct. When I read someone's thoughts, I am not aware of there being a signal. I mean I think I pick up the thought directly. If you assume the telepathic process to be the medium and the thought the message, there is no intermediate element."

"Are you sure about that?" asked Sam.

"I'm trying to remember if I have ever read the thoughts of someone whose language I don't speak. I don't think so. But that would be a case in point, wouldn't it? If I could read the thoughts without understanding the language in between?"

"Possibly, but I wonder how accurate that would be."

"It can be terribly accurate, believe me," Mike said. "You can tell exactly what someone is thinking."

"Exactly?"

"Sure! Exactly what they're seeing and feeling and hearing."

"What would happen if the person whose thoughts you are reading is blind or deaf? Would you then be able to tell what he's 'seeing'?"

"I don't know."

"Or feeling?" Sam went on. "How accurate is a feeling? What is the shape and size and weight of an emotion? This is a very complex process we're discussing now. I take your point that mind reading may seem more direct, perhaps it is, but maybe in this case the intermediate element is the perception, you know, the eye or ear or whatever. Maybe there's a hidden step we haven't even mentioned. Philosophers and linguists have been arguing about this problem for centuries, and I don't think we're going to solve it today.

"I know," Mike said.

But the point of what I'm trying to say is that extraterrestrials may not have the same sensory mechanisms we have. They may not even have any eyes or ears at all, although I think that is highly unlikely.

"And as for feelings, who knows? I mean I am sure my range of feelings is somewhat different to yours or Chuck's or Jan's. It's a question of upbringing and experience and education, plus a number of other factors, probably. But there is bound to be a world of difference between my feelings and values and perceptions and those of an extraterrestrial. So there is no guarantee that thought forms or mental processes will be in any way comparable."

Sam fell silent and seemed to wait for a response.

"Does that mean we can't communicate with the extraterrestrials at all then?" said Chuck.

"No, I think we can. But you are going to have to change all your ideas about communication. In all likelihood, there will be two communication situations, which I am going to call 'long distance' and 'local.' Let's take long distance first. Now, we have no reason to suppose that telepathic transference is able to cover distance faster than radio waves or even light. Of course, it may. We just don't know. But judging by every other known phenomenon in the universe, it would seem unlikely. So we're up against a time problem."

"Light years," Jan said, nodding.

"Precisely." Sam agreed. "Even if telepathic transference operates at the speed of light, it would take many years to reach the closest inhabitable star. At the time I was working at Green Bank, the Royal Greenwich Observatory produced a catalogue of what it called 'candidate stars'—that is, stars capable of supporting life as we know it, and fairly close to earth. It came up with some six hundred stars, all within eighty light years. That's close, by astronomical standards, but if we're talking in terms of communication, it makes dialogue difficult, to say the least. That's what I meant by changing our ideas about communication. In these circumstances, communication ceases to be a two-way process. You can send a message, but you shouldn't really expect an answer, or at least not within fifty or sixty years. But we can and should be sending information into space on the assumption that someone or something, some form of intelligence, is out there somewhere listening."

"Now wait a minute," Mike interrupted, "what language are we going to use?"

"I'm coming to that in just a minute," Sam replied. "Let me first touch on the other situation, local communication. You'll see why. In a local situation, you could expect to communicate with extraterrestrials located in a spacecraft, close to Earth. Now firstly, there would not be the time lag you would have with long-distance communication, and secondly, it might be supposed that extraterrestrials on reconnaissance missions around the earth would have some knowledge of our languages. One could expect them to monitor our radio communications and, God forbid, our radio and television programs. Furthermore, through this contact, they would have some familiarity with our customs and lifestyles and thought patterns. What I am saying is that even without language, they'd be able to grasp our thought shapes and perceptions and maybe even our feelings and emotions. This may answer part of your question, Mike, but only part."

Mike nodded, and Sam went on. "Okay, let's get back to long-distance communication, our one-way information process. And we're back straightaway to the problem of what we want to say and how we're going to say it. You remember over the last four days, we've been trying to get you to project musical frequencies. This is because we're going to turn you into telepathic Morse transmitters."

"How are they going to understand Morse, if they don't understand English?" Jan inquired, looking around with a self-satisfied smirk.

"We won't be using Morse code as you know it but a binary code made up of dots and dashes, or short and long signals, if you prefer. We'll be giving you a series of these signals to transmit telepathically."

"What makes you think this binary code will be understood any better than Morse?"

"Because it's not based on language. You see, binary code is basic to electronics and molecular structures and even the phenomena of electro-magnetism. And of course, it's basic to all computers and computer language. Anyone with any knowledge of advanced science, as we would suppose these extraterrestrials to be, would be familiar with its principle. Now, using the binary principle, you can establish a long string of dots and dashes which when they are added up and interpreted will be seen to express certain ideas."

"Like what?" Mike intervened. "If I'm going to be talking to extraterrestrials, I think I'd like to know what I'm saying."

"Well, there'd be different ideas like, for instance, our number system from one to ten, or the atomic numbers of the basic elements that are important to the carbon-based chemistry of our human life on earth. And then, these dots and dashes can be arranged to form a picture showing the solar system and our position in it. All kinds of things like that, space coordinates, chemical formulae, the DNA molecule, and so on."

"Wouldn't they know all these things already?" Chuck asked.

"Oh, certainly. Most of them. The point is they would give an indication of where we are in space and how advanced we are scientifically. It might be comforting for them to know there are other living beings in space.

"Wouldn't they know that from their space missions?" Chuck insisted.

"They may not be the same beings. You see, there are thousands, maybe millions, of planets capable of supporting life. We don't know who we may reach. And they probably don't know each other either, just as only a few hundred years ago, the people on either side of the Atlantic didn't know each other, and they were only a few thousand miles apart."

"So how are we going to go about this?" Mike asked after a pause. "It seems to me we're talking about several different things at once, different people, different distances, different messages, different directions."

"That's right," Jim intervened in his deep drawl, "and that's why we are going to start working to a very precise schedule from now on. You're going to find yourselves involved in four basic modes which we have decided to call 'long-distance receive,' 'local receive,' 'long-distance send,' and 'local send.' These are radio terms, but I think they are self-explanatory, and there is no possible confusion between them. For each of these modes, you will be given either standing instructions or specific messages or guidelines. You will be working different periods—I don't like the word *shift*—mainly during the day, but I also want to establish a few night operations. We don't really have enough staff to cover a twenty-four-hour period, but we can schedule random watches. It's the best we can do with available resources. I'll be handing round rosters so that you know when you'll be required, but we're not planning to use each of you more than nine hours in any twenty-four-hour period, although these schedules may be modified later, and of course you may wish to volunteer for extra hours if you're not tired. We'll be starting these new schedules tomorrow morning. Any questions?"

The meeting broke up into a general discussion about messages and work schedules, and Mike sat back and thought over what he had just heard. A lot of it made sense, but there were still too many holes, and he could not make up his mind whether Sam was being totally honest with them or blinding them with science. Jim, Dr. Jim, and Sam certainly knew their subject and were making a good job of training them, as far as he could tell. Frank was something of a mystery still. He rarely appeared at the lab, and nobody seemed to know what he got up to, although he never left the station. Mike had asked him once where he worked, but he had been evasive, gesturing vaguely toward one of the huts.

But the big mystery remained Hal Packham. What made him function? What were his motivations? Who had trained him? And why did he have to go to Washington so often?

Chapter 11

Moscow, May 23, 2007. 4:00 p.m.

Katrina had had a very exciting day. After the surprise results of her efforts in the laboratory, Yuri had rushed her off to see Professor Levkov. At first, Levkov was skeptical.

"Ninety-two out of a hundred? That's impossible!"

"But look, Professor," said Yuri, "here are the results. And remember, she guessed your number."

"Hmm. That's true."

"I thought there was something unusual when Katrina complained about feeling dizzy during the precognition tests this morning. Tell Professor Levkov what you felt, Katrina."

"It was like looking at a television set with several pictures superimposed on each other, only all in my head of course. And the more people there were in the cubicle, the worse it became."

"You see, Professor," Yuri went on excitedly, "that must have meant she was picking up the thoughts of the other people in the cubicle."

"Did you feel anything when you were alone in the cubicle?" Levkov asked.

"No," replied Katrina. "That's just it, but as I said, the more people there were, the more confused I felt."

"The only explanation was that she was getting interference from the others. That's why I asked her to do the telepathy tests this afternoon."

"This is amazing," said Levkov. "Would you mind doing another test?" he asked Katrina. "I'll clear the lab, and we can do some really serious work."

They had run three more tests with one of the lab assistants as a sender, and each time Katrina had achieved extremely high scores. And so as they stood in the lab studying the results, they all felt very exhilarated.

"This is wonderful, my dear," Levkov stated with enthusiasm. "It is incredible but wonderful. With someone like you, there is no limit to what we can do. Oh, I can't wait to tell Professor Kamikov."

Katrina smiled to herself. Perhaps she would have the pleasure of telling Kamikov herself this evening. But she still felt puzzled by it all.

"Professor Levkov," she said, "why do you think I can do those tests so easily?"

"Obviously, you're a born telepathist. You have a natural gift, and it's a superb one at that."

"But why haven't I discovered it before?"

"I really don't know. Haven't you ever noticed anything before today? Guessed what people were thinking, for example, and felt you knew what someone was going to say before they said it?"

"No, never."

"Well, I don't understand. Perhaps it's a gift you've suddenly developed. All I know is that you're able to perceive Zener cards telepathically through another subject in standard laboratory conditions with phenomenal accuracy. If we can get Kamikov's approval, I'd like to do some more advanced tests with you and really see what you can do. Let's go to his office now and see if we can see him immediately."

"I think he said he had an outside appointment this afternoon," said Yuri, looking at his watch, "but it's late already. Maybe he has come back. We could try to see if he is there."

They walked down the corridor to Kamikov's office. As they entered, Tanya, Kamikov's secretary, smiled and said, "Oh, Miss Klimenkova, I have been trying to reach you everywhere. I have an urgent message for you from Professor Kamikov."

"So he isn't here then?" asked Levkov.

"No, Professor, he was out this afternoon, and now he's at home working on something."

"Oh well, I'll be able to call him there. Katrina, come to see me tomorrow, and I'll tell you what he said. Come along, Yuri. I want to go over those results again before I call him."

The two men strode out, leaving Katrina behind. She looked expectantly at Tanya. No doubt Professor Kamikov would not be able to see her that evening. That must be what the message was. She sighed and felt a little let down after all the excitement, suddenly realizing how much she had been looking forward to her evening.

"Now," said Tanya, picking up a folder, "the professor has asked me to tell you that he needs this file at home as soon as possible and that he needs to talk to you about it. He's expecting an urgent call and cannot go out. So would you mind running it round to his apartment on your way home?"

She smiled and looked at Katrina with sympathy.

"I hope it doesn't take you too far out of your way."

She handed her a typewritten slip. "Here's the address. Do you know where that is?"

Katrina glanced at the address and nodded. Her spirits lifted. Maybe the evening was not ruined after all. She said good night and hurried down to the cloakroom to change. There was a message on her locker door that said: "Urgent: Please contact Kamikov's office before leaving. Have a good evening! Anna."

Katrina smiled as she smoothed her hair in front of the mirror. Anna was impossible!

Leonid Kamikov lived in central Moscow, not far from the racetrack, so it was still only six-thirty when Katrina walked out of the Byelorussia metro station and turned right along Gruzinsky Val Ulitsa. Kamikov's apartment building was on the corner of Gruzinsky and Presnensky. It was not a very fashionable residential area, although it was certainly central, and Katrina wondered why a man as powerful and influential as Kamikov would choose to live there. Perhaps it was just another indication of his unconventionality.

She had seen enough of him over the last few weeks to realize that he did have an unconventional mind. His approach to the already highly unconventional field of parapsychology was unusual in itself, while in political matters, he was as much a rebel as anyone could be in the Soviet Union, and he got away with it. He was unconventional in other areas too. He worked the oddest hours, took his meals at the most unusual times, and, on occasion, he arrived at the office in Cossack boots and smock which, Katrina thought privately, suited his flamboyant figure very well. She wondered what his apartment would be like.

She walked up the two flights of stairs to his apartment and rang. She had to ring twice before he answered.

"Ah, Katrina. You brought my file. Thank you. Come in, come in! I'll be with you in a moment. I'm on the phone. You arrived just in time with my file. You can wait in there."

He took the folder from Katrina and motioned to the living room. He stepped into a study off the entrance hall. Katrina heard him pick up the phone and continue his conversation. She walked into the living room.

It certainly was unconventional—unconventional for Moscow, that is. Katrina had been half expecting samovars and bearskin rugs, something overstated and larger than life. Instead, she was confronted with cool, contemporary Scandinavian: stainless steel, glass, oiled wood, low furniture, and a thick white carpet. Across one entire wall was a long glass and steel shelf unit, complete with a B&O CD player and perhaps a thousand CDs. A small sculpture stood on a low glass table. It looked like a Brancusi. Could it be? On the shelves were books on art, ballet, philosophy, and religion in Russian, English, German, and French. And seemingly out of place in such a contemporary decor, a splendid bronze of a galloping horse was on a wide mantle above the brick and steel fireplace. Katrina ran a hand over the horse's broad, muscle-knotted back.

"Are you fond of horses?"

She, startled, dropped her hand, and wheeled round to face a smiling Kamikov, who looked bigger than ever standing in the doorway.

"No. Yes. I mean, yes, of course I do—or am, rather. And it's such a beautiful sculpture."

"Yes, it is. Thank you for bringing me that file. I've been fighting the ministry over budgets for the last two weeks. Anyway that's all over now. We can relax. And since you're here, let's have a drink. I have a bottle of French Macon I'd like you to taste. Just sit down and make yourself comfortable while I open it."

He went out and returned a few minutes later with a bottle in an ice bucket and two glasses. He poured a glass and handed it to Katrina, who had seated herself on a deep suede sofa in front of the window. He poured himself a glass and lowered his massive frame onto the sofa next to her.

"Santé, my dear," he said.

They touched glasses and drank.

"Mm! That's good," Katrina exclaimed.

Kamikov drained his glass and filled it again. "Very good. Have some more." Katrina held out her glass. "I wanted to talk to you about your work, ask you how you were enjoying it, and so on. By all accounts, you seem to be doing well. Everyone likes you. You ask intelligent questions. And now, on top of all that, it appears you're a telepathic phenomenon. Levkov telephoned me just before you arrived. You know, he's very excited. So is young Barchenko. They say they've never seen anything like it."

He paused. Katrina did not know what to say.

"I was just as surprised as they were. Professor Levkov said we would be able to do all kinds of important experiments. I feel like I would be doing something useful for the country. And that makes me proud. I've always wanted to do that." She stopped and smiled foolishly.

"Well, it's nothing to be ashamed of," Kamikov said. "It's quite a discovery. You should be happy. Here, have some more wine. We should celebrate."

He filled Katrina's glass again and smiled into her eyes.

"We're going to do great things together," he said softly, raising his glass in salute.

Katrina smiled back at Kamikov across the raised glasses and felt a thrill of excitement run through her. He wanted her. She could feel it. And she could sense a hard surge of desire behind those smiling eyes.

"Professor," she began.

"Leonid, please."

"Leonid, may I ask you a question?" He nodded. "What made you choose to live in this neighborhood?"

Kamikov laughed softly. "You think you're changing the subject, but you're not. The reason I live in this neighborhood is because it's close to two of my three passions in life: horses and ballet. The racetrack is just across the street, and the Bolshoi is only a few minutes' walk down Gorki. So it suits me very well."

He put a large, gentle hand on her shoulder, and Katrina shifted slightly as a flush of warmth spread through her hips. God, it had been a long time.

"You haven't asked me what my third passion is," he said.

"I don't think I need to," she replied.

"That's right, you're a mind reader!"

He moved his hand a little lower down. She tensed and made a soft noise and then reached out and pulled him toward her. After a while, she said in his ear: "Why did you tell Tanya that you wanted to discuss that file with me?"

"I was concerned about your honor," he said.

She giggled. He lifted her in his arms and carried her into his bedroom. He was big and strong and hard, and Katrina let herself be dominated, abandoning herself to his caresses. He was an expert lover, and her body responded, building to a long, straining climax that left her drained and curiously empty. As he turned onto his back, she realized she had felt nothing inside—no love, no affection, no tenderness. In him, too, she had felt no response but only an intense desire which had peaked and ebbed, leaving a cold void. She had often thought of Kamikov as an animal, a powerful male animal, and that had attracted her female instincts. But the union she had vainly sought with Yuri, and other men, still escaped her. Did it exist? She knew it had to. She turned on her side. Kamikov was staring at the ceiling. She put an arm across his huge chest, in a gesture of affection. She could at least pretend! He smiled and patted her hand.

"Well, that was very nice, my dear. We must do it again some time."

She withdrew her arm and sat up.

"What time is it?" she said.

"Eight thirty."

"I have to leave. My father is expecting me."

"All right. I have to go to a reception in a little while anyway."

They both got up. Kamikov threw on a robe while Katrina dressed and made herself presentable. When she came out of the bedroom, he was sprawled on the floor reading and listening to some modern music, with the wine bottle, now almost empty, next to him. When he saw her, he rose.

"Good-bye," he said, putting both hands on her shoulders.

"Good-bye," she replied, reaching up to kiss his cheek.

"You must come again," he said, opening the door.

"Yes, I will."

They both knew she never would.

An hour and a half later, Kamikov walked up the steps of the French embassy, resplendent in full evening dress and decorations.

The entrance was ablaze with light as limousines arrived to deposit or collect guests, and liveried footmen scurried to and fro, bowing and opening doors. Kamikov presented a card and was ushered toward the crowded ballroom.

The occasion was an official visit by the French minister of foreign affairs, who stood in the receiving line next to the French ambassador and their wives.

"Monsieur le Professeur Leonid Kamikov," the usher intoned.

"Ah, Monsieur le Professeur!" His Excellency, the ambassador exclaimed. "So glad you could come."

"Votre Excellence," Kamikov murmured.

"I'd like you to meet our foreign minister, Bertrand de Casteyrand."

"Monsieur le Ministre, I am honored."

The minister made a few diplomatic noises, and Kamikov was about to move on into the ballroom.

"Just a moment," the French ambassador said. "Young Gaudreau, you know, our attaché culturel, wanted to talk to you." He beckoned to an aide.

"Langlois, allez me chercher Gaudreau, s'il vous plaît. Dîtes lui que j'ai besoin de lui tout de suite! Oui, mon cher Kamikov, he wants to talk to you about a meeting of scientists in Paris next month."

Within minutes, Gaudreau appeared, led Kamikov to the bar, gave him a drink, pushed him into a seat, and launched into a long description of the meeting he wanted to the Soviet scientist to chair. Kamikov told him he wouldn't be free and excused himself to join a group of men standing by the window. As he approached, one of the men detached himself from the group and stepped forward to greet him. He was a thickset man with heavy jowls and the long upper lip of the Georgian peasant.

"Leonid Kamikov, old friend."

"Anatol Lopukhin, greetings. I haven't seen you in a long time."

"Let's get out of here and find a real drink," the thickset man boomed. "I need some vodka." He lowered his voice. "Leonid, I only came tonight because I was told you would be here. Levkov tells me you have a new discovery."

"Levkov talks too much," Kamikov said. "But that is correct. I think you should meet her. She's young and enthusiastic. She's highly educated, phenomenally gifted, and ready to do anything for her country."

"She sounds perfect."

"And I'll tell you something else…" He leaned down and whispered in his ear. The two men burst out laughing and walked out, clapping each other on the back.

Chapter 12

Washington, DC, May 28, 2007. 3:00 p.m.

The Eastern shuttle from New York banked sharply over the Potomac River for its final approach into Washington National Airport. Seated on the right hand side of the aircraft, Colonel Henry Packham enjoyed an excellent view of the Pentagon, where he had a number of appointments that morning.

Packham had not come directly from Sullom Voe. He had made a number of stops on the way. First of all, he had stopped in London for a routine meeting with Mike Stanton. He had also held less routine talks with two special advisers at the Norwegian embassy.

Then he had flown to Paris where he had met a man he knew only as Crespin, but whom other men in France referred to as Le Furet—the Ferret. They had met in a stone villa in the once prosperous suburb of Choisy-le-Roi. There Packham had turned over a large sum of money in exchange for a thick file which he had studied throughout the flight across the Atlantic.

In New York, he had stopped for talks with leaders of the delegation to the next meeting of the United Nations Committee on the Peaceful Uses of Outer Space (Subcommittee Three), scheduled to be held in two days' time. Sitting in the offices of the US delegation, right across the street from UN headquarters, he had been briefed on plans to introduce a resolution calling for a united front in the eventuality of contact with extraterrestrial intelligence. The drafting officers were still tinkering with the language, but it would run along the lines of "As champions of the cause of peace and true democracy and as leaders of the free world, etc., the United States calls upon all nations inspired by the same principles, etc., to cooperate fully and join together to present a united front to representatives of civilizations or peoples from space, etc., etc." There were a number of technical clauses concerning the mechanisms and procedures projected to implement the main thrust of the resolution and offering data handling infrastructures and training for those countries requiring assistance.

The resolution was of course intended to perform several functions. While reaffirming the traditional position of the United States as leader of the free world, it also attempted to give the United States a lead role in formulating a worldwide approach to extraterrestrial matters. The offers of training and technical support were calculated to stir interest among the developing nations, thus creating some influence leverage from which to bargain with the Russians over the question of the monitoring mechanisms launched at the last meeting and included as item four on the agenda of the next meeting.

"What a waste of time and effort," Packham thought as he recovered his garment bag and hurried out of the airport where a car was waiting to drive him to the Pentagon.

He spent the morning discussing administrative matters. Since the Sullom Voe project was top secret, there were a number of problems involving payment and requisition codes which he had been unable to clear up by letter or e-mail. Top secret or not, the Pentagon's accounting department wanted some kind of justification for the extra expenditures Packham had incurred. He sorted it all out in the end, not without difficulty, and then had lunch with the assistant secretary for defense, Andrew Fitch, who was technically responsible for the project but who in fact did not know all the details. Not that he wanted to. He was skeptical about the whole question of extraterrestrial life and thought the money expended on the project would be far better spent on a nuclear warhead or a couple of tanks. He had no idea of the oil dimensions behind the project.

"And then all this UN crap," he confided toward the end of the meal. "I sometimes cannot believe that we're spending all this money just to keep a bunch of Russian spies in New York. Everyone knows the UN is riddled with them."

"At least we know where they are like that," Packham suggested gently.

"Okay, maybe. But is that any reason to pay them for it?"

Packham smiled. He had been over this argument so many times, particularly with military people who did not think it was necessarily better to talk rather than to fight or to debate rather than to kill each other. Usually, officials such as the secretary for defense and his assistants played the role of doves against the army's hawks, but Fitch was an exception.

"Anyway," Fitch went on a little more calmly, after drinking some coffee, "that's not your fault. To come back to this project of yours, how long do you expect it to go on? Because I'm having a hell of a time finding unmarked funding. If you're going to go on into the next fiscal year, we're going to have to find some way of getting it in the budget. What do you say?"

Packham had to be careful here, because Fitch did not know the project was already operational, nor did he know what the project was really all about. Outside the White House, very few people knew that.

"It's going to take a while," Packham began. "Once we get started, I expect it'll take us a couple of years to get any results, unless we're very lucky."

"A couple of years? I wasn't told that. I was told it was a short-term project."

"Well, as I say, we may get lucky."

"Does the secretary know this?"

"I don't know. Perhaps you'd better ask him. "

"You bet you I'm going to ask him."

Packham felt sorry for Fitch, who was obviously being kept in the dark about several aspects of the project. Still, that couldn't be helped, and judging from Fitch's outbursts over lunch, perhaps there was very good reason not to entrust him with details.

"Come on, Andie, I'm just doing a job," he said. "Don't get mad at me. I'll walk you back to your office. I'm expecting a call, and I told the switchboard to put it through to your number."

Fitch's secretary had taken the call.

"The White House called," she said, visibly impressed, "confirming your appointment with Scott Brady at three-thirty this afternoon."

Scott Brady, White House Chief of Staff, welcomed Packham at the door of his office, which was just a few doors down from the president's office.

"Come in, Colonel Packham. I haven't had the pleasure of meeting you, but I've heard a lot about you."

Scott Brady, wunderkind of the administration and apple of the president's eye, was a slight young man in his early thirties. His striking good looks, easy charm, and incisive intellect had made him a great favorite with both the press and the general public, but he was disliked by a number of key figures in the Washington establishment.

"You must be wondering why I wanted to see you," Brady said, after they had sunk into a pair of battered leather armchairs. Packham certainly was. He had been told of the meeting by Mike Stanton in London. He knew the White House was aware of the project and had indeed given its approval, but his line of communication had always been with the Pentagon and Defense, in the shape of the secretary of defense himself. So it had come as a surprise that no less a person than Scott Brady wished to meet him during his trip to Washington. He did not feel entirely comfortable about the matter, however, because he was not certain how much Brady knew about the project. It might be embarrassing to have to refuse information.

"I was a little surprised, yes," he said. "What was it you wanted to see me about?"

Brady burst out laughing. "How many things do you think we have to discuss together? Colonel Packham, I admire your tact, but let me put you at ease. I know everything there is to know about your project. Just in case you have any doubts, the top clearance code word is 'Lone Wolf.' Does that make things easier for you?"

"Yes, it does. Thank you." As far as Packham knew, only six people were in possession of the code word, and one of those was the president. It would be natural for the Chief of Staff, particularly since he was so close to the president, to have been given the code word.

"Now we've cleared the air, perhaps you can tell me how the project is progressing."

"Very well indeed. If you have been reading the coded traffic, you will know we recruited this Afghanistan veteran, Mike Marshall. He is turning out to be even better than expected. My senior scientists tell me that he is absolutely fantastic and that he has at least tripled the effectiveness of the team. So I'm very pleased about that. Also, we went operational three days ago. I'm not expecting any immediate results, but who knows? In any case, we couldn't hope for any results until we became operational. So, Mr. Brady, all in all, we are progressing extremely well, and I am confident that if we can establish contact, we'll take the lead on oil production and availability, which of course is what this is all about."

"How far do you think the Russians have progressed?"

"It's impossible to say, of course, but I have no reason to suppose they are ahead of us."

"Good. That's what I was hoping you would say. Colonel Packham, I want you to know that the president is squarely behind this project. We had a talk about it only this morning, and I can tell you that he is very anxious for it to succeed. Now, listen carefully. I cannot stress enough the importance of our being the first to establish contact with the extraterrestrials. It is absolutely vital. I want to make certain you understand why. That is why I asked you to come.

"You can imagine the immense international prestige to be gained from being the first country to communicate with extraterrestrial intelligence." Packham nodded. "The effect would be stunning, as you must be aware. But there are also domestic political ramifications you may not have considered."

"Go on," Packham said.

"Let's say we make contact with the extraterrestrials. Apart from the prestige aspects, there would be a lot of pressure from the international community for us to become the world's spokesman vis-à-vis the extraterrestrials. At some point, the Russians would have to swallow their pride and join in for the sake of international solidarity, universal brotherhood, and so on. They could not afford to be isolated. They would hate it, of course, but the pressure would be too great to ignore. In other words, they would have to negotiate with us. Now, just imagine the bargaining position that would put us in: The president would be able to dictate his terms, up to a point."

"It would certainly put him in a very powerful position," Packham remarked thoughtfully, and then he added with a smile, "and it wouldn't do his popularity any harm either, particularly with the oil cartel, which as you are aware has been very supportive of this administration."

"That's right, but that's not for public consumption of course. As far as the public would know, he'd be able to impose a strategic arms treaty with the Russians that would not only limit but even drastically reduce armaments. In one stroke, he would slash the risk of nuclear warfare and at the same time achieve giant spending cuts. And just think what he could do with the money saved. He could initiate whole new social programs, pour funds into energy research, rebuild the environment, beef up foreign aid. Why, he would be the most popular president ever to sit in the White House."

"I can see why the president is interested in this project," Packham said with a wry smile.

"Then you can understand why it is imperative to succeed," Brady retorted. "I think I have said enough already, and I know you are just as interested as we are in the success of the project, but I want you to spare no effort to make it work. If there is anything you need, give me a call on this number." He scribbled on a slip of paper and handed it to Packham. "This comes straight into my office, and only I answer it. Is there anything you need right now?"

Packham reported the conversation he had had with Andie Fitch and the need to put the project funding on a more permanent footing.

"Okay," said Brady, making a note on a yellow legal pad, "I'll fix Fitch. He's a an idiot. I'll get the secretary of defense to explain to him in words of one syllable what is at stake. Don't worry. That'll be taken care of. Anything else?"

"Yes, I need a car for this evening. I don't need a chauffeur. Just a car. Can you fix it?"

"Sure," Brady said. He put his head back and yelled, "Jack!" A door behind Brady's desk opened, and a strongly built man in shirt sleeves appeared.

"Jack, this is Colonel Packham. Can you swing a vehicle from the car pool for him tonight? Colonel, if you go with Jack and tell him where and when you want it, I'm sure it can be arranged. And if there's anything else you need, just give me a call."

"Thanks," Packham said as they shook hands. "I appreciate it."

"And don't forget what I told you. We've got to get there first!"

Packham spent the rest of the afternoon on routine calls and a few personal matters. When he checked into his hotel, there was already a set of keys in his mailbox with a note telling him where the White House pool car was parked and what to do when he had finished with it. Brady's people were efficient.

That evening, he drove out to a house in Virginia, about thirty miles from Washington. He had wanted to drive himself so that no one would know where he was going. However, as he crossed Memorial Bridge toward Arlington, he failed to notice the gray Toyota that tucked itself in behind him in the Virginia traffic lane and then continued to follow him. The house in Virginia was an old one; it was covered in creeper and set well back from the road in several acres of wooded land. There was an intercom system at the gate, and he had to say who he was before the gate opened. As he talked in the microphone, the Toyota drove slowly past and disappeared round the corner.

There were already three cars standing in the drive in front of the entrance. Packham parked next to them and rang the bell. The man who opened the door recognized him immediately and showed him into a book-lined study, closing the door behind him. Packham blinked in surprise as he looked round the room. Two of the men present were well-known to him. They were neither White House, nor Pentagon, nor State Department. The third he had never met, but he knew his face from a thousand press photographs. It was James Farrel, the president's national security adviser.

Farrel held out his hand. "Colonel Packham. I'm glad to know you."

They shook hands. Farrel motioned with his head. "The others you know, of course. I'm sure you didn't expect to see me here tonight, but there's a reason. I know you had a meeting with Scott Brady at the White House this afternoon." He paused.

"I'm not denying it," Packham said. "There was nothing secret about it."

"I'm not saying there was. Brady told you why it is vitally important for your project to succeed, and he gave you a number of reasons."

Packham remained silent.

"He told you why it was important, and he gave you a number of reasons," Farrel repeated. "Tonight, I'm going to tell you the real reason."

Two days later, a little after ten a.m., Packham walked across to the UN with Jack Schultz, the leader of the US delegation to the Committee on the Peaceful Uses of Outer Space (Sub-Committee 3) which was scheduled.

"Do you think your resolution will go through?" Packham asked as they waited to push their way through the revolving door at the main entrance.

"Oh sure," Schultz replied, "with a little pushing. There'll be some modifications, but no one is going to come out against the need for a united front. Everyone will support all the fancy stuff about democracy and basic freedoms and so on, even if privately they have reservations. As for the technical clauses, we're prepared to negotiate if Lopukhin and his gang agree to back off on their resolution about monitoring signals. Do you remember that? Yes, you were at the last meeting, weren't you? The Russians put forward an agenda item on the verification of signals. Well, since then, they've sent a detailed resolution to the committee bureau which sets out monitoring procedures. It really boils down to another attempt to control broadcasting."

"Oh my God," groaned Packham, "not again!"

"I'm afraid so." He hesitated and consulted a sheaf of papers in his hand. "It's in S31. We have to go down one."

The conference room was already pretty full, and Bhongar, the outgoing chairman, called the meeting to order promptly at ten-thirty.

"Ladies and gentlemen, the first item on the agenda, and my last act as chairman of this subcommittee, is to proceed to the election of a new chairman. The bureau is ready to receive nominations."

The meeting settled down into a comfortable squabble for the chair between the Arab group and the African group. The Africans finally carried the day after a roll-call vote, and the new chairman, Dr. Tobias Mensah of Ghana, took his place on the rostrum. Beaming broadly, Mensah tackled the second item on the agenda, which was "approval of the agenda."

"I, ah, believe that there are now six items on the agenda. The first was of course the election of the new chairman, and I, ah, wish to thank you all for your confidence. Item two is what we are dealing with now. Item three is a presentation of the results of the questionnaire sent to member states concerning the dangers of space debris falling to earth. I, ah, believe that so far only seven replies have been received. Is that correct?"

He looked down the rostrum table to the committee secretary, who removed his glasses and nodded.

"Yes, that is correct, Dr. Mensah, and I would like to take this opportunity to remind delegates that the closing date for replies is fast approaching and that we would like to receive as many as possible before drafting our report."

"The, ah, next item, item number four," Mensah resumed, "is the item introduced by the Russian delegation at the last meeting." Here, he nodded gravely at the thickset figure of Anatol Lopukhin, who was busy with his notes and did not even notice.

"And I, ah, believe that this item is to be accompanied by a resolution which I see is already being circulated. Good. Item five is a new resolution put forward by the US delegation. It was received by the secretariat yesterday and is now being duplicated. It should be available by the end of the morning."

"Point of order, Mr. Chairman," said the delegate sitting next to Lopukhin. "The US resolution has not yet been formally proposed."

"Mr. Chairman," said Jack Schultz, raising his hand.

"The distinguished delegate of the United States of America has the floor."

"I wish formally to propose the inclusion of Resolution Number SP/POL/OSP/SC3/ll.8 as item five on the agenda."

"Seconded," called the Australian delegate, raising his name board.

Mensah beamed and continued. "That is settled then. The final item on the agenda is preparation of the secretary general's report. That will take up most of our time, so I suggest we close the agenda there if there is no objection."

The day dragged on with much heavy debate on the Russian resolution. The United States succeeded in having all reference to control removed, but there were so many amendments to the original text that it was sent to a drafting committee for a substantial rewrite. Debate on it would be resumed the next day or the day after. This just gave time for the US delegation to introduce its resolution and for the Russians to fire an initial broadside before Mensah adjourned the meeting and the secretary reminded everyone that the Ghanaian delegation was hosting a reception at the UN Plaza Hotel at six-thirty to mark the election of the new chairman.

At the reception, while eating African finger food and drinking Black Label scotch, Packham observed Lopukhin at close quarters. A sturdy figure, he was recounting some obviously doubtful story to a trio of giggling Ghanaian beauties who had been handing round drinks. Packham noted though that despite the wide grin and the jovial manner, the eyes never smiled.

"Jack," he said to Schultz, who was standing next to him, "do you think you could introduce me to Lopukhin?"

"Well, I don't think it would look very good for the leader of the US delegation to do that. Why don't you just walk over and join the group? I want to talk to the Australians anyway."

He disappeared and Packham sauntered over to where Lopukhin had just finished another story, and the girls were falling about, politely hiding their laughs with their hands. Lopukhin looked round at Packham as he approached.

"Why, Colonel Packham," he exclaimed, "I have been looking forward to meeting you." The girls excused themselves discreetly. "Well, well, well. Colonel Henry S. Packham, or may I call you Hal? That's what your friends call you, isn't it?"

"That is correct," said Packham, searching in his mind the details of the file he had studied so carefully on the transatlantic flight.

"You are quite right, Anatol, or should I call you Tola, like your friends?"

Lopukhin smiled and extended a hand.

"I hope you are enjoying the meeting. I appreciated your resolution."

"Really?" said Packham in a disbelieving tone.

"Yes, don't think we are fooled by it, but it is always good politics to suggest a united front. It is good to seek cooperation. It is good to work together on all things, don't you agree?"

"Maybe not all things," Packham said.

"Perhaps you are right, but it is always good to have allies, outside of official positions, if you see what I mean. It is not always good to be, how do you say, a lone wolf?"

Chapter 13

Sullom Voe, June 1, 2007. 1:30 p.m.

Mike sat on a high stool in Lab 2, with his eyes closed and his mind scanning emptiness for a possible signal. He was working a local send-and-receive shift. They had finally wound up calling their work periods "shifts," despite Jim Gardner's initial reservations. He was sitting on an uncomfortable stool because he found that was the best way for him to concentrate. The others had developed their own postures. Chuck preferred to lie flat on his back on top of a bench, while Jan favored an ordinary chair or occasionally assumed a lotus position on the floor. As Mike concentrated, Chuck sat on one of the lab benches quietly reading an American tennis magazine.

This type of shift, worked in pairs, was divided into thirty-minute segments, with thirty minutes send, thirty minutes off, thirty minutes receive, thirty minutes off, and so on. The segments were short since a great deal of concentration was required. It was necessary to switch off completely and rest between them. At first, there had been a problem of interference. The resting partner had found himself picking up the send signals of the active partner, and this had proved to be exhausting since their telepathic faculties never relaxed.

They had discussed the problem at length, and after a few experiments, Jim had come up with a very effective technique to blot out the interference. The same technique also provided a screen against unwanted mind reading. This was a very welcome spin-off since some of them had felt uncomfortable in the presence of so much telepathic talent, never knowing if their most private thoughts were being shared by others. This had led to a certain wariness, and when Jim's mental screen was shown to be effective, the group was able to relax and work more closely together in the knowledge that their thoughts were safe from prying minds.

In reality, there was no need to use the screen all the time since their telepathic abilities usually remained dormant unless deliberately brought into use. Mike still had his occasional flashes of insight, but he had learned to control his mental processes much better.

Just as each of the telepathists had developed different physical positions when concentrating, they had also adopted individual mental configurations. Jim had encouraged them to visualize their minds in action, and he gave them a geometric form on which they could focus their concentration. They had all created their own symbols. When he was in a receive mode, Mike visualized his mind, and indeed his whole being, as a large curved dish slowly tilting and turning to sweep the cosmos. To complete this image of a receptacle, Mike found himself cupping his hands in front of his chest like a beggar appealing for alms. His configuration for sending was more complicated. He envisioned himself as a touchstone—a body formed of two pyramids joined at their bases and offering six points from which his signals could be projected in six different directions at once. How he arrived at this configuration or the dish symbol, he did not know. They seemed to have emerged spontaneously as he forced his mind to grapple with the mechanisms of thought projection and reception.

Chuck turned a page, glanced at his watch, and looked at Mike, still immobile on his lab stool. It would soon be time to relieve him and start his own send segment. Another three minutes yet. He finished the article he was reading, put his magazine down, and gently called, "Mike." Mike's eyes opened immediately.

"Time?" he asked.

"Uh-huh. My turn."

Mike stretched and stood up. "I think I'll get some air. I'll be back in half an hour."

"Okay. Be good."

Chuck arranged himself flat on the bench, with his head resting on an oriental neck pillow. Mike went out quietly, closing the door behind him. In the control room through which he had to pass to reach the exterior sat two of the technical assistants who always remained on duty whenever any work was being done. Dr. Jim and Jim Gardner were in Lab 1 helping Jan to memorize a long binary message written by Sam for a long-distance send. Each of the three telepathists had been assigned a different message. Mike and Chuck had already learned theirs after many hours of effort. They were formed of a seemingly endless sequence of long and short signals, which, in binary code, expressed various formulae, coordinates, and descriptions.

After experimenting with the rosters first proposed by Jim, the four basic modes, local send, local receive, long-distance send, and long-distance receive, were dealt with in the following manner. Local send and receive were grouped into a two-man shift which usually lasted for four hours. While this shift was being worked, the third member of the team concentrated on long-distance send and long-distance receive, with much more emphasis being placed on send than receive since the receive mode was partly covered by the local receive anyway. After four hours, the telepathists were switched. At first, it had seemed unfair to have two on local and only one on long distance, but all three men agreed that the long-distance send mode was the easiest since they were merely projecting a set message. It was a procedure that rapidly became automatic. With local send, on the other hand, more concentration and effort were required to project a series of thoughts based on the themes of "welcome," "peace," "brotherhood," "love," etc., worked out by "the management," i.e., Packham, Jim, and Sam.

So far, they had had no success. They had often picked up stray signals, but they had always turned out to be of local origin of thoughts, messages, even sometimes lengthy sequences unconsciously projected by people around the station or in the vicinity. They looked on these signals as static or, as Sam put it, cosmic background noise at close quarters. Still, as Jim pointed out, even if they had not achieved contact with extraterrestrials, they had proved that their methods were right and that their team's telepathic abilities were beyond doubt.

Mike sauntered across the compound and watched the helicopter land on its daily visit. It came in every day at four with supplies and occasionally ferried personnel to and from the mainland. The pilot set it down neatly, jumped out, leaving the rotors idling, and hurried into the station office with a pouch of mail. Two soldiers emerged and unloaded some small crates. The pilot would check if there was anything to load and if not would be airborne again in minutes. Mike ran a professional eye over the helicopter. It was the same one that had brought him out from Aberdeen, one of the old Hueys. It seemed strange for him not to be flying. He wondered if any of his clients had tried to get hold of him and, if so, what they had been told by the embassy officers detailed to monitor his phone.

The pilot came out of the hut accompanied by Baker who threw a large package into the chopper and closed the freight door. The pilot waved, climbed in, and clattered off over the hill and back to Aberdeen. Baker watched it go, turned to reenter the office, caught sight of Mike, and gave him a friendly salute. Mike raised his hand in response. He was no longer afflicted with Baker's constant presence. After the first few days on the station, Packham had obviously come to the conclusion that Mike was not going to be a security problem after all and had returned Baker to normal duties. This was a relief for both of them. Mike had disliked the arrangement intensely and had said as much to Packham, while Baker himself found it boring in the extreme.

Since then, relieved of what could only be a strained relationship, the two men had become quite friendly, and they sometimes talked together at length after dinner. Baker nourished dreams of one day becoming a lawyer. He was taking correspondence courses, and when he discovered that Mike held a law degree, he frequently sought him out to ask his opinion about some of the points he was studying. Mike found this new relationship stimulating, and he was sometimes surprised to discover how much he remembered from law school.

He walked round the compound, smelling the heather-laden air blowing up from the Sound, and he watched a small flock of sheep wander aimlessly through the derelict huts farther up the hillside. He felt good. The daily outdoor exercise, the regular meals, and the undisturbed nights—all so different from his normal life—were doing wonders for his physical well-being. He glanced at his watch. It was time to get back and relieve Chuck. He waited until the thirty minutes were up before opening the lab door and interrupting Chuck's concentration. Chuck stretched and said he too would get some air. Mike settled down for a period of local receive.

He established his mental "dish" image, tracking back and forth and sweeping the space he felt receding away from him in all directions. Suddenly, there was a flutter on the edge of the dish. It was like feeling something out of the corner of his mind. He stopped the dish and swung back toward the flutter, striving to focus his concentration on it. The flutter grew in intensity and became identifiable as mental long and short signals. Mike's mind faltered and then locked back onto the signal. Binary code! He relaxed and smiled. Of course, it must be Jan sending from the other lab. But no. He stiffened again. In his present position, Jan would be behind him and to his right. This signal was coming from directly in front of him. He tried to think. What direction was he facing? Yes, the signal was coming from over the hill, from the northeast. It couldn't be Jan. What the hell was it? He forced his mind back onto the signal. Yes, there was no doubt. It was binary code. Now that he had locked onto it, the signal was coming in strong and clear. What should he do? Call Jim? Try to respond? Try to take down the signals? He hesitated. Then the signal stopped. Dammit! He concentrated all his efforts in the direction the signal had been coming from. Nothing.

He wiped the sweat off his face and said, "Get hold of Jim. Tell him I've got something. I need him here right away." All the labs were wired with live microphones, and he knew that the technical assistants outside in the control room would already be trying to locate Jim. He forced himself to relax and tried to assume his dish configuration again. Had the signal stopped, or had he lost concentration? He scanned across the whole northeastern sector, but it was in vain.

The door burst open, and Jim rushed in, followed by Packham.

"I've had a contact," Mike said. "Binary code with a strong signal from the northeast."

"Binary code!" Packham exclaimed.

"Why not?" said Jim. "If we think they're advanced enough to understand binary, why shouldn't they think the same of us? It's logical, but why didn't we think of it before?"

"So what do we do?" said Mike. "What do we do if they start again? Respond?"

"I don't know if there's much point. If they're sending binary, the odds are it's coming from a distant source, light years away. So no dialogue would be possible. No, I think what we have to do is try to record it and see if we can make any sense out of it."

"This is wonderful, Mike," Packham said. "It's a breakthrough. I'm going to call Washington right away."

"Now wait a minute, Hal," said Jim. "I'd like to make a little more certain about it first."

"But, Mike, you're certain, aren't you? You did pick up a signal?"

"Oh yes, I'm sure enough. But I think I'd go along with Jim on this. We're dealing with something we know very little about.

I feel sure I got something, but as far as I know it might have been my mind playing tricks on me. It's difficult to be certain about anything. I suggest we wait until we have a confirmation, preferably by Chuck or Jan."

Packham looked disappointed, but he finally agreed it might be more prudent to wait for a second contact. By this time, Chuck, Jan, and Sam had joined the group, and everybody wanted to know details of the signals, such as what they felt like, how strong they were, and so on. The discussion went on for an hour before Packham broke it up. He declared they could take the rest of the day off and invited them all over to his quarters for a celebratory drink.

After this "breakthrough," as Packham still insisted on calling it, they all began the next day with renewed enthusiasm. Chuck was convinced he was going to be the next to achieve a contact, and he couldn't wait to get started. The day passed, though, with no new contact, and it was a dispirited team that gathered in the evening to compare results.

Two days later, Mike had another contact that was strong and clear and straight out of the northeast again. He grabbed a pad and started to scribble down the long and short signals. Mike had decided, whatever anyone else thought, that he would attempt to respond if he had a new contact. As soon as the signals came to an end, he put down his pad and started to send his standard binary message, beaming it as far as he could toward the northeast. After a minute, he stopped and waited. There was a pause, then, feebly at first but with growing strength, he detected a thought. Not a signal but a definite thought!

Who are you? the thought said.

Mike's mind raced. What could he answer?

A friend, he sent back. *Who are you?*

A friend too. Where are you?

Sullom Voe, Shetland.

There was a long pause, and then came another thought. *Are you an earth dweller?*

Yes, Mike replied. *Are you an extraterrestrial?*

No. I'm an earth dweller too.

Mike gasped. What the heck was going on? Who was this contact? An earth dweller!

My name is Marshall. Who are you, and where are you?

I am called Brebin. I am in Finland.

Mike had a sudden intuition.

Are you Russian?

Yes. Are you American?

Yes. There was a very long pause, and then Mike sensed a strong feeling of anxiety.

We should not be communicating.

Why not? said Mike.

We are on different sides.

So what? Listen, don't you think it's amazing that we are communicating at all? And we don't even speak the same language.

Yes, it is most interesting. Are you trying to contact extraterrestrials?

Yes. Are you?

Of course. Now, I must stop. This is dangerous.

Dangerous? Why?

It is, believe me. Good-bye.

No, wait. Brebin. Listen, let me tell you about us here. We are an American team on the Shetland Islands trying to establish communication with extraterrestrial intelligence. So far, we have had no success. I thought you were an extraterrestrial.

I thought you were too. We are running a similar operation on Mount Haltia.

Where's that?

In northwest Finland. It's the closest we can get to the North Sea.

Are you trying for UFOs too?

What's that?

Alien spacecraft?
Yes. I must go.
Wait, wait, Mike said desperately. *Do you have another name? My name is Mike.*
Yes. Sergei Brebin. I have to leave you. This is too dangerous.
Listen, can we communicate again?
Perhaps.
When? How about tomorrow at ten o'clock?
There was a silence.
Sergei! Brebin!
There was no reply. Mike mopped his face and went in search of Packham. He found him in the station commander's office.
"Hal, can I see you for a moment?"
"Sure. Come over to my place."
They walked across to Packham's quarters.
"I've had another contact," Mike started.
"Great. Have you told Jim?"
"No. I wanted to talk to you about it first. You'll see why. They're not extraterrestrials. They're Russians!"
"What?" Packham exploded. "How do you know?"
"I had a conversation with them, or at least with one of their telepathists."
There was a shocked silence during which Packham stared at Mike in disbelief. "Wait a minute," he said finally. "Start again. Tell me what happened."
"Well, it was like the other day. I picked up a signal—binary code again. I noted it down, and then I sent back a signal. I thought, 'What the hell, it can't do any harm. If by chance they're close, they might respond. If they're light years away, it doesn't matter anyway.' And he responded—this guy of theirs."
"Go on," said Packham.
"At first, we both thought the other was an extraterrestrial. Then I asked him where they are and told him where we are."

"*You did what?*" roared Packham. "You told him where we are? Are you out of your mind? This is supposed to be a top-secret project. You must be crazy. Telling the Russians—telling them where we are!"

"Well, we know where they are now. Listen, Hal, just calm down, will you? I don't think he'll even tell his people about our contact."

"What do you mean?"

"I think he'll be too scared to tell them. He kept saying it was dangerous to communicate with me. If there is any danger, it can only be from his own people. So I don't think he's going to go around boasting about it."

Packham smiled, with his anger fading. "You know, I think you may be right. That would be absolutely typical of the Russians. And you found out where they are?"

"Yes, in Finland."

"You can give me the details later. Do you think you'll communicate again?"

"I don't know. I told him we'd try again tomorrow, but he may be too scared."

"Okay. Listen, Mike. This may be a break. I want you to try to contact him again tomorrow. I want you to try to find out everything you can about their project. Meanwhile, I'm going to prepare a full briefing for you on what you can say about our project and what you can't. Most of it won't be true, of course, but there'll be just enough truth to make it sound credible. Now, there's one more thing. You are not to mention this to anyone, not even Jim. You will report directly to me and only to me. Do you understand?"

"Sure, but why?"

"Do you think I want everybody to know we're communicating with the Russians?"

Chapter 14

Sullom Voe, June 3, 2007. 8:15 a.m.

"So you say the message came from the northeast?" Frank Mambrino panted as they jogged over the brow of the hill and began their descent to the station a mile farther down the track.

"Uh-huh," Mike said, still out of breath from the long incline.

"And the source wasn't moving?"

"No. Not as far as I could tell."

"Mm."

Ever since they had started on their morning run, Mambrino had been plying Mike with questions about his "contact." He had not been around when Mike had received his first binary message, but he had obviously heard about it from the others. They slowed to a walk to cool down a little before reaching the station.

"And you haven't had another contact since?"

"No," Mike lied.

"Peculiar."

"What is?"

"The whole thing," Mambino said. "You're so certain of the direction, which makes me think the source must be either on or close to earth. If the source were a distant planet, you wouldn't have had such a clear idea of direction. The message would have been reaching you at a much wider angle, if you see what I mean. But you're quite definite about the direction. So that can only mean a source close enough to earth to give a clearly identifiable bearing. And what could that source be? A spacecraft? But why would a spacecraft be sending binary code? I can understand a binary message from a distant star, but surely a spacecraft trying to communicate with us would make some attempt to use a more easily understandable form of language. And it didn't move."

"So?" Mike said after a pause.

"So, I think your message is coming from the Russkies! We've all been assuming it was a message coming in, but why couldn't it be a message going out? A binary message from the Russians directed into space. And you just happened to pick it up, by accident. Why not? We know the Russians are up to something very similar to our operation. And what lies northeast of here? Norway, Finland, and the Soviet Union."

Mike was impressed by Mambrino's reasoning. Perhaps there was much more behind that easy smile than anyone suspected. He would have to be careful.

"So, what do you think?" Mambrino insisted.

"Well, I suppose you could be right," Mike said "Let's hope we get another message, and then perhaps we'll be able to tell."

The duty security guard checked them in at the gate, along with the other members of the morning's jogging party, and they split to go to their own quarters.

Mike took a long shower, and as he dried himself, he thought about his talk with Mambrino. He wondered if any of the others had come to the same conclusion. But then what difference did it make if they had? They didn't know about Brebin. He walked through to the bedroom to look at his watch. It was still only eight-thirty. He had plenty of time. He had said he would try to contact Brebin at ten. He was curious to see whether he would respond. He went back into the bathroom and started to shave.

As he lathered his face, staring into the mirror, Mike felt something stir in his mind. He blinked, shook his head, and picked up his razor. There it was again! It was a thought, an identity. Brebin! He put down his razor and concentrated.

Marshall, this is Brebin, came into his mind.

Brebin, this is Marshall. I am receiving you, he projected.

Good, came the reply, with what felt like relief.
It is not yet ten.
I know. Pay attention please. I have little time. I cannot communicate at ten. It is too dangerous. During the day, I am watched by telguards."

Telguards? Mike queried.

Yes, telepathists trained to monitor us. I was lucky not to be detected yesterday. We had just finished a session, and the telguard was out of the room. But we're wasting time. I will communicate tonight at about eleven. Be ready. Someone is coming.

The communication broke off, and Mike found himself still staring into the bathroom mirror, with soap all over his face. He picked up his razor again, wet it, and started to shave. Brebin's thoughts had been as strong and clear as a telephone message, but they had been tinged with anxiety and fear. Why was he so frightened? What would happen to him if he were caught, and why had he run the risk of communicating if it were so dangerous? Perhaps he would find out more tonight.

He dressed, breakfasted, and walked over to the lab for the morning session. Normally, he was scheduled for local send and receive with Jan, but since his contact the other day, Jim had put Mike on a special program of his own, concentrating on local and long-distance receive. Chuck was still convinced he was going to be the next to get a contact and started off each morning with the same touching enthusiasm. As far as Mike knew, Packham had told no one about his contact with Brebin.

The morning passed uneventfully, although at one point Mike thought he had the faintest of flutters on the periphery of his awareness, like a yellow moth on the edge of a pool of darkness. Jim, who was sitting in on every one of Mike's sessions now, became very excited, but despite repeated efforts, Mike could neither bring it closer nor make it any clearer. Furthermore, Mike could not give it any direction, which was interesting in the light of what Mambrino had been saying earlier that morning.

Mike mentioned their conversation to Packham after lunch. He also told him of Brebin's early morning contact and complained about the position the situation place him in.

"I don't like it," he told Packham. "I don't mind communicating with Brebin, but I don't like all this secrecy. What harm would it do to tell the others? We're all under security wraps here anyway, and it makes me very uncomfortable to have to lie to someone like Mambrino. What do you know about him, by the way? There's something a little strange about him. He's not a spook, is he?"

"His file has been double- and triple-checked. Of course, if he is with the company, that wouldn't necessarily show in his file, but I'll have it checked again. And look, I know this situation is difficult for you right now, but believe me, it's better to keep the whole thing secret, even inside this station. Now, what I really wanted to discuss with you is what you're going to tell Brebin about our operation."

He handed Mike a sheet of paper. "These basically are the facts I want you to slip into your conversation, and you will also see the questions I would like you to ask, if you get a chance."

Mike glanced at the tightly written sheet. There was a list of names and code words he had never seen before.

"How much of all this is true?" he asked.

"More than you might think. The operation code name, for example, is Lone Wolf. That's true, and it's top secret. Or rather was."

"What do you mean?"

"I happen to know that the Russians found that out."

"How do you know?"

"That's unimportant."

Mike thought for a moment. "Then, what's the point of telling them, or rather telling Brebin? In any case, he's scared, scared for his life maybe, and judging by his behavior, he doesn't want anyone to know he's in contact with me."

"Because if he does tell them, or if he's forced to tell them, they'll recognize the code name. They'll know it's correct and, hopefully, they'll assume all the rest of the information is true."

Mike stared at Packham. "This is just a game for you, isn't it? You don't care at all about the people involved, do you?"

"That's not true. These are just elementary precautions. That's something you have to learn to live with."

"Or die with?"

"Now come on, Mike! I think you're overreacting to this. These are routine procedures. You mustn't worry about them. Just see what you can do with Brebin. And relax!"

That night after dinner, Mike sat in his room and waited for Brebin to establish contact. He tried himself to reach Brebin, but there was no response. Then, at eleven precisely, Mike picked up Brebin's already familiar thought shapes.

Marshall, this is Brebin.

Sergei, this is Mike, he responded. *How are you?*

Well. There was a puzzled pause. *Why do you ask?*

I was concerned about you. You seemed frightened, and you said communicating with me was dangerous.

It is. It is, Brebin came in emphatically. *Now listen. I want to ask you some questions. You say you are American. I want to be certain. Who was the first president of the United States?*

George Washington, of course. Everybody knows that.

What was his wife called?

Martha.

What are the last two lines of the national anthem?

This is ridiculous!

Do you know?

Of course. Mike sighed. *"And the star-spangled banner in triumph shall wave, O'er the land of the free and the home of the brave."*

Which state were you born in?

Rhode Island.
Capital?
Providence.
What is the name of the street with all the old houses?
You mean Benefit Street?
Yes, good.
How do you know all this, anyway? You're not American.
I'm a professor of American history and geography. I wanted to be a little more certain about you. Of course, I cannot be completely certain.
Don't you trust me?
How can I trust you? I don't even know you.
You must trust me. We are special people.
I have learned not to trust anyone. And you too would do better not to trust anyone.
Not even you? Mike interrupted.
Perhaps. You don't know anything about me either. Don't trust anyone. Don't trust your own people. I don't. It is too dangerous. Wait. Just a moment.

There was a long pause. Then Brebin came in again. *I thought there was someone outside the door.*
You keep talking about danger. What is the danger?
Our project is top secret, as I suppose yours is too. If my masters thought I was communicating with anyone, they would be very angry. I dread to think what would happen if they knew I was communicating with an American!
Why are you communicating with me? You told me not to trust you.
Good, good. You are right. Don't forget that I did not originally set out to contact you.
That is correct, but you have reestablished contact with me twice now. You didn't have to.
No, I didn't. But I did. Why? Because I'm worried. Because I'm frightened, and since we have something in common—you said we were special people—I thought I could share my fears with you. I'm frightened by what I think my countrymen are trying to do. The leaders

of this project are seeking to establish contact with extraterrestrials in order to steal their technology with which they believe they can dominate the world. I think that is wrong. But what can I do alone? I feel the extraterrestrials should be warned. They should be made to understand that not all men are evil.

That is precisely what we want to do, Sergei. That at least is what Packham had always said. *We want to show them that we are peace-loving beings, that we have no evil intentions, that we are willing to cooperate, and that their knowledge can perhaps help us to cure disease, do away with poverty, and put an end to conflict.*

Mike Marshall, if you believe that, then you are more naïve than I thought. I have heard there is something to do with oil. I told you, do not trust anyone, not even your own people.

The next three nights, Mike spent many hours in communication with Sergei Brebin, discussing their respective projects, comparing political ideologies, and speculating about the possibilities of achieving contact with the extraterrestrials. Their conversations were absorbing, broken only by manifestations of Sergei's anxiety. Mike had come to like Sergei very much. He was astonished at the Russian's knowledge of American history and culture. Of course it was his profession, but even so, Sergei's familiarity with the details of everyday life in the United States never ceased to amaze him. And there was a human warmth about him that Mike felt close to. Contact between the two had become very easy, and Mike always knew immediately when Sergei was trying to reach him. His thought shapes were quite distinctive; they were full and round and a deep shade of burgundy red. When Sergei was anxious or fearful, as he often was, his thought shapes shrank into jagged blotches, pulsating at high speed. His own thought shapes, according to Sergei, were hard and linear, with sometimes a metallic blue and sometimes a sharp green.

He told Sergei all about the project at Sullom Voe and the progress, or lack of progress, they had made so far. At first, he felt unwilling to talk about it, not wanting to reveal too much but at the same time not wanting to resort to Packham's briefing sheet. For some reason, he could not bring himself to be dishonest with Sergei. Finally, he decided he would trust him—despite Sergei's own warnings—and told him the truth, although he did not tell him that Packham had wanted him to give him some different information. Sergei, surprisingly, was quite willing, even eager, to describe the Russian project, as if to convince Mike of his good intentions. At first, Mike was suspicious of this but in the end determined that Sergei was being truthful too.

According to Sergei, the Russian project was much bigger than the American operation. Housed in a former meteorological station, close to the top of Mount Haltia in the extreme northwest corner of Finland and only sixty miles from the North Sea, the project involved more than a hundred people. There were ten telepathists, including Sergei, and an equal number of telguards. These were really second-line telepathists whose job it was to monitor the work of Sergei and his colleagues. Mike wondered why this was necessary, and Sergei told him it was standard procedure. There was always someone watching someone else. Even the watchers were watched. Mike began to understand some of Sergei's anxieties.

Apart from the telepathists and their telguards, there was a team of forty or fifty scientists, technicians, and statisticians, plus a large support staff. The project was run by a man called Lopukhin, whom Sergei described as ruthless and inhuman, obsessed by the task of establishing contact with extraterrestrial intelligence as soon as possible, and ready to crush anyone or anything that stood in his way. He was continuously pressing for results and became more irritable and unpleasant as the days went by.

As for the Russian telepathists, very few of them believed in what they were doing. Some doubted their own capabilities. Some were not really convinced of the existence of extraterrestrial life. Others, like Sergei, suspected the motives of the project leaders.

Sergei himself felt certain that sooner or later, they would achieve contact with extraterrestrials, but he was fearful of the result. Lopukhin would do anything to get his hands on their technology.

We must warn them, Sergei kept telling Mike. *But how? If ever I achieve contact, I'll be so heavily monitored, I won't be free to say anything. It may be up to you, Mike!*

Every day, Mike reported to Packham on the previous night's conversation. Under Packham's questioning, he gave full details of the Russian operation's location, personnel, structures, and schedules, but he remained reticent about Sergei's inner thoughts because he felt instinctively that Packham would not approve of the closeness of the relationship the two had developed. On the first morning, he had tried to talk about Sergei's conviction that the Russians only wanted the extraterrestrials' technology to dominate the world, but Packham had had a very strange reaction. He had jumped to his feet and started shouting, saying that such a conviction was ridiculous, that there was nothing to support it, and that you could never believe what a Russian told you.

"Never trust a Russian," Packham had bellowed.

"Don't trust anyone!" Mike could still hear Sergei saying.

By now, the excitement over Mike's first contact had died down somewhat. However, Mike was still kept on a special receive schedule, and Jim still insisted on attending every session. Mike had become so used to communicating with Sergei that he half expected to pick him up during one of these sessions. But he did not.

After three full days of special receive sessions and three nights of lengthy conversations with Sergei, Mike was beginning to feel very tired. During the afternoon session, he almost fell asleep on his stool, and Jim sent him out for a cup of coffee and a breath of fresh air.

The coffee revived him, and he felt much better as he walked across the compound. The weather had turned cold that morning, and there were a few drops of rain between the gusty squalls, but the air tasted clean and sweet. The supply helicopter clattered in over the station, and Mike turned to watch it land. *Must be four o'clock,* he thought, and he glanced at his watch. *Yes. Right on schedule.* The pilot put the chopper down neatly, and Mike turned back toward the lab.

"Feeling better?" Jim said.

"Much, thanks," Mike replied truthfully.

"Okay then, want to try the northeast again, or just scan?"

"I'll just scan. You know, when I picked up the signal I was scanning, I wasn't concentrating on any particular direction."

"Okay, anything you say."

Mike perched himself on his stool, closed his eyes, and assumed his dish configuration. He tried to keep his mind off Sergei and began a slow, circular scanning movement. His mind tracked across the inner darkness of his perception, reaching out into the emptiness of space. He felt calmer now and more alert as his faculties probed the velvety blackness around him, stretching out like a slender beam to brush the gates of infinity.

The beam stumbled. There was a glow out there, a faint glimmer, like a lighthouse seen from miles out at sea. He tried to relax, letting his Alpha rhythms take over, and then he returned to the glimmer. It was gone. No, there it was again; it was a flutter, a yellow flicker against the darkness. He had seen it before. It was the yellow moth he had half glimpsed the other day. He tried to focus on it, but the more he tried, the farther it receded. He forced himself to relax again, and as he relaxed, it became clearer, stronger. Yes, it was the yellow moth, tiny and distant, but indistinct as it was, he definitely had an impression of wings fluttering in a patch of light. Once again, no effort, or lack of effort, could bring it closer. It remained as elusive as ever. However, as Jim pointed out when he discussed it with him, it was a signal he had picked up twice—an image he had recognized. It must be something. It must have some significance, unless it was purely the fruit of his imagination. Jim suggested they should ask Jan and Chuck whether they had ever experienced anything similar, and privately, Mike made a note to mention it to Sergei that evening.

The evening passed pleasantly enough. Elated by the new development, Jim was on great form at dinner, with a seemingly inexhaustible fund of anecdotes about ESP and J.B. Rhine's early lab experiments. Dr. Jim matched them with some surprisingly earthy stories from his medical student days. Chuck drank them in with wide, shining eyes and guffaws of delight. Frank Mambrino smiled and smiled. Even Jan seemed a little less solemn than usual. Only Sam Goldman failed to join in wholeheartedly. He sat at one end of the table, smiling thinly at the stories and occasionally pushing up his spectacles with a thoughtful air. After dinner when Mike took a drink outside to enjoy the air, he was soon joined by Sam.

"Interesting, what Jim was saying about your moth," he said.

"Uh-huh," Mike responded, waiting.

"What makes you think it's a moth?"

"Well, nothing really. I only used the word because it seemed to describe the fluttering movement I was getting, but you must understand the image was so faint and indistinct. Why do you ask? Do you have an idea what it might be?"

"No, on the contrary. In all the literature I have read about extraterrestrials and possible traces they may have left on earth, I have never come across a moth symbol. Wheels, yes. Geometrical shapes, humanoid figures, birds, spaceships even. But moths, never! That's why I asked you whether you're sure it's a moth."

"I'm not sure at all. If I see it again, maybe I'll get a clearer image."

"Okay, just try and keep an open mind."

With that, Sam bade Mike good night and withdrew, looking just as thoughtful as before. Mike shrugged and reminded himself again to put it to Sergei. He finished his drink and went to his quarters to wait for Sergei's communication. So far, Sergei had been remarkably punctual, coming in almost exactly at eleven. It was not quite eleven yet, so Mike glanced through a magazine, keeping his mind alert for Sergei. At eleven, he put his magazine down and sat quietly waiting. There was no signal. He continued to wait. Still no signal. He looked at his watch. Five minutes after eleven. He frowned and then smiled to himself, reflecting how quickly the human mind became accustomed to a habit. Five minutes late and he was already wondering where Sergei was! He smiled again and shook his head.

Ten minutes later, there was still no signal from Sergei. Something must have delayed him. He picked up his magazine again and finished the article he had started. No signal. He undressed and took a shower. No signal. He got into bed and read for another fifteen minutes. At twelve he decided that Sergei was not going to contact him. It was already one o'clock in Finland. Surely he wouldn't still be tied up unless they were working night hours, but Sergei had not mentioned it. Then why hadn't he communicated? Was there something wrong? He began to project, *Sergei, this is Mike*. Perhaps Sergei had fallen asleep. If he had, would he be able to wake him?

After ten minutes, he stopped projecting. Either Sergei was asleep, or he was busy doing something else and was not free to communicate—unless something had happened to him. He felt very uneasy but then decided there was nothing he could do. He read for another thirty minutes and then settled down to sleep. Sleep was a long time coming.

Suddenly Mike jolted upright in bed, with his eyes staring, his nerves knotted, a convulsing scream echoing round his head, and a long shriek of agony cutting into the raw flesh of his senses. The scream doubled in intensity, rose to a teeth-gritting peak, and then suddenly faded, leaving only ripples of whimpering pain washing against the walls of his mind. Sergei! They were Sergei's thought shapes! That agony, the finality of that scream. Sergei!

He knew with a suddenness that took his breath away that Sergei was dead. That scream was Sergei's last projection and his last agonizing appeal to the world of the living as his being was hurled from life into death. They had killed him, Mike knew. They had killed him because he had communicated with the other side, because he had dared to question their motives. But that meant he had been right about the Russians. They did want the technology of the extraterrestrials. They did want it to dominate the rest of the world. Sergei had been right. And they had killed him for it. He jumped out of bed, threw on some clothes, and ran over to Packham's room.

"They've killed Brebin," he told a startled Packham.

"What? What do you mean? Now be quiet and come in, quickly!"

"They've killed Brebin. I know. I heard his death scream. They killed him because he knew too much. Because he knew they wanted to dominate. Is that what we're doing too, Packham? Is it?"

"Calm down. You're overwrought. Come on. Calm down. Let me fix you a drink."

He walked over to the bar cabinet and poured Mike a generous drink.

Sergei was right. Mike continued to think. *He was right about the Russians. Was he right about the Americans too?* "Don't trust anyone," Sergei had said. "Not even your own people!"

Chapter 15

Sullom Voe, June 12, 2007. 9:30 a.m.

Life had settled down into a steady routine again. Mike continued to have occasional glimpses of the yellow moth, but it never did anything different or came any closer, so Jim decided to put everybody back on their old schedules. Since the disappearance of Brebin, Mike had had little to do with Packham. There was no longer any reason to report to him, and Mike now felt uncomfortable in his presence. In any case, Packham kept out of his way.

The raw experience of Brebin's death had shaken Mike, and for a few days he remained very listless and depressed. His depression seemed to be shared by the others, even though they knew nothing of the Brebin incident. They became stale and restless. When they started to snap at each other, Jim thought it was time they should have a break. He persuaded Packham to let them organize a day's outing to Scalloway, a little fishing port farther down the coast.

The day before the outing, however, the monotony was broken when Frank Mambrino had to be flown out with a suspected gall bladder attack. At breakfast, he had complained of severe shooting pains in the upper abdomen and back. Dr. Jim examined him and said that while it was impossible to be certain, the pains seemed to be coming from the gall bladder. Perhaps Frank had gallstones and did not even know it. Without an X-ray, there was no way of telling. It could just go away in a few days, or it could flare up and perhaps even rupture. In his opinion, it would be wiser to put Frank under observation for a while. Arrangements were made with the Aberdeen General Hospital, and Frank left on the four o'clock helicopter looking better already and smiling bravely.

The outing to Scalloway was a great success. They drove over in two vans and strolled along the quay heading, looking at the fishing boats and admiring the squat, weather-pocked houses huddled round the picturesque little harbor. In winter, the westerly gales came roaring onto the coast, literally rocking the houses on their foundations. But in summer, with their brightly painted window sills and door mounts, they looked peaceful and almost pretty.

For lunch, they drove a little way up the coast and grilled steaks on driftwood fires, watching the gulls wheel and squabble over the wake of a trawler slowly working the banks a mile offshore. It was a perfect day, almost hot, and after a huge lunch, they sat around on the rocks and reminisced about childhood summers. Even Packham mellowed and spoke about a vacation in Maine. A little later, Chuck showed everyone how to do handstands, and Sam Goldman revealed himself to be an expert at skipping pebbles. Mike loosened up a little and managed to shake off his depression. Listening to Jim tell a long, involved story about a mermaid and a lighthouse keeper, he even found himself smiling.

At four, they drove back into the village and spent a couple of hours browsing round the few shops, examining fishing supplies, cheap, sturdy work clothes, and plastic kitchen utensils. Chuck bought some souvenirs: a glass float used to hold up fishing nets, a ship in a bottle, and a giant crab shell. Some of them wanted to send postcards, but Packham vetoed that on security grounds. He had warned everyone before the outing that they were to be careful what they said to the inhabitants, but the people of Scalloway, while remaining open and friendly, proved to be singularly incurious.

At half past six, Dr. Jim suggested they should sample the local beer, so they all piled into the Fisherman's Cove, right on the harbor. Dr. Jim, who had lived in London for a number of years, said he was an expert on English beer and would advise them on what to drink. The landlord, who had overheard this comment, said rather pointedly that he only stocked Scottish beer, implying that English beer might be good enough for the English but that Scots deserved something better. Dr. Jim placated the landlord by saying that he had heard nothing but praise for Scottish beer, and what would he recommend? Within minutes, they all found themselves holding pint mugs of best bitter, a tangy, oak-colored ale drawn straight from the wood. It slid down just fine, and they ordered more.

A few fishermen came in and joined them, chatting in broad, guttural Scots. They watched the fishermen play darts, and after a while, Chuck challenged them to a game. They formed teams and agreed to play for the beer. The fishermen drank a lot of free beer that night, while the Americans made it a point of pride to keep up with them. By nine-thirty, they were pretty drunk, and they sang all the way back to Sullom Voe. It had been a lovely day, they agreed, as they said good night. They had really enjoyed it.

Leonid Kamikov was enjoying himself too. Sitting in his usual box at the Bolshoi, he watched the company's new production of *Petrouchka* with a critical and knowledgeable eye. It was good, he thought. It was vigorous but not too vigorous to overwhelm that delicate touch of traditional elegance he liked to see in Russian ballet. It was altogether very satisfying. He applauded briskly, and when the lights came on for the intermission, he walked out into the foyer for a glass of champagne. Before he reached the bar, however, a large man in street clothes approached him and said something in a low voice. Kamikov made a gesture of protest, jerking his head in the direction of his box and pointing at his watch. The man shrugged and said something else. Kamikov frowned, pursed his lips, and then followed the man out of the theater.

"This is too much." He continued to protest as they climbed into a large government car. "You could have chosen a more convenient time."

"I apologize, comrade," the messenger said, "but don't tell me. I only execute orders."

The car sped through central Moscow to one of the offices listed as the Kremlin but actually outside the walls of the old citadel. The messenger produced a pass, and the car was allowed to enter the courtyard. Kamikov was taken upstairs and pushed into an office.

"Tola!" he exclaimed when he saw who was in the office. "What the hell is all this about?"

"Good evening, Leonid. Thank you for coming so promptly. You are looking well."

"Tola, you old fox. Would you mind explaining? Dragging me out of the ballet in the middle of a performance. I hope it's urgent. And what are you doing in Moscow? I thought you were on mission somewhere."

"I was, Leonid. I still am. I'm only in Moscow for a few hours. That's why I had to interrupt your evening. Please forgive me. And it is urgent. I have been given step-three priority by our friends across the street. Something has happened, and I need more telepathists. As many as you can give me. And I need them damn quick. How many can you let me have?"

"I don't know offhand. I'll have to consult with Levkov."

Lopukhin pushed a telephone toward him. "Levkov has been driven to the institute. He doesn't know why. He's sitting in his office, waiting. Call him and explain. I need these people in forty-eight hours." He smiled. "If you're quick, you'll be able to catch the last act."

As it turned out, Kamikov did not finish until two in the morning. After talking with Levkov, he had to draft a number of memos and get them approved by the Kremlin night staff, which was no easy task at the best of times. When he finished, he reported back to Lopukhin, who had spent all of the intervening time on the telephone.

"I knew you could do it, Leonid," he said. "Sorry you couldn't make the last act after all. Have some champagne." He motioned toward an ice bucket on the desk.

"What's happened, Tola, to make everything so urgent?"

"I can't tell even you, Leonid, I'm afraid. Top secret." The phone rang. "Now, if you will excuse me, I have a lot to do before morning."

Kamikov strode out angrily. He refused the offer of a car, hoping to walk his anger off. He was still angry, however, when he turned into Presnensky, too angry to notice the dark figure that had followed him all the way home and which now melted into the doorway of the apartment building next to his.

In Washington, DC, a gray Toyota pulled out of a garage entrance in Chevy Chase and drove carefully down Connecticut Avenue. After a while, it turned off onto Rock Creek Parkway and continued to Memorial Bridge where it moved into the Virginia traffic lane. Thirty minutes later, it pulled up in front of an old house covered in creeper and set well back from the road in several acres of wooded land. The driver got out and pressed the button on the intercom by the gate.

"Hello," he said, smiling into the intercom, "this is Frank."

In Murmansk, Captain Gregory Ponotiev paced the bridge of his ship, the *Leningrad,* one of the largest oceanographic research vessels in the Soviet Union. As he paced, he muttered to himself. It was three in the morning. It was cold, and he was very tired. He had been on his feet now for almost thirty-six hours, ever since he had received a call from Moscow instructing him to assemble his crew, make his ship ready for sea, and lay in provisions for an extended voyage with one hundred and twenty passengers on board. The passengers would be arriving by various routes any time after midnight on the following day, and they would expect a meal.

Ponotiev peered through the mist along the deserted wharf, wishing he had turned in for a few hours instead of waiting to greet them. But his curiosity had proved too strong. He wanted to know what this was all about, where he would be taking his vessel, and what kind of work they would be doing. There was still no sign of them. He walked across to the other wing of the bridge and looked aft across the flat sweep of the main working deck, with its multiple lifts and winches and the raised helicopter platform on the stern. They had only completed three scientific cruises under his command and had just been repainted. The mist had wet the superstructure, and under the harsh dock lights, the paintwork glistened like new. He nodded with satisfaction. Everything looked clean and orderly. It was a ship to be proud of. And he was proud of it.

There was a sound of engines and a clattering noise from the end of the wharf. He turned and walked back to the other side of the bridge and looked forward. There were lights coming down the wharf. Five buses ground along the cobbled surface and pulled up at the foot of the gangplank with much hissing of compressed air. The doors opened, and people started to climb out, clutching bundles and boxes and staring at the ship towering above them.

More lights appeared at the end of the wharf, and a large car bounced past the buses and came to a halt. Two men got out and started up the gangplank. The one in the lead was a thickset man with the long upper lip of the Georgian peasant.

"Public transportation for downtown Washington will be leaving shortly from the East wing," the loudspeaker system intoned. Packham strode out of Dulles International Airport into the glaring heat and looked for an air-conditioned taxi. There was one only three places back, and he was soon on his way into DC.

Stanton had told him that Scott Brady wanted to see him as soon as possible. He wondered what the hurry was. There were no new developments in his project as far as anyone knew. He had not reported Marshall's first binary message, and he had certainly never breathed a word about the whole Brebin episode. He had however reported Lopukhin's use—deliberate or otherwise—of the "Lone Wolf" code name and had demanded renewed security checks across the whole project. The checks had proved negative, but they had given the project a new code name as a matter of routine. The leak, if there was a leak, could have come from a dozen sources. Things were never really as secure as people liked to believe.

Packham found a message at his hotel telling him Scott Brady would expect him at the White House around five. That gave him time to walk across to the Hertz office on L Street and rent a car. He would need it later.

Scott Brady was just as affable as ever, but he looked tired, with fine lines of fatigue beneath his eyes. There had been another Mideast crisis recently as well as a series of press attacks about some of the president's more blatant war decisions. The strains of his duties as White House Chief of Staff were beginning to show.

"Good to see you, Colonel. How's the project coming?"

"Well, to be frank, I do not have anything to report. We have picked up a few things but nothing with any meaning or pattern. However, I do feel that we now have a strong, well-trained team in top condition. If there is anything to be achieved, I am confident they will be capable of achieving it."

"Is there anything else that can be done to speed things up? More money? More people?"

"Well, if we could find any more telepathists, we could increase the amount of time spent monitoring and projecting. At the moment we are working shifts, but there's a limit to what the men can do."

"Do you know how we could find any more?"

"It would require a lot of time, or money, or both, but I suppose it would be possible to work out a recruiting program."

"Can you get me the details tomorrow? I'll see what I can do to find the necessary funding."

"Tomorrow's a bit soon. Give me a couple of days."

"Tomorrow, Colonel!" Brady said firmly, rubbing his eyes. "If you need any assistance, you can have it. But I don't want to waste any time. We need you, Colonel. We need your project, and we need results. Not in three months, but now."

Packham got Brady to make a few phone calls to people who could help him put together a recruitment program in record time. The calls produced results. Personal calls from the White House Chief of Staff usually did.

He returned to his hotel, made a few phone calls of his own, and then drove out to Virginia. James Farrel was not there this time, but the other two men were. They lost no time in idle conversation.

"Well, Colonel," the taller of them said, "you've been hiding things from us."

"What do you mean?" Packham said, wondering what they were referring to. There were several pieces of information he had not passed on to them.

"Don't give us that," the shorter man snapped. "We're talking about the binary signal Marshall received. Why didn't you report it?"

"I didn't report it because I was hoping to have it confirmed by another signal. We never did have another signal, so we assumed it was just a fluke. If we ever do, I'll let you know."

"I hope you will, Colonel," the taller man said. "It's important that we be kept fully informed at all times. Now I gather Brady wants you to double your personnel."

Packham nodded. *My God, they certainly were well-informed.*

"That's good because we have received news of increased UFO sightings in West Africa. I'll give you the details in a moment. Furthermore, we have reason to believe the Russians are beefing up their operation too. Colonel Packham, they must not be allowed to get ahead of us. They must not be allowed to win. I do not need to remind you that this is not an ordinary race. You know what is at stake."

An hour later, Packham drove back to Washington looking very thoughtful. He had learned a lot in the last hour, but he still did not understand how they had known about Marshall. Thank God they did not know about Brebin. Or did they?

In Sullom Voe, Mike and Chuck were resting between two sessions.

"I wish I could get a contact." Chuck sighed. "This whole thing is turning into a huge yawn. If I got something, I'd feel encouraged to go on—even something like your yellow butterfly. Have you seen it again recently?"

"No, not for a couple of days. But it doesn't do anything. It just sits there and flutters. It's a mystery, really. I think Jim is right that it must have some meaning. But what? If only I could get closer to it."

"It's a pity we can't help you somehow," said Chuck earnestly. He looked at his watch. "Anyway, time to get back to the treadmill. You're up."

Mike stretched and climbed onto his lab stool, settling down almost automatically into his receive position. He swept his mind clear and began tracking. Thirty seconds later, he had a signal. A strong, remarkably strong, signal from straight out of the northeast.

Brebin? No, it couldn't be Brebin. He was dead. Or was he? With an effort, Mike pulled himself together and concentrated. No, it wasn't Brebin. Behind the signal was a thought quality that was quite different. No, it was definitely not Brebin. He would have recognized him anywhere. Then who was it? Whoever it was, he was damn good. The signal kept coming in like a strong, steady beat. No, this was something else—something quite different. Coming from the northeast, it had to be another Russian. But that strong? Could it possibly be an extraterrestrial?

The signal continued loud and clear. Mike could feel the thought shapes throbbing behind it. They were calm and confident, which were so different to those of Brebin. And there was another difference. Mike could not put his finger on it. What was it? The signal came to an abrupt end, and Mike was left groping in the void. He wanted to respond, but should he? He still felt responsible in a way for what had happened to Sergei. But this was different. The whole personality felt different. And then, it might not be a Russian; it might be an extraterrestrial.

The signal suddenly began again with the same strong, steady beat. He hesitated to call Jim. If it was another Russian, presumably Packham would not want anyone to know, but then Packham was still away in Washington. What if it was an extraterrestrial after all? Mike frowned. He would have to respond. He could not run the risk of missing a genuine contact. He waited for the signal to come to an end, and then, turning toward the northeast, he projected, *Who are you? Please reply!* as hard as he could.

There was a pause, a moment of confusion, and then, in a sudden surge of excitement, a wonderfully clear response.

Yes. Hello. I can hear you. I can hear you.

Without the binary message, the thought shape was totally different.

Hello, Mike responded. *Who are you? Are you Russian?*

Yes, came the delighted reply. *How did you know?*

I am American. I am not an extraterrestrial. My name is Marshall. Mike Marshall. Who are you, please?
You are American?
Mike was fascinated by the thought shapes. They had a unique quality about them.
Yes, he said. *Tell me your name.*
Klimenkova. Katrina Klimenkova.
Mike knocked his knuckles against his forehead. Of course. A woman. That's why he had been puzzled by the thought shapes.
Katrina, listen. Do not be afraid of me. Are you being watched?
Watched? Why? And why should I be afraid of you?
Are you sure you're not being watched?
Of course. What did you say your name was?
Mike.
Mike, this is wonderful. Actually communicating with someone by telepathy, so clearly and simply. I wouldn't have thought it possible. Wait a moment. I must tell my supervisor.
No! Mike intervened. *Don't do that, please!*
What is it? I can feel you're very tense, very nervous. This was ironical, he reflected. Now it was he who was being told not to be afraid. How could he tell her that she was in danger?
Katrina, he began, *I don't think your supervisors would like you to be communicating with an American. They might get angry with you. If you're supposed to be working right now, they might notice something. Why don't we agree to communicate later, when you have finished working?*
I agree. I have to start sending again, anyway. But how will I contact you?
Just beam southwest and call "Mike."
All right. It'll be around seven.
Mike relaxed as the signal disappeared. What a coincidence. Another Russian. Although, he reflected, it was logical if you thought about it for a moment. In fact, it was surprising that neither Chuck nor Jan had picked up Russian signals or that

the Russians had not picked up any of them. Of course, the Russians may have. Maybe they had and had been instructed not to respond.

In any case, Katrina seemed much more relaxed about it than Sergei had ever been. Was that because she was more sure of herself? Did she know something Sergei didn't, or was she just plain naïve? After all, there was a danger. It was not imaginary. Sergei had been killed; he was sure of it. But how could he warn her if she did not think there was any danger? If she did not want to be warned, he couldn't help it. Maybe he was just trying to make up for Sergei's death, for which he continued to feel partly responsible. Maybe he felt responsible for her too, because she seemed so naïve and vulnerable. He told himself not to be ridiculous. He didn't know anything about her. Perhaps she was tougher and more self-reliant than he was and didn't need any of his help. He wished he knew more about her. In any case, for the moment, he wasn't going to tell anyone at Sullom Voe about his new contact.

For some reason, he found it difficult to wait until seven. He finished his session with Chuck and went over to his room and tried to read, but he couldn't concentrate. He took a walk round the compound. *It is beginning to feel like a concentration camp*, he thought, and he dropped into the mess for a drink.

Frank Mambrino was sitting there, eating a plate of spaghetti. He had flown back the day before, after his observation period in hospital. They had found nothing wrong with him apparently, but he claimed to have lost a lot of weight. Mike certainly couldn't see any difference, and in any case, the way he was stuffing spaghetti into his mouth, he would soon put back anything he had lost.

At seven, Mike was back in his room, waiting. He did not have to wait long. At few minutes after seven, he sensed his name being projected. It felt good. He could not say why, but the way it was being projected filled him with pleasure. There was something about it which conveyed a feeling of softness but at the same time an image of strength and simplicity. Finally, he responded.

Yes, Katrina. I am here.

Oh good. I was afraid I wouldn't find you again.

I was afraid you might get the hours confused.

What do you mean?

Isn't there still an hour's difference with Finland?

What are you talking about? Are you in Finland? It had not occurred to me that you could be anywhere else other than America!

Now wait a minute, Mike said, *aren't you in Finland?*

No. What gave you that idea? We are on a ship somewhere in the North Sea. I'm not quite certain where. So where are you then if you're neither in America nor in Finland?

Mike told her a little about the American project, including where it was, how many people were involved, and what they were trying to achieve.

Why that's wonderful! she exclaimed. *That's exactly what we're trying to do here. And isn't it wonderful that we're able to communicate in this way? Without any language problem? I never thought that would be possible. You see, I'm a linguist by training, and part of my work has been trying to discover the importance of language in telepathic communication. Now I see there is no problem. Language does not seem to make any difference at all!*

Katrina, Mike cut in, *did you know a man called Sergei Brebin?*

No. Who was he? Russian, obviously.

He used to work on your project.

How do you know this?

Because we used to communicate together, just like you and I are communicating now

No, I don't know him or didn't know him, rather. What became of him? You talk about him as if he's dead or something.

He must have been taken off the project, Mike said squeamishly, not wanting to tell her what he knew. *The project used to be located in Finland. That's why I kept talking about Finland. You seem to have made many changes. Tell me, is Lopukhin still in charge?*

Yes. He is. He's still here.

Behind the words, Mike thought he could detect a feeling of disgust.

Don't you like him?

No, he's a pig!

What makes you say that?

Well, you're not a woman. You wouldn't understand. But he has a way of looking at you that makes you feel dirty. And my best friend, Anna, says he has tried to molest her. I don't like him.

Katrina. I want you to be very careful with him. I think he's dangerous.

Sorry, Katrina, he went on, *I didn't want to give you advice like that. I'm sure you can look after yourself.*

Don't apologize, Mike. I like it. I mean, I'm sure you're trying to be helpful. And it's flattering, in a way.

Mike, do you mind if I ask how old you are? He felt a certain warmth in Katrina's question.

I'm thirty-three. And you?

Twenty-six. There was a slight hesitation. *Are you married? Sorry,* she rushed on without waiting for an answer, *this is starting to sound like a silly novel!*

No, I'm not married. Are you?

No. I was though.

There was a pause, and then Mike continued. *Look, about Lopukhin. I don't want to scare you, but I meant what I said. Be careful. From what Brebin told me, he can be very dangerous.*

All right, Katrina agreed softly. *I'll be careful. Thank you for the warning.*

Katrina's thought shape at that moment was very strong. It came across as a slender, peach-colored oval with an iridescent blue edging. To Mike, it was both exciting and immensely peaceful at the same time. In an odd way, it seemed distant and yet very familiar. He wanted to explore it further, but reluctantly he forced himself back to immediate matters.

From what you tell me, your project seems to have changed a lot. What's the point of the ship, and what kind of ship is it anyway?

It's an oceanographic research vessel, the captain told me. It's called the Leningrad. It's one hundred and twenty meters long, and it can cruise at fourteen knots. The reason we're on it is to get closer to the alien spacecraft sighted over the North Sea oil rigs.

That makes sense. Now you mention it, I'm surprised no one here thought of that. Do you still have ten telepathists?

Oh no. We have more than that. There are twenty of us.

And how many telguards?

Telguards? I don't know what you mean.

They used to have those before you started, Mike said hastily. That's why she was not being watched or at least thought she was not being watched. Perhaps Lopukhin had converted the telguards into fully operational telepathists. According to Katrina, there were now twenty of them. Yes, that was probably what had happened.

They used to monitor the telepathists to see if they were sending the correct message, he continued.

Well, that would be useful, Katrina commented gravely. *Some of the telepathists we have are not worth much anyway. Certainly not as good as you. You have a very clear signal. What a pity we can't be working together. We're both working for the same objectives, after all. Don't you think it's admirable that our two countries are both seeking to extend a hand of friendship toward beings from beyond our planet? Isn't it wonderful that our two countries are working together for once?*

I think that would be wonderful, if it were true.

Isn't that what you just told me? Didn't you tell me that you were trying to contact extraterrestrial intelligence so as to bring new technology to the world's problems?

Yes, I did, Mike said.

Well. So are we.

Mike did not know what to say. How could he begin to explain what he thought the real situation was? He didn't want to alienate her, but he couldn't let her go on thinking the way she did.

Listen, Katrina, he began, *I don't know how to say this. I told you what our project is supposed to be doing and what people have told me it is supposed to be doing. But I'm not certain of that. I don't know whether it's true. It's sad to say, but today one has to be suspicious of things that sound too good to be true, and this does. You believe your project is firmly based on noble ideals. Maybe it is. But I have reason to believe it may not be. There may be other hidden objectives which are not so noble.*

No, you are wrong! Katrina retorted. *You are only saying that because you do not trust Russians. You Americans are all the same. Only you can be right. You do not know Russia. You do not know what it is capable of. It can be strong and noble and good. The Russian people are noble and good. How can you doubt it?*

Katrina, please. I am not saying that we Americans are right. I am saying that I suspect our own motives too. And I am merely suggesting to you that yours may not be all they appear to be. I am not asking you to reject your country and to turn your back on your people and your beliefs. Someone once told me, "Don't trust anyone, not even your own people." He was right, but I didn't believe him then. He had to die to convince me!

Mike, Mike, what is it? I can feel you are very hurt. What happened? Won't you tell me?

One day, perhaps. Meanwhile, I do think you should be careful. Don't mention our contact to anyone. It can serve no purpose to do so. He paused, hating to break the communication, but he did not want to expose Katrina to any more danger than was necessary. He couldn't believe Lopukhin had allowed all monitoring to be dropped.

Mike, we are going to communicate again, aren't we?

Yes, but I think we should only do so when you are certain there is no danger of being overheard. We could communicate tomorrow night.
How about early tomorrow morning?
All right.
Don't you want to?
Yes, I do, Mike said, realizing he meant it.
There was an embarrassed pause.
Well, good night then, Mike said.
Good night. And Mike…
Yes.
I enjoyed communicating with you.

Chapter 16

North Sea, June 14, 2007. 2:45 p.m.

On board the *Leningrad,* Captain Ponotiev laid off a new course on the bridge chart table and waited for his second-in-command to come on watch and relieve him. The new course would take them slightly to the north of the Frigg oilfield. This would become the pattern for the next few weeks. Lopukhin had instructed him to take the vessel as close as possible to the oilfield, without being too obvious. Ponotiev had pointed out that even if they were out of sight, they would still appear on the rigs' radar screens and that far from being invisible, they were going to be very obvious sitting a few miles away doing nothing.

"Why do you think I chose an oceanographic research vessel?" Lopukhin had retorted icily. "If anybody becomes curious, we are engaged in oceanographic research which requires us to stay in the same area for an indefinite length of time. No one is going to question that. I would advise you to keep a few instruments or sample trawls on deck ready to go over the side if ever we are approached. Your job is to keep the ship out of trouble and as close to the rigs as possible. We'll be changing fields from time to time too, but I want to concentrate on Frigg and Ekofisk. That's where most of the spacecraft have been sighted."

Ponotiev snorted. What a crazy, wild goose chase! Aliens from outer space and telepathists! Well it didn't make any difference what Lopukhin and his bunch of tame ghost hunters thought; he had his job to do, and he was going to do it. He was responsible for the safety of his ship and everyone on it, and no one was going to make him get too close to those damn rigs. It might be all right in summer when the weather was fair, but when the autumn gales started, it would be a very different matter. He had seen a rig get out of control once and knew what a menace they could be. That's why his new course, and all the other courses he would lay from now on, would put the ship on the other side of the world. He did not want to get downwind of the rogue rig!

His first mate came on the bridge, and he gave him the new course, explaining why he always wanted to be upwind of any danger. The weather was good now, but it could change very quickly in the North Sea.

"It has been remarkably good," the first mate agreed, glancing at the sea and the sky, "but it won't last for ever. I pity all our poor passengers when it breaks. You know how much this ship rolls, particularly if we're just station keeping, wallowing around the same spot."

"It'll serve some of them right!" Pontiev said with a grin. "Particularly that damn Lopukhin. He's really got a way of irritating me."

Thirty feet below, in a small cabin on the port side of the ship, Katrina and Anna Gan were also talking about Lopukhin.

"I thought he was going to explode!" Anna giggled, referring to a meeting they had attended that afternoon when Lopukhin had assembled the whole team and warned them that he was not going to tolerate any slacking. "This is not a pleasure cruise!" he had said. Someone had laughed, and that had made him furious.

"I think he's ridiculous," Anna went on, "but he frightens me. He's always trying to paw me around. Not that I usually object to that!" She added with another giggle, "But he's so—ugh—oily! I can't stand him to touch me!"

"Well, you be careful," Katrina said, remembering Mike's words. "He could be dangerous."

So far, she had not told Anna about Mike. He had repeatedly warned her against saying anything to anybody, but she would have dearly loved to tell Anna all about it. She was glad Anna had been included on the team at the last minute, when one of the lab assistants had dropped out. She was a good friend, and it was very pleasant to have someone to talk to, particularly in such a closed community in which no one knew each other.

The move from Moscow had been so sudden. One day they were working in the lab, and the next they were sitting in a bus bound for Murmansk. They had been allowed twenty-four hours to pack and settle their immediate affairs, without knowing how long they would be away. Several weeks, at least, they had been told. All they knew was that they had been recruited for a top-secret mission of the greatest national interest.

"You should be proud," Levkov had told her. "Not everyone has the chance to serve her country in such an important way."

At first, they had found it difficult to adapt to life at sea, particularly in such cramped quarters, and once again Katrina was thankful that she was able to share a cabin with someone she knew. But they had settled down quickly enough. Anna had been a little seasick the first two days, but the ministrations of a handsome ship's doctor had put her on her feet in no time. When they were not working, they spent as much time as possible on deck, enjoying the sea air.

The work itself was boring. There were seven-and-a-half hours of projection or reception every day, and that meant seven-and-a-half hours in a stuffy hold converted into a lab. Despite her conviction, Katrina was beginning to find the whole project too monotonous for her active brain, until her contact with Mike provided some relief and the certainty that telepathic communication at a distance was a workable reality. Not that she had ever really doubted it, but it was good to have proof!

"You never did tell me what really happened with Kamikov," Anna said unexpectedly, filing her nails.

"Well," Katrina began carefully, "I think it's true to say we discovered we had very little in common, and he's far too old for me. You know what I want from a man, Anna. I've told you before. Kamikov doesn't have it. I don't think I've met a man yet who does. Unless…"

Anna squeaked and put down her nail file.

"Katrina Klimenkova! You're hiding something from me. What is it? Who is he? Tell me, quick!"

"No, I can't, Anna, I can't."

"Oh yes you can," Anna said, jumping across the room and starting to pummel her. "And you're going to, even if I have to beat it out of you!"

The two women pushed and pulled each other, rocking with laughter. Finally, Anna dragged Katrina to the floor and sat on her, bouncing up and down on her stomach.

"Now will you tell me?" she said, bouncing.

"Stop! Stop!" Katrina gasped between bounces. "I give in. Stop. I'll tell you!"

Anatol Lopukhin reread the long e-mail from Moscow. He swore and slammed it down on the desk in his stateroom. *Those interfering fools*, he thought. *They'll ruin the whole project if they're not careful.* Apparently, some high officials wanted to leak news of the project to the Western press so as to establish the fact that the Soviets were the first in the field and that their motives for contacting extraterrestrial intelligence were as pure as driven snow! Damned meddling idiots! He paced up and down the length of the stateroom, cursing. This world would be a better place without politicians!

There was a tap at the door.

"Yes, come in!" he shouted.

Three men and a woman filed in and accepted his invitation to be seated. Lopukhin pushed the cable to one side and sat on the desk in front of them.

"I sent for you because I want to be quite certain you understand your duties. Volkov and Zeludev—" he nodded at two of the men "—you were on the old project, so you know more than the others. But I want to stress that your duties will be different here. First of all, you will not be known as telguards. In fact, you will not be known at all. You will be operating incognito, as it were. Your job will be to monitor the work of the telepathists, but I want you to do it discreetly. If they know of your existence, they will be wary of you. You have all been picked for your telepathic abilities, but there are not enough of you to assign one to each telepathist. So you are going to have to be selective. However, I want to make certain that every telepathist is monitored from time to time. I'll leave it to you to work out schedules and subjects, and make sure you don't miss anyone. Any questions?"

The woman raised a finger, and Lopukhin nodded.

"What are we supposed to be monitoring for?" she asked.

"Anything that does not correspond to an official signal. You can get copies of the day's signals from the duty officer. Anything, I repeat anything, that deviates from those signals must be reported. Now, I know that some of the telepathists may occasionally communicate between themselves. It does happen, accidentally. But I don't want you using your discretion. You may not recognize the importance of what you pick up. Everything must be reported—to me personally. Is that clear?"

They all nodded.

Mike and Katrina continued to communicate two or three times a day. Mike had learned to look forward to these encounters. In one way, he felt that he had always known Katrina, so closely did their thoughts match, but in another way, he was convinced he would never be able to know enough about her. Every time he opened a door in her mind, it was like entering a whole new world, a world he wanted to linger in and explore, but he knew that there would always be another door, and another.

They had told each other about their lives. Mike was curious to know when her telepathic abilities had first revealed themselves and whether they had troubled her as much as his had him. He was very surprised to learn how late they had appeared.

You mean you never had any flashes or any sudden insights into people's minds? he had said. *Not even—* he hesitated but soon went on, knowing he could never hide anything from Katrina now *—not even in moments of great intimacy? For example, with your husband?*

No, no. On the contrary, she had replied with no embarrassment, *it always seemed that those were the moments I was the most cut off from everyone, particularly my husband. I think that is probably why I didn't fight to keep our marriage together.*

You must have felt close to him at times.

Oh yes, of course. But we were very young. Our closeness never went very deep. We were like affectionate puppies, clumsily falling over each other, full of life and youth but unable to communicate beyond a certain level of animal attraction.

Mike was invariably astonished by the clarity of her thought and by her disarming leaps from profundity to mischievous fun poking. She was always teasing him about his love life.

You must be very ugly if you never managed to find a wife, she said and then went on to ask him what he looked like. He tried to describe himself but felt he was not doing a very good job.

You sound nice, she said. *Those silly American women don't know how to appreciate you!* Mike, for once, did not know whether she was teasing or not. He asked her to describe herself.

Well, I have two eyes, a nose, two ears, she began. *Oh, how can I describe myself without seeming conceited or hypocritical? I think I'm pretty. Several men have told me that, but I wouldn't know. You'll have to wait until you see me!*

Do you think that will ever happen?

Who knows?

One subject they constantly returned to was their work and the question of whether they would one day succeed in contacting any form of extraterrestrial intelligence.

It sometimes seems like it could take forever, Mike said once.

I know what you mean, Katrina put in, *and I've only been doing this for a few days. But I can't believe we'll do this for the rest of our lives.*

No, not if we do establish contact. What are you going to do after this is all over?

I suppose I'll go back to working at the institute. But, of course, things may be very different. If we do succeed in communicating with extraterrestrials, I expect our lives will be changed. Particularly for people like ourselves, who have been involved in this communication process. Just think of all the follow-up work that would have to be done. If we did not establish some form of communication other than telepathy, then we'd be very busy handling the flow of information back and forth. We would become machines—human transmitters and receivers.

I'm sure we'd be able to work out a more direct form of communication, Mike said. *It wouldn't make sense otherwise.*

Oh, I agree with you. But then, assuming that we did, think of all the research that would result. We'd be busy for years exploring new applications for telepathic communication, without mentioning all the other things we would probably learn from the extra-terrestrials.

Yes, it would be true in every technical field, I suppose. That is, if the extra-terrestrials are indeed more technically advanced than we are. We have always assumed that, but of course they may not be, or at least not in everything. They may be more advanced in space travel, we could safely assume that, but that doesn't mean to say they know more than we do about medicine, or chemistry, or agriculture, things that would help us solve our problems.

No, and even if they did, their agriculture or their medicine might not be suitable at all for human applications. In any case, Mike said after a pause, *the world would be a very different place. Just the fact of knowing that there is extraterrestrial intelligence, that we are not alone in this universe, that there are things bigger than us, might jolt us into realizing that war and ideological conflicts are ridiculous. Maybe even our politicians would get the message! Maybe they would at least see the virtues of trying to live together peacefully instead of always wanting to bomb the hell out of each other.*

Maybe, Katrina picked up, *maybe they would learn enough about communication to be able to converse the way we are. But, Mike, what is going to happen if we do not succeed in establishing contact with the extraterrestrials? Perhaps they don't want to communicate with us. Perhaps they don't know how. Perhaps, contrary to what we believe, they don't use binary language. How are we going to tell if they are trying to communicate with us? I mean, we pick up signals all the time. How are we going to know if it's them?*

What signals are you talking about? Mike asked. *You mean local conversations, thoughts, feelings, what we call "static" here?*

Yes, I suppose so, but there are others too. For example, there's one recurring signal I get which doesn't seem to mean anything, except that it keeps coming back, and that makes me think it must have some meaning.

Oh? said Mike, suddenly very alert. *What signal is that?*

Well, it's difficult to distinguish really. It's usually very faint and distant. I think it's a golden bird.

A golden bird?

Yes, I think it's a bird. At least I think it has wings. I can see them fluttering.

Did you say "fluttering"? Mike asked excitedly.

Yes, that's why I think it's a bird, and it's a light golden color. So I call it my golden bird.

Is it right on the edge of your perception, and every time you try to get closer, it recedes?

Yes, yes. How do you know? Have you been picking up the same signal?

I don't know. I think so. Only I call it my yellow moth. But now I think about it, you're right. It's not a moth. It's a bird, and it is more golden than yellow. You're absolutely right. It's a golden bird.

What does it mean?

I don't know. But this is amazing, Katrina. I too thought it had to have some meaning since it keeps coming back, but now I know you're getting it too, then it must *have a meaning.*

Mike, said Katrina, *are you thinking what I'm thinking?*

You know I am. And you're right. It can only be one thing. It's what we've been waiting for!

Everyone agreed that Packham had been impossible since his return from Washington. He had stalked round the labs, something he had never done before, exhorting them all to greater efforts. This irritated the three telepathists intensely, since there was nothing more they could do. It was frustrating enough as it was, projecting signals without knowing whether there was anyone to listen, or endlessly scanning for messages that never came.

Even Jim and Sam were annoyed since they felt Packham was disturbing their charges. Dr. Jim never gave any sign of annoyance, but then he never gave much sign of anything. Only Frank seemed genuinely untroubled by Packham's words, but then he was very busy with a new array of electronic gadgetry he had ordered for monitoring UFO activity. So, for various reasons, everyone groaned when Packham called a general meeting. The last thing they wanted was another pep talk.

Packham sat scowling and nervously tapping a pencil on the bench in front of him when they all filed into the main lab. They sat down in silence, and Packham scowled round the group.

"All right!" he began. "Something has happened which does not make me feel very happy. There has been a security leak, and it had to come from someone on this station and, I'm pretty certain, from someone in this room."

He glanced angrily round the group again. They returned his gaze with differing degrees of astonishment or resentment. Jim Gardner was obviously very put out and looked as if he was about to protest, but Packham raised a hand, and he remained silent. No one else spoke. Chuck squirmed in his seat, unable to support the cold anger in Packham's eyes.

"I don't know who it is," Packham continued, "and I don't know why anyone would want to compromise the project in this way. Perhaps it was unintentional. Anyway, whatever the case, or whatever the reason, I have decided that no one will leave the station on any pretext whatsoever. No more outings, no more jogging. Nothing. Anyone have questions?"

Dr. Jim raised a hand and said, "Yes. Are you certain there has been a leak?" Packham nodded. "How did you find out?"

"I'm not going to tell you. But there is no doubt in my mind that there has been a leak, and I cannot run the risk of its happening again. This project is too far advanced. There is too much at stake. We are now approaching a point where success may be just around the corner. You are beginning to work well together as a team. We may be getting some more people on staff here. I say 'may.' I'll believe them when I see them. And as Frank will tell you in a moment, never have there been more sightings of UFOs in the area. The time is ripe. This project is too important to jeopardize, and I am not going to allow any more—" here, he looked angrily round the group again, finally letting his gaze settle on Mike "—I am not going to allow anyone to destroy it."

He is losing his grip, Mike thought. *He's paranoid. If there had been a leak, what was the point of telling everyone about it? All he had succeeded in doing was to sow a grain of panic and disorder while possibly alienating one of the key people on the project, Jim Gardner. What had happened to make him act in this way? Something pretty serious,* he conjectured. After a long pause, Packham motioned at Frank Mambrino.

"Tell us what you've got, Frank."

Frank stood up and waved a multi-leaf computer printout.

"This came in last night, on the chopper," he began with a wide smile, which contrasted with Packham's overbearing scowl. "It's a compilation of all UFO sightings over the last two weeks. There are thirty-seven of them, sorry, thirty-four of them," he paused for emphasis, tapping the sheaf of paper with his finger, "thirty-four of them over North Sea oilfields. Gentlemen. They're here. The extraterrestrials are here. If we're going to communicate with them, now's the time!"

"Okay," Mike interrupted, "I believe you. But what difference does it make? What can we do now that we haven't been doing already? What do you want us to do now, Packham, stand on a ladder and wave, singing 'America, America'?"

Packham scowled at Mike. "That's not funny, Marshall. Just let Frank finish." "Yeah, I know, fellas," said Frank. "You've all been doing your best, but I think this may make your job easier. Listen, what I'm going to do is try to establish a pattern from all these sightings. I can probably work out the best time for you to be operational. What direction any UFOs may be coming from, how long they'll stay around, speed, distances, and so on. Would that be useful for you? Jim, Sam? I'm only trying to be helpful."

"Sure, Frank, we appreciate it," said Sam. "I think that would be most useful. Let us know when you have some suggestions for us."

"Okay then," Packham resumed, "get back to your work, all of you. And just let me be clear on this point again. There is to be no communication—" he pounded the bench with his fist for greater emphasis and stared hard at Mike "—no communication of any kind with anyone outside this station."

Mike thought he detected a certain manic glint in Packham's eye. Was all this directed at him? Was Packham referring to his previous contact with the Russians? Did he think the leak had come from him? Packham was in deadly earnest. A thought occurred to him that suddenly left him feeling cold. Perhaps if they thought he was endangering the project, Packham and his superiors would not hesitate any more than the Russians to get rid of him.

Chapter 17

Sullom Voe, June 28, 2007. 11:30 a.m.

Despite the pleasure and satisfaction he derived from his now frequent contacts with Katrina, Mike felt increasingly jaded and depressed. Since Packham's last meeting, he had become more than ever convinced that the motives behind the American project were not all they claimed to be, or else they had changed. Packham certainly had changed. At the beginning, when Mike had first met him, he was very friendly and open, at least superficially. But now he seemed to be permanently irritable and aggressive. And every time he went to Washington, he became worse. Mike sometimes wondered who Packham reported to. In any case, Packham never spoke any more of bringing the virtues of American life and political thought to the attention of extraterrestrial intelligence. His sole concern now seemed to be the speed with which results could be obtained.

Mike also felt that he was standing still. When he discovered that Katrina was picking up the golden bird, they were both elated and filled with excitement. It was all coming true. They were going to succeed. The extraterrestrials were trying to establish contact. But since then, neither of them had managed to move an inch further forward. The golden bird stayed where it was, just out of reach, never really fully perceived, floating tantalizingly on the edge of awareness. They talked about it often. How could they get closer or bring it closer? It was a maddening situation, and Mike was grateful for someone with whom he could share his frustration—someone who understood. It had to have a meaning, they told each other repeatedly. Otherwise, why would it exist?

Why would they both be able to perceive it? At times, Mike began to doubt whether it had anything to do with extraterrestrials.

Two days after Packham's meeting, however, he received some positive encouragement when he discussed it with Sam Goldman. By now, Mike saw the golden bird practically every time he started receiving. He could choose to ignore it if he wanted, and he did if he was scanning for other signals, but it was always there in the background, on the brink of darkness. Once a day, under Jim's promptings, he spent half an hour trying to come to grips with the elusive image but never with any success. He had continued to refer to it as his yellow moth, since that was what they had always called it, but that morning, after another fruitless session, he drew Sam to one side.

"Sam, do you remember asking me about my yellow moth? Whether I was sure it was a moth? You said you had never come across a moth symbol in connection with extraterrestrials. What about a bird? A golden bird instead of a yellow moth?"

"That would be much better," said Sam. "Yes, of course. Why didn't I think of it? A golden bird. Yes, now that would fit much better. The bird is of course a very frequent symbol, representing space and flight, but it is often given godlike or supernatural qualities too. Let me see now," Sam continued, pushing up his glasses and pulling his upper lip. "Yes, I can think of several examples in Latin American vestiges, in Polynesian folk tales, and even of course in ancient Egypt, although the connection there may be tenuous. You've got the Bird Men of Easter Island and Lake Titicaca, the flying creatures of many African legends, all unexplained. And you find winged deities up and down the fables and mythologies of almost every civilization. Now that I think about it, there are endless examples, with many in areas or near sites associated with what is believed to have been extraterrestrial activity."

"What about the color?" Mike asked.

"Well, it could be color, or it could be the precious metal, both of which are highly symbolical. The color is often associated with light and by extension with knowledge or wisdom. It could also be representative of power and majesty. If it has any connection with powered flight, then propulsion jets or flames may be intended. As for the metal gold, it too has always been associated with deity and royalty and in many cases also carries a meaning of purity and immutability. Now another thing you have to consider is the kind of bird. The meaning would be different according to whether it's an eagle, a hawk, a dove, or a condor, for example."

"My God, Sam! I didn't realize you were such an expert."

"Oh, well," Sam replied modestly, "it's a hobby of mine. Anyway, I think you've got a much better symbol there than your yellow moth."

"Do you think it might have anything to do with extraterrestrials?"

"It's possible. In fact, it would be a perfect symbol of extraterrestrial life, having already had some contact with Earth or wishing to establish contact with us."

"But then why aren't we getting anywhere with it if they want to contact us?"

"Mike, if we knew that, we'd be home and dry. But we don't. And there must be some good reason why we can't understand it."

"There has to be a way." Mike fumed. "There has to be some way of understanding it. Otherwise, it doesn't make sense."

"Patience, patience!" said Sam. "But I have an idea. I want to talk to Jim about it first. If he agrees, we can try it out this afternoon."

A few hours later, Jim and Sam explained to the three telepathists what they wanted them to do.

"It appears that Sam and I have been thinking along the same lines," Jim began. "We realize how frustrating you all feel about not achieving any results or, in the case of Mike, receiving a signal but not being able to make any sense out of it. It was something

Chuck said one day that set my mind working. He said: 'If only we could help Mike somehow. We're supposed to be a team, but we're not working as a team. Mike is all alone, and we're not giving him any support. He's like a star football player. He's got the ball and he's ready to go, but he cannot get anywhere without our support. How can we give him the support he needs?' That was a very good question, and I've been trying to find an answer. Then, this morning, Sam came to me with a suggestion. Sam, why don't you explain?"

"Sure," said Sam. "I got to thinking about this because I suspected Mike's problem was one of signal strength. Incidentally, for your information, we've decided it's a golden bird, not a yellow moth. Maybe he wasn't getting any further with his signal because it wasn't strong enough to reach him. Now in telecommunications terms, what do you do when a signal is not strong enough? You amplify it. How do you do that? You beef up the receiving equipment. Okay. How about telepathy? You three are our receiving equipment. How can we link you up? Put you together in such a way as to make you more powerful? In an electronic circuit, we would wire you together in a particular way. We can't do that, so what we want you to do is make your own connections, stand in a circle, and hold hands. Now this may sound ridiculous, but we know that currents do flow from person to person and that handholding is often used in many collective religious rites to increase group spiritualist participation. It's used in some forms of hypnosis, in spiritual séances, and even in singing round the old campfire. The idea of forming a chain is almost as ancient as religion itself. Anyway, we'd like you to give it a try. What do you think?"

"We can give it a try," said Chuck. "It's better than doing nothing."

"I agree," Jan added, "although I'm not certain how we're going to do it. Whether we each have to scan outwards at the same time or try to go through Mike's mind."

"Well, I'm not certain either, believe me!" said Sam. "I think the idea to begin with is to try to form a collective mind, if that doesn't sound too ambitious or too weird. But I really don't know. What do you think, Mike?"

"Let's just try and see what happens. As you know from previous discussions, we all have our own individual configurations for sending and receiving. They may not fit, or they may even conflict. I think we've just got to start and see what we feel."

"Very sensible," said Jim. "Sam and I will leave you, but we'll be right outside."

When Sam and Jim left, the three telepathists stood in the middle of the lab, and, rather sheepishly at first, they formed a circle and held hands.

"Let's just try to feel each other's minds to begin with," Mike suggested.

It was a strange sensation. They were all familiar with each other's thought patterns, having done countless training exercises together, but this was the first time all three of them had come together. Mike could feel Chuck's angular shapes, warm and willing. Jan's softer, more complex shapes stayed a little detached. Mike was not certain, but he thought he detected a touch of resentment there.

"What's wrong, Jan?" he said. "I can feel some resistance. Mad at me for some reason?"

"No, I'm not mad at you," Jan said, and then she added with devastating frankness, "but I think I may be a little jealous of you—jealous of your having received a signal before me. I'm disappointed not to have been first."

"That's very honest of you," Mike said.

"I think I have to be. I think I have to bring this out into the open so that it will no longer be an obstacle. I wouldn't want it to spoil the project. So I admit I have been jealous, and I suppose I resented the idea of going through your mind, instead of retaining my individuality. I know it's ridiculous, but I can't help it. Perhaps now I've talked about it, it will disappear."

"Thank you, Jan. I appreciate your openness. Let's try again."

They linked hands once more, and Mike immediately felt a difference. Jan's thought shapes were calmer now and less aloof. Chuck was still as willing as ever. Mike opened up his mind, gradually assuming his dish configuration, not without difficulty though, since he felt the other two tugging in different directions, no doubt unconsciously seeking their own individual configurations.

Very quickly he found the golden bird, or rather, it appeared on the periphery of his perception. There it was, fluttering gently. He took a deep breath, squeezed the hands of his companions, and adopting a now familiar technique, he tried to focus out of the corner of his mind, looking without looking. That was the only way to begin to see the golden bird. If you tried to look at it directly, it went away. He relaxed and tried to pull the other two into his awareness. He squeezed their hands again, hoping to encourage them. The golden bird continued to flutter, neither receding nor becoming any closer. After a few minutes, Mike relaxed his grip and let the golden bird recede into the distance.

"Well, did you get it?" he asked of the other two.

They both shook their heads.

"Dammit, it was there!" Mike said. "Let's try again, but this time, relax! The harder you look, the less you'll see."

They settled down again. Mike located the bird, and this time Chuck suddenly squeezed his hand. "I've got it," he whispered. "I think."

Mike relaxed even more and tried to bring Chuck closer to the image. Chuck squeezed his hand harder. After a while Mike broke contact.

"You saw it?" he asked Chuck.

"Yes, I'm sure."

"You, Jan?"

"No, nothing."

"Let's try again."

Again, Chuck squeezed his hand as soon as the bird appeared. Again, Jan saw nothing. They tried changing positions, but Jan still failed to see anything.

"Okay," said Mike, "try on your own now, Chuck."

Chuck concentrated then relaxed, but after several minutes, he broke the silence and looked at Mike in puzzlement.

"I've lost it."

"Try again, with me."

They tried together, and Chuck immediately saw it again.

"You know what," said Jim a few minutes later, after they had given up and called a halt, "Chuck is seeing the golden bird only in Mike's mind. He's merely picking up the image locally. That's better than nothing, though," he went on encouragingly, "since now Chuck at least knows what it looks like. He'll be able to recognize it if he sees it alone. It's another step forward, however small. So don't feel bad about it. Anyway, let's forget it for the moment. We'll just have one last session on local receive, and then we'll call it a day."

Mike now looked forward to every communication with Katrina. Over the last few days, he had realized that she was becoming an important part of his life. There was something so soothing and satisfying about their contacts that Mike knew he would find it difficult to do without them. He also realized that he was becoming increasingly anxious about their length and frequency. Despite Katrina's assurances, he knew that she was running a risk in communicating with him, and although he hated himself for it, he had to insist upon keeping their contacts down to a reasonable length.

Their "relationship" had now progressed far beyond a simple friendship, if such a relationship could remain simple or straightforward in the circumstances. They now knew practically everything there was to know about each other, and given the nature of their relationship and means of communication, it would have been difficult to hide anything for long, even if they had wished. This made their contacts uniquely direct. At first, they had attempted to preserve a few areas of private thought, but their telepathic communication was so clear and so intense that they soon decided it was simpler to be completely open. As soon as they realized how much easier it was not to hide anything, they found they could relax and be themselves. This too was unique, and both of them found it enormously refreshing not to have to pretend.

All this had brought them very close together, and in other circumstances, they both knew their relationship would not have remained as it was. It would have inevitably blossomed into something deeper. This, Mike realized, was why he was so anxious about Katrina's situation. Of course she knew this and often teased him about it.

You old worry bear! she used to say. *Nothing is going to happen to me.*

Mike told her about the experiment he had been doing with Chuck and Jan.

Sounds like a good idea, she said. *Anything is worth trying.*

Yes, but I don't think it's going to work. Chuck is merely seeing the image reflected in my mind, not the original, and Jan is too hostile to be able to connect with me properly. There are too many obstacles between us all, human relationships being what they are. I think, in order to work, you'd probably need people who are so close to each other that there wouldn't be any barriers, brothers and sisters perhaps, or twins.

Or husbands and wives? Katrina asked softly.

I thought you told me husbands and wives aren't necessarily close, Mike said jokingly.

I mean husbands and wives like us!

Mike knew that Katrina had stopped joking. There was a sober seriousness about her now which made him catch his breath.

Katrina, he said very gently, with nothing or everything to say, finding pleasure and comfort in merely formulating her name. *Katrina, my dear.*

Mike, came the soft reply. *Mike, listen. I don't know what to say. These circumstances are so confusing. I have never seen you. I have never touched you. And yet…I want you. Can you understand?*

Yes!

There was something happening that they had never experienced before. They both felt as though they were moving closer together, almost able to reach forward and touch each other.

I wish I could touch you, Katrina thought to Mike, *if only for a few moments.*

I know, me too.

I've never felt like this before. It's like we're connected, like we're meant to be, you know?

Yes, I feel so very close to you too. Closer than with anyone I have ever known. Katrina, if only I could hold you!

Perhaps you can!

Mike held out his arms.

I'm holding you, Katrina, he said.

I know. I can feel your arms around me. Mike, I love you. How can I say this? I must be losing my mind!

No, I think we both know that we have been in love for some time. I love you too, Katrina. You are the only woman I have ever known with whom I feel at peace and at one with myself and everything around me.

They gave themselves up to a long, caressing embrace, in which their beings touched and mingled, flowing into and around each other, merging and parting, melting, breathing, and pulsing together. For a moment, they were out of space and time, suspended in a void of calm, slowly gyrating and twisting like unborn twins in their mother's womb, clutched to each other, un-separated, inseparable, one.

Mike, Katrina murmured, *take me!*

And Mike knew that he could, physically separated as they were. He pulled her closer, feeling her shoulder bend to fit against him. With infinite gentleness, he caressed her neck and shoulders and then, with a suddenness which left them both dizzy, he felt his soul drawn into a vortex of love, deep into the whirling nothingness of the primeval molecule from which they both sprang and in which they were now reunited. Weightless, they floated in a sea of serenity, basking in the warmth and contentment of total inter-penetration. Then slowly, very slowly, they returned to their senses, still merged and still clinging to each other.

Mike, Katrina thought, after a while, *what's going to happen to us? I don't want to lose you.*

How can we ever lose each other? If we can be this close, we'll always be together, wherever we are, together with our golden bird.

Do you think together we can reach our golden bird?

We can try.

Without any further discussion, knowing what to do as if by instinct, they let their minds open very gradually and naturally. It was like pulling back successive curtains in a darkened room, with each new curtain letting in a little more of the golden glow that lay behind them. And then, as the last curtain parted, they saw the golden bird, no longer on the edge of their vision but this time soaring above them, still very distant but now clear and luminous, dazzling, and beautiful, lazily winging its way through space, timeless, eternal! They could not say anything. They merely stood and gazed, filled with awe and wonder.

At last, Katrina spoke. *Mike, it's beautiful!*

Yes, it's the most beautiful thing I've ever seen. It's like looking at peace.

Mike, look. Am I imagining things? It's coming closer!

The golden bird was still very far away, but as they looked, it seemed to grow very gradually, wheeling from side to side and circling and rising, but it was unmistakably slowly moving toward them.

Suddenly, the image was torn, and Mike felt a stab of alarm from Katrina.

Katrina, he called, *what is it?*

There's someone at the door. Someone is knocking at the door. Mike, I have to answer. I hate to leave you now, but I must answer.

Be careful! he called.

Katrina's image faded, and Mike was left feeling lonely, cold, and very empty. The suddenness with which he and Katrina had been torn apart was numbing. The golden bird was still an echo in his mind, and he could still feel Katrina's presence, but he was alone—alone and worried. Now, more than ever, he was concerned for Katrina's safety. He could not trust Lopukhin. What if anything happened to Katrina? He could not stand the thought of losing her. He had told her that they could not lose each other, but now he was not so certain.

He rose and paced up and down his room, with his mind in a whirl. He forced himself to think calmly. "Just take it easy," he told himself. "Stop getting all worked up over nothing. Someone had knocked on her door, that's all. It could have been anyone."

Gradually, he reassured himself. There was nothing to worry about. It was just that after his experience with Katrina, he was particularly sensitive. She would try to contact him again soon.

It was two hours before Mike picked up Katrina's signal. By this time, he was very worried.

Katrina, where have you been? Are you all right?

Oh, Mike! Her thought shapes were twisted, jagged, hurt.

What happened? Tell me, Katrina!

Lopukhin has found out. He sent for me. There were guards at the door. He wants to know everything about you! What am I going to do? Her thoughts were still jumbled, confused, painful.

Katrina, tell me, did he hurt you?

Not much. He slapped me around a bit. But he's going to send for me again, I know.

Listen. Tell me what happened from the beginning, and calmly.

Katrina told him that the guards had hustled her off to see Lopukhin, who was in an uncontrollable rage. He had hit her two or three times in the face and called her a traitor, telling her he knew all about her communications with Mike.

They hate you Americans, Mike. He said they were looking forward to getting the technology of the extraterrestrials so that they could crush you and the rest of the world. You were right. They're not interested in peace or understanding. They just want to rule the world. What can we do?

Tell me the rest.

He said he was going to squeeze me dry, to find out everything I know about your project. And he'll do it. I know he will. He was going to start on me then and there, but he was called to the bridge for an urgent radio message from Moscow. Then when he came back, he said he had things to attend to but that he would look forward to resuming our conversation tomorrow. What am I going to tell him? I don't know what to do. I cannot betray you. And what about the extraterrestrials? We've got to warn them!

You're right. But, for the moment, that's secondary. The most urgent thing is you. If he interrogates you, just tell him everything. It's not important.

He said that, but he knew that as soon as Lopukhin had got all the information he wanted, he would kill her, just like Brebin. He had to do something. He couldn't leave her in the hands of Lopukhin. How could he get to her?

Mike, we have to let them know!

Wait, Mike said, *just let me think.* A plan was beginning to take shape in his head. It was a crazy, desperate idea, but it might work. It would have to!

Katrina, he said. *I'm going to come and get you! I can't leave you there. You're in too much danger, and you're right, we must warn the extraterrestrials. I'm convinced now that neither of our countries is interested in anything but their technology or their weapons. We are the only ones who can warn them, but we need time, and we need to be together.*

What are you saying? We're hundreds of miles apart. You're on land. I'm on a ship. How can you come and get me?

In a helicopter! But I cannot come until tomorrow afternoon. You're going to have to survive until then. Listen, there's a helicopter that (which) comes into our station every day at four. I've watched it arrive and land many times. I know I can fly it, and I think I can steal it.

But how are you going to find me?

I think we're much closer than you think. You told me you'd heard you were cruising off the Frigg oilfield. Well that's not more than eighty miles east of Sullom Voe. The field will be easy to recognize with all the rigs, and the Leningrad *will be the only large vessel in the vicinity except for supply ships. If the visibility is good, there should be no problem. If it is bad, you're going to have to guide me. But we'll worry about that when we get to it. Now, for the moment, I want you to think about the ship. It's an oceanographic research ship, you told me. All right, then it must have a large flat work deck I could land on. Is that right? I don't want to have to pick you up in the sea.*

There is a large deck. But wait a minute, now I remember, there's a helicopter platform on the stern. I've never seen it used, but one of the crew told me what it was.

Even better. I wasn't very happy about landing on a deck. This might work! The only problem now is how are you going to keep out of Lopukhin's way until tomorrow afternoon? Is there any way you can get out of your cabin?

Oh yes. It's not locked. There's not even a lock on the door. The guards know I can't go anywhere.

Thank God for that. Mike sighed. *That makes things a lot easier. What you must do now is hide somewhere—somewhere they can't find you. Can you think of anywhere?*

Yes, I'll think of something.

Find somewhere safe and go there now. You never know when Lopukhin will come looking for you. Now, we must stop this communication. I hope no one is monitoring it.

I don't care, Katrina cut in, *I had to talk to you. I had to feel you again.*

Are you better now? Mike asked gently.

Yes, I can't wait until you come! Be careful.

You be careful too, Katrina. Now, one last thing, bring warm clothes and food if you can. We may have to go to ground for a few days. They'll all be looking for us. I'll be in touch tomorrow afternoon about four. Until then, we must maintain silence. Otherwise they will find you.

Chapter 18

Sullom Voe, June 29, 2007. 6:30 p.m.

Mike sat staring in front of him, weighing the enormity of the task that lay before him. He had tried to make it sound simple to Katrina, but he was painfully aware of the difficulties and dangers involved. Assuming that he could make off with the helicopter, would he be able to locate the *Leningrad*? Would he be able to land without interference? Would Katrina be able to find a safe hiding place and get to the helicopter without being captured? And assuming all that, where would they go once safe? He was certain that both the Americans and the Soviets would try to track them down. Initially, they would not have much choice. They would be able to go only as far as the helicopter would take them, and that would not be very far, depending on the amount of fuel on board.

Mike started to work out the options. He rummaged through a pile of books and pulled out a map of Shetland and the North Sea he had bought on their outing to Scalloway. He spread it out in front of him. He could assume the helicopter would have enough fuel to get back to its base in Aberdeen, a distance of over 100 miles, and it would no doubt have some in reserve, so he could count on a minimum range of, say, 150 miles. The Frigg oilfield lay some seventy-five or eighty miles East South East of Sullom Voe, so after picking up Katrina on the *Leningrad*, that would leave him with about the same number of miles in hand. distance in hand. Where could they go with that? He looked at the scale on the map. They could just make Aberdeen, or they could return to Shetland or the Orkney Islands forty miles farther south. Or, they could continue on east to Norway.

Mike grimaced. That did not make many options. Of course, if the helicopter had more fuel on board, he could think of Denmark or even Germany, but for the moment, he could not count on it. All things considered, of the options open to them, he preferred Norway. Shetland was out of the question. The Orkneys were too barren and inhospitable, and once there, there was no way of getting off again without the helicopter or a boat. Eastern Scotland was promising, but it was densely populated, at least along the seaboard, and they might not have enough fuel to go far inland. The Norwegian coast, on the other hand, was within reasonable flying distance, and it was sparsely populated; once the heat died down and they knew what they were doing, it was close enough to civilization to provide alternative lines of retreat. He was not altogether satisfied with it, but by the look of things, it was going to have to be Norway, assuming everything else went according to plan. He ran a hand over his brow. It was a lot to assume!

When Mike cut off their communication, Katrina turned and smiled at Anna who was standing on the other side of the cabin, staring at her in awe.

"Is that how you do it?" Anna asked. "Were you talking to him, just like that?"

Katrina nodded and drew in her breath sharply. Her face hurt where Lopukhin had hit her, not bothering to open his hand.

"Here, let me take care of your face," said Anna, springing into action. "That brute! Come and sit down."

Katrina obeyed and closed her eyes as Anna held a cold compress to her jaw and cheek.

"I can't believe that's how you communicate," Anna chattered on. "It looks so easy. What did you say?"

Katrina told her of Mike's plan and the need to find a safe hiding place.

"Yes, you can't stay here. Lopukhin will be hunting for you first thing in the morning, Now, let's think. You need somewhere safe—a place where no one will think of looking. And ideally, it should be not too far from the helicopter platform on the stern."

"But everything is so exposed there," Katrina objected. "I can't think of anywhere that affords any kind of cover. There is nothing but those storage bins under the platform, and they're probably all locked. Of course, there's the sick bay, but that's no use."

"Wait a minute!" said Anna. "The sick bay. That's it!"

"That's no good, Anna. People go in there all the time. And it'll be locked anyway. I couldn't get in."

"Don't you be so sure," Anna said with a grin. "You remember when I was seasick. I went to see the doctor several times, so I got a good look at the sick bay. In fact," Anna went on coyly, "he showed me all over the place. Now in the back is a room reserved for emergency operations. It's usually kept locked because there are all kinds of drugs and instruments and things, so no one ever goes in there. And there's even a bed, so you could rest."

"But how am I supposed to get in there? Unless you have the key, of course!" Katrina added sardonically.

"No, but I can get it!"

Katrina stared at her in astonishment.

"And how do you propose to do that?"

"You remember how attractive the ship's doctor is?"

"Go on," said Katrina, beginning to understand.

"Well, he thinks I'm attractive too, and he's been trying to get me into his little operating room ever since I recovered. I have been on the point of giving in for days. Now, I think enough time has gone by for me to be able to surrender with grace! I'm going to ask him for the key and tell him I'll meet him there tomorrow night. Simple!"

"Would you really do that for me?"

"With pleasure. And I mean it! Now why don't you lie down with your compress and try to get some rest. Tomorrow will be a busy day. I'll go and visit my favorite ship's doctor right now and tell him I can hardly wait. It will drive him out of his mind. I'll see if I can get some food for you too while I'm gone."

She made Katrina lie down in her bunk, and she covered her with a blanket and crept out.

As Anna left Katrina to rest, Mike folded his map, extinguished the lights in his room, and slipped outside. At one in the morning, most people were asleep, and the compound was in semidarkness. Only a few lights shone over the entrance gate and the office hut. It was getting late enough in the season for the sun to have gone down for a real night. In fact, it was getting late enough in the season for the weather to start breaking up. There was a fitful breeze stirring, and when Mike glanced at the sky, he could see ragged clouds moving swiftly against a bright background of stars. The local fishermen could have told him that this meant wind, in all probability a southerly gale, and it was nothing serious like the great northwesterly storms that would make them think twice about going too far offshore.

Mike walked quietly across the compound to the mess. He wanted to see if he could find some provisions. The door was unlocked, and Mike groped his way across the recreation room toward the kitchens. They ate well on the station, and there were usually large stocks of food available, but a lot of it was frozen and would not keep for long out of a freezer. What Mike wanted was either canned goods or food that would keep for several days without refrigeration. He picked his way through a cupboard of dry stores and one of the large cold boxes, assembling a collection of suitable items, which he stuffed into a large plastic garbage bag. He then looked around for other useful articles, collecting a can opener, some matches, and a couple of kitchen knives.

With all this under his arm, Mike crept back across the recreation room, quietly opened the door, and stepped out.

"Going somewhere?" a voice said softly not three feet away. Mike whirled toward the voice. It was Frank Mambrino, leaning against the side of the hut next to the door.

"Frank!" Mike exploded. "What the heck are you doing there?"

"Just looking for UFOs—and other strange phenomena," Frank replied, grinning broadly, with his teeth gleaming in the semidarkness. "I might ask you the same question."

"Well," Mike said, his mind racing, "I came over to grab a snack. I couldn't sleep."

"Looks like you got pretty hungry!" Frank said, eyeing the plastic bag under Mike's arm and grinning more broadly than ever.

"Oh that?" Mike muttered. "Yes. I, er, broke a bottle of beer in the bathroom, so I took some paper towels to clean it up."

"Really?" Frank smiled disbelievingly. "My, my! You're certainly having a busy night!"

Mike laughed. "Yes. Well, I must get back and clean up my bathroom."

"Yes, you must."

"Well, good night then."

"Good night," said Frank, still grinning.

Mike turned and walked across the compound, trying to look casual but knowing how odd his behavior must seem. Frank watched him go, with a thoughtful expression on his face. He was not grinning anymore.

Katrina could not sleep. Her jaw hurt, and in any case, she was too keyed up by recent events and the thought of what might lie ahead to do more than close her eyes and attempt to rest. Lopukhin had frightened her. She had never met real violence before, and Lopukhin's anger and hatred had left her hurt and bruised, as much emotionally as physically. She was frightened of what Lopukhin might do to her again, but she was curiously confident that Mike would somehow manage to come and take her away. She wondered about that. Why did she have such confidence in a man she had never met? She knew she loved him. She was certain of that now. She loved him in a way she could love no other man, because only he could fill the emptiness within her. She longed to see him, to look at him with real eyes, to touch him with real hands, to feel him hold her with real arms. Yes, she loved him, but would he come? Could he come? She sighed and held the compress closer to her face.

She was still resting when Anna returned, clutching a canvas bag and looking very dishevelled. Katrina sat up in her bunk.

"Anna, are you all right?" she asked.

"Oh yes," said Anna, "very much so! That Alex! I had quite a job persuading him to wait until tomorrow night! I had quite a job persuading *myself* to wait until tomorrow night! However—" here she reached inside her blouse and produced a key "—I did. And we now have the answer to your problem: an operating room all to yourself."

"Wonderful! No one will think of looking in there."

Anna pointed at the canvas bag. "And in there, my dear, is enough food for a small siege, including a bottle of vodka."

"How did you get all that?"

"Well, I am friendly with one of the cooks. He's dying to try out some new recipes with me!"

Katrina burst out laughing. "You're impossible! But I'm very grateful for everything you've done. What would I do without you?"

"It's nothing," Anna said airily. "Now, it's time to get you installed in that operating room. The sooner you're in hiding, the better I'll feel. I don't trust Lopukhin!"

Katrina gathered together a few essentials and followed Anna along the corridor toward the stern of the ship. When they reached the aft companionway, Anna motioned for her to wait while she went on deck to make sure no one was around. She returned in a few moments and beckoned her to follow. It was cold on deck, and a strong wind was blowing. The two women hurried across to the sick bay, and Anna let them in, opening first the office door and then the door to the operating room, a small, windowless cubicle with wheeled emergency equipment around the walls and a narrow, hard-looking couch in the centre. Anna prodded it and grimaced.

"Not the most comfortable bed in the world," she said, "but at least you can rest a little. It's going to be a long wait." Anna looked at Katrina, and suddenly her eyes filled with tears. They hugged.

"I don't know when I'll see you again, Anna. Thanks for everything."

"Let me know what happens." Anna sniffed, wiping her eyes. "I want to know how you make out with the extraterrestrials. And I want to know all about Mike!"

They hugged again.

"Take care, Anna," Katrina whispered. "I hope everything works out the way you want it."

Anna left and Katrina locked the door of the operating room. Anna opened the door of the sick bay and peered out. There was still no one around. She carefully closed the door behind her and made for the companionway. On the bridge, Captain Ponotiev turned just in time to see a small female figure slip across the deck and disappear from sight. He shook his head and smiled. That oversexed ship's doctor was at it again! What a stallion! But he ought to be more discreet. He would have to talk to him about it in the morning. He continued his pacing and resumed his observation of the elements. Yes, they were in for a blow. The wind was already beginning to whip the tops off the waves, and the sea was shortening from the south. The sky remained clear though, and the barometer was dropping only very gradually. Perhaps it would not be much, just a friendly warning tap before winter really rolled its sleeves up, but it was enough of a slap to give his passengers a foretaste of what the North Sea was capable. For the moment, the ship was behaving well, but if the wind persisted, they would get bounced.

Mike managed to sleep a few hours and awoke fairly refreshed. His first thoughts were for Katrina, but he had to force himself not to contact her immediately, as he usually did. It would be too risky. It was astonishing how quickly he had become accustomed to her contact, and he was suddenly aware of how painful it was to be deprived of it. She gave him a completeness he had never experienced before, and he knew now, with aching certainty, that he would never be able to live without her presence. He looked at his watch. Seven-thirty! How could he wait until four o'clock?

A sudden thought struck him. He leaped out of bed and tore back the curtains. It was a brilliant sunny day, but he could see the wind flattening the coarse grass in violent gusts. He could even hear it buffeting the hut. Rats! The helicopter! If there was too much wind, the helicopter would not be able to come. He dressed quickly and went outside. The wind was as strong as it looked, gusting up to thirty or thirty-five knots, he estimated. If it did not get much stronger, it might be all right. He had flown choppers in more than that, but they were notoriously dangerous in strong winds, and he did not fancy landing on the pitching deck of a ship in such conditions. He cursed. Today of all days! It had been fine for weeks. He cursed again and strode over to the station office. Perhaps they had a weather report.

The duty sergeant told him that they had not received the official military report yet but that the BBC had put out a gale warning in their early morning shipping forecast.

"Bit windy. But it's a lovely day," said the sergeant looking out of the window.

"When do you get your weather report?" Mike insisted.

"Not until after ten when the radio operator comes on. Stop by around ten if you're interested."

Mike thanked him and walked over to breakfast. What would happen if the helicopter did not arrive? Nothing. Precisely! But then what would become of Katrina? If he did not go and get her, how long could she stay in the same hiding place? How long before she was discovered? How long before Lopukhin got his hands on her? Mike tried to put it out of his mind. It was going to be a long day!

At ten-fifteen, toward the end of a receive session, he told Jim he had a headache and needed some fresh air. Outside, the wind was still very strong in patches. He would have preferred a stronger wind if it had fewer gusts. It was the gusts that were dangerous for a helicopter. In the station office, the weather report had just arrived, and the sergeant gave Mike a copy.

"It says winds up to forty-five knots," he told Mike. "But it still looks nice outside."

Mike read the report. It described a typical high-pressure system with a cold front moving in quickly from the west. Initially, winds would be from the south with gusts of up to forty-five knots and would then shift to the southwest as the front came through, bringing a few rain clouds and a chance of poor visibility. *It could be worse,* Mike thought. *But it could be a whole lot better!*

It was one of those borderline situations. Everything would now depend upon the weather in Aberdeen and the humor of the pilot. If he decided not to come, that was it. There was nothing Mike could do. Feeling very powerless, he went back to the lab and pretended to take an interest in the morning's work.

On board the *Leningrad*, locked in the operating room of the sick bay, Katrina was very aware of the ship's motion, which was gradually becoming more violent. Although there were no windows in the operating room, she guessed that the weather must be deteriorating. She was lonely in her hiding place and prayed that the time would pass more quickly. She looked at her watch for the tenth time in as many minutes. Eleven o'clock. *Another six hours,* she told herself. She had spent a very uncomfortable night perched on the operating table, but she was grateful for the safety of her hiding place. At least she hoped it was safe. She had heard voices in the sick bay next door a little earlier, but for the last hour, no one had been near the place. She wondered whether they were looking for her. If they were, would they think of searching the sick bay?

She did not know it, but Lopukhin had already ordered a complete search of the ship. He had sent for her at nine o'clock. When she could not be found, he had flown into a terrible rage and told his men to search every corner of every deck and hold. Even now, as she nervously consulted her watch, search parties were systematically combing the vessel, starting at the bow and gradually working their way backward toward the stern.

At lunchtime, the weather was no better, and worse if anything, and Mike knew the chances of seeing the helicopter that afternoon were growing slimmer by the hour. He sat through lunch and went back into the lab feeling very despondent. He did however arrange with Jan to be off at four. As four o'clock approached, he grew more and more apprehensive, and finally, at fifteen minutes before the hour, he could not stand it any longer and handed over to Jan, saying he was going outside for a few moments.

The weather looked about the same still, with heavy gusts of wind sweeping in from the south. Mike started to walk over to his quarters to pick up his bag of provisions and a few spare clothes. He might as well have them ready, just in case. Then before he had gone ten paces, he froze as he heard the unmistakable beat of a helicopter. It was coming! And it was early! He would have to act quickly. He ran over to the station office and stood against the wall. Time was going to be vital. As soon as the pilot landed and walked into the hut, he would have to sprint for the helicopter. If all went well, he could be away in seconds with the bag of provisions in hand.

The helicopter came in over the hill, bucking and swerving in the gusts. It looked rough up there, Mike thought, but the pilot seemed to know what he was doing. He jockeyed the ship over the station, hovered for few seconds between gusts, and then, as the wind eased, dropped quickly to the grass, landing with only a slight bump. Mike waited for the door to open, but the pilot stayed where he was. What was he doing? The note of the engine dropped, and then Mike knew. He was shutting off the engine! Why? He always kept it running. He had been counting on that.

The rotor slowed to a halt, and the engine died. By this time, the duty sergeant had emerged from the hut and stood watching. The pilot jumped out of the helicopter which was rocking in the gusts, and he shouted to him.

"I'm not going back in this weather. We've got to get something to tie the ship down. Do you have anything we could use for weights?"

The two men went inside. Mike knew it was now or never, with the engine running or not. He sprinted to the helicopter and climbed aboard. He ran an eye over the instruments. He threw the contact switches, waited a few seconds for the feeds to pump, and then hit the start button. There was a whining noise and the engine started, gradually picking up speed. The pilot and the duty sergeant came out of the hut and stared at him. The pilot waved his arms and shouted, but Mike could not hear what he said. He threw the rotor in gear and slowly, painfully slowly, the tips of the rotor started to turn. The pilot was running to the helicopter. The rotor was beginning to turn a little faster, but he still needed more revs before he could lift. The pilot ducked under the rotor and reached for the door. Mike slammed the pitch in, and the helicopter bucked, throwing the pilot off balance.

Mike gritted his teeth. More revs! He needed more revs! The pilot was reaching for the door again. Mike threw the pitch and held it in. The helicopter bucked again, reared, and then was caught by a gust that picked it off the ground and hurled it sideways. Mike gunned the engine, and the 'copter somehow stayed in the air, swaying sideways and then miraculously rising and righting itself. Mike missed the flagpole by inches and skipped over the wire fence, breathing again for the first time in minutes.

He steadied the helicopter, banked east, and skimmed over the hill toward Lerwick. The helicopter was handling well despite the wind, and it felt good to be in the air again and good to be doing something, at least. He looked for the fuel gauge. It stood at about two-thirds full. He seemed to remember these choppers had a range of about 280 nautical miles. Yes, that would be about right. If it had come up from Aberdeen, that would have been 120 miles, which with a strong tailwind would have used about a third. So he had fuelled for something like 180 nautical miles. That would be enough. Just. If he did not have any problems and if he did not lose too much time finding the Leningrad.

He looked around the cockpit for charts. There was the pilot's course chart on the seat next to him, showing the route taken from Aberdeen to Sullom Voe. He took it out of the transparent plastic case and unfolded it, but all it showed was Northern Scotland, the Orkneys, and the Shetlands. It did not go far enough east to take in Norway. Too bad. He would have to fly by guesswork. He turned a little so as not to fly directly over Lerwick and set a course east-southeast, in the general direction of Frigg. As he left the shelter of land, he could feel the wind more, and he adjusted his course a few degrees further south to compensate for the added drift. The wind was a little less gusty, but it was strong enough to make the helicopter difficult to fly, and it was beginning to kick up quite a vicious looking sea. The weather was still crystal clear, with no sign of the rain clouds forecast. If the visibility held, Mike knew he would be able to see the oilfield from a considerable distance. He guessed the whole trip would take about forty-five minutes, so before long he should be able to see the first drilling platforms.

Packham stood in the station commander's office, staring incredulously at the duty sergeant and the pilot.

"You mean you just let him take off?"

"I tried to stop him," said the pilot, "but he handled that ship beautifully. He's some flyer!"

"Does anyone have any idea where he is going?"

"He flew off east toward Lerwick. But that does not mean anything. Perhaps you should put out an alert."

"That's what I'm going to do, just as soon as I've spoken to London."

"Well, he can't get very far," the pilot said. He seemed to be enjoying himself. "He doesn't have a whole lot of range. He's got a lot of guts to go anywhere in this weather."

From a height of 200 feet, Mike spotted the oilfield at a distance of forty miles. It was a fantastic sight, with twenty or thirty platforms rising like trees out of a brilliant silver carpet. It looked very peaceful, and it was hard to believe that each platform was a hive of industry with gangs of tool pushers working round the clock and anything up to two miles of pipe thrusting down beneath it into the seabed. The wind was still rising, and as Mike approached the first rigs, he could see heavy seas breaking against their legs, sending gouts of spray high into the air. The rigs themselves looked as steady as rocks. They were built to take anything the North Sea could throw at them, and this was child's play.

Mike looked around for the *Leningrad*. There were more ships in the area than he would have imagined. Most of the platforms had small supply vessels keeping station a few cables away or patrolling the anchor buoys to check for possible drag. The *Leningrad* would be a larger vessel, presumably well outside the field. Mike did not want to waste time and fuel flying all the way round the field. He would have to take a gamble and fly over the field, hoping to catch sight of it. He was now several miles south of the field, and there was nothing in that area. He would fly due north and see if he could spot the *Leningrad* on the way.

Ten minutes later, Mike was beginning to wonder if he had the right field. There was nothing there that looked like an oceanographic vessel. The last platform was looming larger in front of him and beyond that, nothing. He had guessed wrong. It must be on one of the other sides. He altered course to fly east, and then as he did, he caught sight of a ship that had been hidden by the last platform. Another supply vessel, he supposed. But no. Wait a minute! This was bigger, and unlike the supply ships, it had a high built-up platform on the stern. This had to be the *Leningrad*.

He turned north again and thought of his plan of action. First of all, he had to establish contact with Katrina and tell her he was almost there. He began to call, "Katrina, this is Mike!"

Katrina was standing in the operating room, listening to the voices in the sick bay.

"No, there is nothing in there," a voice said. The handle on the door of the operating room rattled, making Katrina jump back. "See, it's locked. It's kept locked all the time."

"We have orders to search everywhere," said another voice. "You must open it."

"I don't have the key," said the voice Katrina assumed to be that of the ship's doctor.

"Where is it?"

"I have mislaid it."

"Well, we are going to have to open it somehow."

"Perhaps the captain's office has a duplicate."

"Possibly. Stay here until we come back."

Katrina breathed again. Where was Mike? She looked yet again at her watch, and then she heard!

Yes, Mike! Where are you?

I'm here, Katrina. About five miles away. Now listen. I'm going to be landing in a few minutes. Can you get to the helicopter platform?

I think so, but I have to get out of here first. If they see me, they'll try to stop me.

Where are you exactly?

In the sick bay, right underneath the helicopter platform, but there is someone in the room next door, and there's a search party looking for me. It'll be coming back in a few minutes. You must hurry!

All right. Just wait. Stay in contact. I'll tell you when to break for it.

The *Leningrad* was facing south, with its bows crashing into heavy head seas. As Mike approached it, he realized how much it was pitching. Landing on that platform was going to be difficult. He would have to pick exactly the right moment. He hoped he would get the helicopter down without damaging anything. He flew down the length of the ship, intending to go beyond it, make a turn, and then approach the ship from downwind. As he passed the stern, he looked for the sick bay. There it was, underneath the platform.

Katrina.

Yes, Mike.

I'll be landing in about sixty seconds. Listen carefully. When you get outside, run forward and you'll find a steel ladder going up to the platform. As soon as I land, keep low and run toward the helicopter. Now, go!

Katrina picked up her canvas bag, unlocked the door, and walked into the sick bay. The ship's doctor stared at her, openmouthed.

"Oh, I must have lost my way," said Katrina, and she made for the door.

He continued to stare, eyes wide, as Katrina walked past him, opened the outside door, and ran for the ladder. There was a shout behind her as the returning search party saw her leave the sick bay and run across the deck. Mike pulled the helicopter into a tight turn and sped back toward the stern of the *Leningrad*, keeping as low as possible to take advantage of the shelter afforded by the ship. At the last minute, he hauled the helicopter up over the stern, stopped almost dead as he hit the wind, and set it down with a thud. He saw a slim, blonde figure climbing up the iron ladder, clutching a canvas bag. Katrina!

Then his heart leaped as he saw a group of men running across the deck toward the ladder. Katrina reached the top and stumbled. A large hand came over the top of the ladder and seized Katrina's ankle. Mike threw open the helicopter door and fired the distress flare pistol he had found in the cockpit. The man, who was now standing at the top of the ladder, clutched the hole in his chest and toppled backward, crashing to the deck below. Mike ran forward and grabbed the canvas bag in one hand, and with the other, he pushed Katrina toward the rocking helicopter. They scrambled in and with the next gust, the helicopter lifted and flipped sideways over the stern. It dipped, trailed its skids in the water for a second, steadied, and then gradually gained height, the beat of its rotor soon lost to those who stood on the deck of the *Leningrad* and watched it slowly disappear toward the east.

Chapter 19

North Sea, June 30, 2007. 4:45 p.m.

Fighting the wind, Mike took the helicopter up to fifty feet and set a course due east.

"Well, we've done it!" he shouted above the noise of the engine and grinned at Katrina.

"What?" she shouted back, cupping a hand to her ear. Mike grinned again, put a finger to his lips, and reverted to thought transfer.

We've done it! he repeated.

I can't really believe this is happening, Katrina responded, turning in her seat and leaning back in order to see Mike better. *I can't believe this is me. I can't believe you are Mike, the Mike.* She ran her eyes over Mike's face, studying every detail.

I like what I'm seeing.

I like what I'm seeing too. He smiled and held out a hand. *And touching.*

Is this really you? Have we really escaped?

For the moment, yes. I don't know for how long. They're going to come after us, that's for sure.

Why? You've said that before. Why won't they leave us alone? We are not going to do them any harm.

They think we are. My people don't know where I am or what I'm doing. They don't know we've been communicating, but they do know I've run off with one of their helicopters and that I know all about their project. That's enough to make them very anxious to see me. As for your people, they've just seen you disappear in a US military helicopter, so God knows what they're thinking. They know we've been communicating, so they'll suspect you've been persuaded to defect. It almost certainly hasn't occurred to them that I have run away too and that it was me flying the helicopter, so they probably assume that the whole thing was engineered by the United States. If they think you've defected, they may not be interested in getting you back, but... Mike left his sentence unfinished.

I know what you were going to say, Katrina put in grimly. *If Lopukhin thinks I've defected, he'll try to track me down and kill me. He's a monster. He's capable of anything.* She fingered her jaw.

Let me look at that, said Mike, gently pulling her face round. There was a dark bruise on her jaw and an angry welt running across her cheek to the corner of her eye.

Yes. Mike breathed, caressing her cheek. *If he can hit a woman like that, he is capable of anything.*

Katrina caught his hand and pressed it. She leaned across and stroked the back of his neck. *Don't be angry. It isn't worth it. The important thing is that we've escaped and that we're together. Together, we may be able to warn the extraterrestrials to stay away.*

Thank God they don't know about that. If they did, we'd have them all on our backs. But you're right, of course. If we can contact the extraterrestrials in time, we may be able to stop our governments from getting the technology to blow us all out of existence. Not that they don't have it already. Doesn't that make you angry? We may be on the brink of contacting extraterrestrial intelligence and opening our lives and minds to all kinds of wonderful advances, and all our crazy leaders can think of is how they can use them to get the advantage of each other.

I know, Katrina said. *I wouldn't have thought it possible. But now I know that people like Lopukhin exist, and they must exist in every government.*

I don't think it's people like Lopukhin or Packham who are ultimately responsible. They are just cogs in a machine, obeying orders. I'd love to know who Packham is reporting to. I don't even think it's our presidents or prime ministers. They are often manipulated too by elements within a government. Inside every government, there are hawks and doves. Sometimes the doves carry the day, sometimes the hawks. Right now, we're suffering from the hawks.

For a moment, they sat in silence, watching the sea sweep past beneath their feet. The waves were bigger now with breaking crests. The wind was still gusty, but it was slowly veering round to the southwest, and Mike thought the visibility was deteriorating. Perhaps they would get rain after all.

Where are we going? Katrina asked.

Norway, Mike replied glancing at the fuel gauge. It now showed less than a third full. *If we get there!*

There was still no sign of the Norwegian coast. Mike estimated it to be sixty or seventy miles away.

I think we'll just have enough fuel, he said.

What are we going to do when we get there?

I don't know. It depends where we can land, but I think we should go into hiding for a few days, until we're safe. After that, we can think again. Do you have any ideas?

No. The most urgent thing is to try to contact the extraterrestrials. If we can do that, I'll feel much happier.

What if we can't?

We'll just have to keep on trying.

I agree. I hope we can find somewhere suitable to hole up. We'll need shelter and food. He pointed to the canvas bag. *Is that what that is?*

Katrina nodded. *I hope there's enough.*

God. I didn't have time to collect my belongings. Why don't you look around in the back to see if there's anything that might be useful.

Katrina nodded again and climbed over the seat. She returned in a few minutes holding a first-aid box and an emergency axe.

That's about all I could find, but there's a container marked 'Survival Kit' next to the life raft.

That's good. There's bound to be some food and drink in there.

He put out a hand to steady Katrina as the helicopter tilted in a particularly strong gust. *And we may need the life raft if we don't get there soon.*

Katrina smiled then pointed ahead. *I don't think we'll need it.*

A long gray line appeared on the horizon. Mike heaved a sigh of relief and smiled at Katrina. Yes, that was the Norwegian coast. They'd be over land in a matter of minutes. They watched as the coastline come nearer, and Mike pointed out a large town.

That must be Bergen. The wind's stronger than I thought. It's pushed us pretty far north.

Can we land in Bergen? Katrina asked.

We could, but I don't want to.

Why not?

Because Packham has probably put out an alert by now, in which case all major airports in the area will be looking out for us. But even if he hasn't, the Norwegian authorities would be very curious about a US military helicopter, particularly flown by two civilians without any official papers. They'd certainly detain us for questioning. And what would we tell them? That we're on the run from both the Americans and the Soviets? Because we want to warn extraterrestrials? By telepathy? They'd lock us in the nearest psychiatric hospital and throw away the key. Besides what would we do in a city?

By this time, they were only a few miles offshore, and Mike altered course again to take them well north of Bergen. Mike looked at the fuel gauge. There still seemed to be some fuel left.

I suggest we fly up the coast a little and see if we can find a place to land, well away from any houses.

North of Bergen, signs of civilization quickly disappeared, apart from an occasional farm, and the terrain became wilder with small fjords cutting jagged indentations into the coastline. It had started to rain, and the visibility was rapidly dropping. Mike brought the helicopter down lower, and they flew over another farm.

Wait! Katrina exclaimed. *Can we go back over that farmhouse? I think it may be abandoned. It looks like it's had a fire.*

Mike turned back, and they flew slowly over the farmhouse.

You're right, he said. *Look how overgrown everything is. It must be abandoned. I think this is it.*

Packham paced across the floor of his office and turned and glared first at Dickinson, the station commander, and then at the helicopter pilot.

"He could be anywhere by now," he said angrily.

"Well, London's put out an alert," Dickinson said soothingly. "What more can you do? They'll be picked up if they try to land. And he's got to land some time."

"Only if he lands at an airport, which I doubt very much. That alert's a waste of time, in my opinion."

"He can't have gone very far," the pilot put in. "I've been trying to work out where he could go with the fuel that was on board, and there are not that many places. I calculate he had a range of a hundred and seventy miles, maybe more, maybe less, depending on the direction he went. Don't forget there's a strong wind. So—" he strode over to the wall map behind Packham's desk and made a circular motion with his hand "—he must be somewhere within this radius. And a lot of that is sea. When you come right down to it, there are only two places he could be: Scotland and Norway."

"Great!" said Packham sarcastically. "All we've got to do is search Scotland and Norway!"

"Now wait a minute," said the pilot. "We can do better than that. If we assume he's not going to use airports, he's still going to have to land somewhere within this radius, and on land. That's not a very wide area. He'll avoid cities and built-up areas and look for open country. A helicopter's pretty easy to spot from the air—that is, if it's out in the open. When we get that Black Hawk that London's sending us, we'll be able to search the whole area in a day. We'll get him."

"I'm not convinced," Packham said and looked at his watch. "And why the hell doesn't Washington call back?"

"They're all out to lunch, I suppose," said Dickinson deprecatingly, looking at his own watch.

"What I want to know," Packham went on, "is why he left. What made him suddenly up and go like that? I know he's a rebellious son of a gun, but if he had had enough, which he obviously had, and if he was prepared to steal a helicopter, which he obviously was, he could have gone at any time. So why didn't he?"

He shook his head then turned to the pilot. "You can go now. You'd better start preparing a flight plan for when the new chopper arrives."

"When will that be?" the pilot inquired.

"Sometime tomorrow morning. They'll let us know from Aberdeen when it stops for refueling."

The pilot left, and Packham turned back to Dickinson. "It makes me nervous to think that Marshall's out there on the loose, knowing what he does."

"I've always thought he was a bad security risk," said Dickinson waspishly. "Right from the start. But what do you expect he'll do?"

"God knows. Maybe nothing. All I know is that as long as he's out there, he's a potential danger to this project. And that means we've got to do something about him."

There was a knock on the door, and the duty sergeant appeared. "I've got Washington on the line, sir. Do you want me to put it through here?"

"Yes, Sergeant. Dickinson, if you wouldn't mind, I'd better take this call alone."

Dickinson left, and Packham picked up the phone.

"This is Packham," he said.

"One moment please," said a voice. He listened to the connections being made then heard the line go hollow as the scrambler was switched in.

"Colonel," another voice said, "this had better be urgent to drag me out of an official luncheon."

Packham explained what had happened and then listened to a prolonged tirade from the other end. His eyes widened as he listened to the flood of words. One of the words that kept recurring sounded like "Mambrino."

Frank Mambrino stormed into Packham's office without knocking.

"What's this I hear about Marshall running off with our helicopter? Is it true?"

Packham nodded blankly.

"I knew it." Mambrino went on. "I knew that son of a gun was up to no good. I knew he must have been talking to the Russians, ever since that first contact he had. It had to be the Russians. And now the son of a gun has defected. Christ! That's all we needed."

"Defected? What makes you think he's defected? He might just have run away."

"Are you being serious? Of course he's defected. It's obvious, isn't it? He's been got at by the Russians!"

"Yes," Packham agreed, deciding not to say anything about the Brebin episode. He had never told anyone about it, and to mention it now would make it look as if he had been deliberately hiding information, which of course he had. "Yes, I suppose you're right. That's what Washington thinks too."

"When did you talk to Washington?"

"Just now." Packham paused and stared coldly at Mambrino. "They also told me about you, and I want to say right away that I don't approve of having a spy mixed up in my project."

"Well that's the way it is, and it's not going to change now. Certainly not after a defection!"

"They said that you were to handle the Marshall business personally and that I was to take orders from you until it was settled. I don't like it. I don't like it at all!"

"Don't take it too badly, Hal. No one needs to know. I'll be discreet. I don't want the others to know what I'm up to. And once it's settled, I'll probably be taken off the project anyway. Now, what action have you taken so far?"

Packham explained what he had done, mentioning the helicopter that London was sending, the pilot's ideas about where Marshall could have gone, and the general alert they had put out. Mambrino nodded his approval.

"We're going to have to move fast though," he said. There was a knock at the door, and Dickinson came in looking flustered.

"Colonel, the radio operator says there's someone calling you up on short waves. Someone calling himself 'Dollar.'"

"Dollar?" said Packham, perplexed. "Dollar? I don't know anyone…" He broke off. Could it be? Tola! "I think I'd better come," he said.

Mambrino followed Packham into the radio room. The operator handed Packham a microphone.

"Just press on the button to talk, sir. I've got reception on the loudspeaker."

"This is Colonel Packham here."

"Hal?" Lopukhin's voice came over the loudspeaker. "Tola. Remember?"

"Yes." He looked across at Mambrino, who raised his eyebrows questioningly.

"Can they hear with the button off?" Packham asked the operator.

"No, sir. It's a cut-off switch."

"Okay. Frank. These are the Russians."

"*What!* What do they want?"

"How do I know?" He pressed the button and spoke into the microphone again. "Tola, what is this? Why are you calling? This is very unprofessional!"

"Believe me. I wouldn't be doing this unless I had to. But it's urgent. Tell me, Hal. Are you missing someone? A man named Marshall?"

"Jesus Christ!" Mambrino exploded. "I told you. He has defected."

"Keep quiet, Frank!" Packham said sharply then turned back to the microphone. "Tola, why do you ask that?"

"Because that damned fool has stolen one of our best telepathists."

"Brebin?"

"Brebin? What do you know…" There was a pause. "No, not Brebin. A girl!"

"I don't know anything about this. We thought he had gone over to you."

"Well, when I saw a US helicopter land on my ship and make off with the girl, I was convinced she was defecting to the West."

"Now wait a minute," Packham said after staring in puzzlement at Mambrino. "Let me get this straight. You said a ship. What ship?"

"All right. You probably know as much about our project as I do about yours, so let's not waste any time beating about the bush. We both have too much to lose. In case you don't know, I'm running my project from a ship now, not so very far from you. Marshall flew in today, landed, and left with Klimenkova, a girl he has been communicating with for some time. At first I thought she'd been talked into joining you, but then I learned from her roommate that she and Marshall want to contact the extraterrestrials and tell them to keep away, because of some half-baked idea they have about our governments' motives."

"I don't understand," Packham said weakly. "How did Marshall know where you were or—"

"Let us not waste any more time on mere details," Lopukhin interrupted. "The important thing is that two of our finest telepathists have escaped and have the ability to warn off the extraterrestrials. If that happens, neither you nor I have a project left. Whatever our governments' motives, you and I have a job to do, and that is to establish contact with extraterrestrial intelligence. If those two get there first, then we fail. Hal, we have to stop them!"

Packham was nodding in agreement. "We have to find them first. How do you propose to do that?"

"We have a very good idea where they are. When they left, we tracked the helicopter on our long-range radar, so we know they are somewhere on the coast of Norway. Now, we also have another means of finding their position more accurately. We have had someone monitoring Klimenkova, and he says that if she starts projecting, he can probably get a bearing on her. And since they want to contact the extraterrestrials, we can assume they will be projecting."

"What do you want us to do?" Packham asked. "If you know where they are, why do you need us?"

"Because you have more of a chance of getting close to them in Norway than we have. If it had been Finland, I wouldn't even have called you. But in Norway, the United States has more room to maneuver than Russia. I told you, I don't like approaching you in this way, but there just isn't time to be too particular. We've got to stop them. It's in both our interests. So I'm making you an offer. If you help us in Norway, we'll take you to them. What do you say?"

"Just a moment," said Packham, and he switched off the microphone. "What do you think, Frank?"

"Well, I don't know whether we can trust those Commies, but if they can lead us to Marshall, it'll make all the difference between stopping him and losing him. It's a chance, but we can't afford not to take it. Besides, what do we have to lose? The important thing is to get to Marshall and this girl before they do any damage."

"Sure, but I don't see how we can really help them in Norway. I'd hate to get the Norwegian government involved in this. Washington would kill me!"

Mambrino had been pacing up and down the room. Now he stopped and faced Packham. "I'll tell you what we're going to do. We'll offer to share our helicopter with them when it comes. We'll pick them up and take them with us. Like that we don't let them out of our sight. We call the shots, and there's no chance of a double cross. Furthermore, we don't have to get the Norwegian authorities involved. It's the only way. If we don't control the situation somehow, the Russians will screw us. Whatever happens, we must not let the Russians get their hands on Marshall and the girl before we do. That must be avoided at all costs. Now perhaps you'd better get back to the Russians and make arrangements to pick them up. When you've finished, I want you to call Stanton for me. I'll be in your office." Packham spoke to Lopukhin for a further ten minutes and then went back to his office where Mambrino was scribbling a list on a sheet of paper.

"Everything all right?" Mambrino inquired.

Packham nodded. "We'll pick them up on their ship tomorrow morning as soon as the helicopter arrives. Meanwhile, they're going to try to get a fix on Marshall."

"Good," said Mambrino, handing Packham the list. "Now I want you to call Stanton in London and get him to make sure this is on the helicopter when it leaves Aberdeen."

Packham glanced at the list and then stared at Mambrino. Mambrino picked up the phone and handed it to him.

Mike threw a few more branches over the helicopter. It was not perfect, but it might do. Unless anyone had a specific reason to search that particular area, they would be unlikely to spot the half-camouflaged helicopter from the air. It would have to do. He picked up the pile of wood he had just split with the emergency axe and walked back toward the farmhouse. One end of the house had been completely gutted by fire, but the other end contained a large kitchen which still had a roof over it and which almost looked as if it had just been abandoned. It still had a few pieces of furniture, some pots and pans, and even a couple of thick woolen rugs in front of the wide stone fireplace in which Mike had already lit a fire. As he pushed open the door, Katrina was unpacking the contents of her canvas bag. She smiled at Mike.

"We have enough food here for three or four days, and I haven't even opened the survival kit yet."

Mike stacked the wood close to the fire to dry and held his hands to the flames for a few moments.

"It's wet and cold out there, but it's getting very cozy in here now."

Katrina came over to the fireplace with the bottle of vodka Anna had packed and a large cup.

"I have just the thing here to keep out the cold…and celebrate our new home. It'll be like, how do you say? A housewarming party."

"Your English is really amazing. I can't believe how good it is."

"Perhaps a little better than your Russian!"

They both laughed. Katrina poured vodka into the cup and offered it to Mike. He drank a little and passed it back to Katrina, who held it in both hands and took a sip. Mike put his hands round hers and smiled at her over the cup.

"Welcome home," he said.

"I'm glad to be here," she said gently. It was a magical moment. All the thoughts and feelings and emotions they had shared were now heightened by a sense of expectancy. "Mike," Katrina whispered after a while, "this is so strange. Everything about our relationship is strange. I feel like I've known you forever, and yet in some ways we are strangers. I've never even kissed you."

Very slowly, still holding the cup between them, they leaned forward, and their lips met in a light, brief kiss. Instantly, they felt a current run through them, adding a physical dimension to their harmony. Katrina pulled away, set down the cup, and put her arms round Mike's waist.

"Listen, Mike," she said, "but right now I want you more than anything else in the world. I want the next few hours to belong to us alone. I want to shut out the rest of the world and be alone with you. I want to take the time to love you. I want to laugh and hold you. I want you to want me. I want to drink some more vodka and have some food, and then I want you to make love to me like no woman ever has before."

Mike pulled her very close and kissed her long and hard. They stood swaying in front of the fire for a moment, and then Mike pulled away and held her at arm's length.

"Katrina, you are beautiful. I loved you before I ever set eyes on you, but now that I have seen you and felt you in my arms for a moment, I love you even more and want you very, very much. Now," he went on lightly, "see what you can find for supper while I build up this fire and try to close the shutters."

When they had finished these tasks, Mike poured them both some more vodka while they sat in front of the fire and toasted bread.

"Here's to the golden bird," said Mike, raising his cup.

"Yes, I was thinking about that too," said Katrina. "I'm certain we can get nearer to it. Remember, it was starting to move closer?"

Mike nodded. "Yes, it has to be the key. I'm sure the closer it comes, the closer we'll be to contact. We must also try to project a response. I have the feeling that together we'll be able to project a stronger signal."

"I do too," Katrina agreed. "But first things first. Supper's ready."

They ate slowly, taking their time, savoring their closeness, and enjoying the delicious feeling of wanting each other. When they could bear it no longer, they sat on the rugs in front of the fire and slowly undressed each other. And when they finally came together, it was like the inevitable merging of twin particles too long held apart by force. For both of them, it was the ultimate experience of love. Their bodies, responsive in themselves, were like fine membranes over their innermost feelings, and as they merged and remerged, they both knew in their completeness that nothing could ever come between them again.

As they returned to time and reality, still holding each other and their thoughts still merged, they felt rather than heard the beat of a wing, and they both knew instantly that the golden bird was there, waiting. Their senses unfolded, and above them soared the golden bird, superb, luminous, and majestic, still distant but moving closer with every beat.

Chapter 20

North Sea, Aboard the Leningrad, June 31, 2007. 9:15 a.m.

"Yes, our man picked up some definite signals this morning," said Lopukhin into the microphone of the *Leningrad's* radio transmitter, "but not enough to get a very accurate bearing. Apparently he was confused at first since he was used to Klimenkova's thought shapes, and now that Marshall is projecting with her, the shapes are different. Anyway, he's identified them now, and the next time they start projecting, he should be able to pin them down. When do you expect the helicopter?"

"In about two hours," said Packham's voice over the loudspeaker. "We know it has landed in Aberdeen, so it will not be long. We should be on our way by twelve. We'll radio you once we're in the air. Incidentally, we want to refuel on board the *Leningrad* so as to have maximum range when we leave. We'll bring our own fuel, but if you could have a couple of mechanics standing by, it would save time."

"That can be arranged," said Lopukhin. "We'll expect to hear from you around noon."

"Okay," said Packham, "we'll call you later."

The set went dead, and Lopukhin nodded in satisfaction before handing the microphone back to the radio operator. He turned to Captain Ponotiev, who was standing next to him.

"Captain, this is very fortunate. The refueling operation will give us more time than we expected. I don't want to give them any excuse to leave someone behind with the helicopter while we discuss tactics below."

"I'll take care of it," said Ponotiev, "but I don't like it. I don't like a lot of things that have been happening on this ship. I don't like the way you treated my ship's doctor, and I certainly don't like what you did to that Gan girl!"

"Captain, what you like or don't like is immaterial. Kindly carry out my instructions. If not, I'll have you relieved of your command. I can and I will. Now have Silvanin sent to my cabin. I want to know if he's made any progress."

Mike and Katrina stood facing each other, with their hands linked, eyes closed, and minds united as they watched the golden bird fly closer. After a while, they sighed and opened their eyes.

"It's still getting closer," Katrina said.

"Yes, it gets a little closer each time. It looks as if soon we'll be able to touch it!"

"It's so beautiful. I could watch it for hours. It's so peaceful and calm and…loving, somehow. When I see it, I am happy, and I feel completely at one with the world, with you, with everything around me. Why do you think it's taking so long to reach us?"

"I don't know," said Mike thoughtfully. "I don't know whether it's because of the distance or because it's taking all that time to penetrate our minds. In any case, it's almost here now, and I think we should spend more time projecting toward it. Do you agree?"

"Yes. But let's have a rest now." She reached up and gave Mike a quick kiss.

"Let's think about something else for a minute. I want to think about last night."

They had spent many hours exploring each other and enjoying what they found. They had slept a little, occasionally waking together to merge and merge again in a flow of love and understanding. And always above them soared the golden bird. They had woken early, hungry and eager to start a new day. The gale had blown itself out during the night, and the morning was clear and fresh with bright sunshine. The farmhouse was built on a cliff overlooking a small fjord, and when they went outside to smell the sparkling morning air, they could not resist the temptation to climb down to the fjord and bathe. The water was stingingly cold, but afterward they felt like new people, like the first man and woman on the first morning of the creation.

They had eaten a large breakfast and discussed how they were going to attempt to contact the extraterrestrials. They had decided to spend as much time as possible on scanning and projecting during the day while they were still fresh, and they would save the evening for themselves. They had begun projecting early and had just completed another session with the golden bird. After a rest, they resumed projection, now achieving instantaneous mind contact and automatically assuming the mental pyramid configuration which seemed best to fit their collective sensibilities. Kneeling on the floor, they held each other by the shoulders and concentrated, thrusting their minds upward in a slender cone and repeating over and over again the same message: *Please come. We await you. We wish you well! Please come. We await you. We wish you well!*

The big Sikorsky Black Hawk dropped out of the sky and landed neatly in the middle of the compound. The pilot killed the engine and climbed out while the rotors were still idling to a stop. Packham and Mambrino waved, and the pilot walked over to where they were standing on the steps of the station office hut.

"Colonel Packham?" he said, looking first at one then the other.

"Yes," said Packham.

The pilot threw a salute. "Lieutenant Garry Whitehead, sir."

"Welcome, Lieutenant. Have a good trip?"

"Yes, Colonel. So what's all the hurry? I was told to get up here as fast as possible."

"Did you pick up a load of fuel and other stuff in Aberdeen?" Mambrino asked, ignoring the lieutenant's question.

"Yes, it's all on board."

"Good," Mambrino went on, "we'll be leaving immediately."

Whitehead looked inquiringly at Packham.

"That is correct," Packham said. "If you're too tired, we have another pilot standing by. Take your choice."

"If I can get a cup of coffee and a sandwich first, I'd rather stay with my ship, sir. But I've been flying since two this morning."

"Okay. Make it snappy," said Mambrino. "We'll give you five minutes. Hal, we'd better get our things."

Five minutes later, the helicopter was airborne again on a course radioed by Captain Ponotiev and calculated to put them over the *Leningrad* in less than an hour.

"Where are we going?" the pilot asked several times, only to be answered with a laconic "You'll see!" But now, as they flew over the northwestern edge of Frigg oilfield, he could contain his curiosity no longer.

"Would somebody mind telling me what this is all about and where we are going?" he said angrily into the intercom. Mambrino grinned and pointed ahead at a vessel rolling gently in the swell left by the blown-out gale. Whitehead put a thumb up and smiled too, but as they came closer to the ship, he suddenly turned and stared at Mambrino.

"That's a Russian ship!" he said. "You've made a mistake!"

"No," said Mambrino, "that's where we're going."

Whitehead turned to Packham, who nodded his head several times and motioned to continue.

The pilot shrugged. "I hope you know what you're doing," he murmured. They flew low over the ship and saw a sailor standing in the center of the landing pad and slowly waving two green flags.

"Looks like they're expecting us," said Whitehead.

"They are," Mambrino confirmed. "You can land."

"I don't like this at all," Whitehead began. "This is contrary to all standing procedures."

"For God's sake, stop worrying and land!" Mambrino snapped.

Whitehead set the big 'copter down on the deck of the *Leningrad*, and Mambrino told him to stop the engines.

"We'll be refueling here," he explained.

Captain Ponotiev appeared on the platform being flanked by four seamen dressed in dirty overalls. He saluted stiffly as Packham climbed down onto the deck, followed by Mambrino and Whitehead. There were brief introductions, and then when Whitehead had shown the Russian working party how to start refueling, Ponotiev ushered them off the platform.

"Comrade Lopukhin wishes to see you in his stateroom to discuss your plan of action. Meanwhile, I'll stay here and personally supervise the refueling operation." He snapped his fingers, and a rating ran across the deck and sprang to attention. He spoke to him rapidly in Russian then turned back to the three Americans and motioned them to follow.

The rating led them downstairs and along a corridor before knocking at a door. Lophukin himself answered and greeted them effusively.

"Welcome, welcome! Come in. I want you to meet Andrei Solvanin, our telepathic bloodhound, and this is Dimitri Pallitov, a very resourceful and reliable member of our team whom I am sure you will all learn to appreciate."

There were introductions all round, and then Lopukhin spread a map of Norway on his desk and pointed to a large red circle some miles north of Bergen.

"They're somewhere in that circle," he said. "Solvanin here has had several good contacts now, and he has been able to work out a fairly accurate bearing, give or take five or ten degrees."

Mambrino was looking at the scale of the map. "How big is that circle? Ten, twenty miles? It should not take us too long to search an area that size. Once we find them, how do you suggest we operate? I have my own ideas, but I'd like to hear yours first."

While Lopukhin explained his plan of action, refueling continued on the helicopter platform. It did not take long to fill the tanks, and as soon as the operation was completed, Ponotiev dismissed the working party. Two minutes later, three men appeared, with two of them carrying a long narrow crate and the other a heavy wooden box. All three climbed aboard the helicopter with their loads. After a while, two of them reappeared empty-handed and walked off, leaving Ponotiev alone on the platform. He was still alone when Lopukhin, Packham, and the others climbed up the iron ladder and made for the helicopter.

"Everything completed?" Lopukhin asked, looking hard at Ponotiev.

"Everything completed," he replied in an expressionless voice.

"Good, then we might as well be on our way."

Mike and Katrina sat on the steps of the farmhouse munching apples and looking out over the fjord. It had turned into one of those truly perfect days only to be found in northern latitudes. After the previous day's gale, the sky was a light washed-out blue with a few flecks of high cloud. The air, flavored with the tang of the sea, still carried the lazy softness of summer, but out of the sun, it gave more than a hint of the cold to come. Beyond the tufted edge of the cliff, the sea shone and gleamed with an occasional white horse, and they could hear it crashing gently on the beach below.

They rarely spoke now. Their thoughts were so intimately mingled that speech seemed superfluous. Communication was instantaneous. Emotions, feelings, and perceptions were shared as much as thoughts. Every moment that passed brought them closer together, and at the same time, they felt curiously involved in the sights and sounds and smells around them, as though they were all part of the same expression of life.

For once, Katrina broke the silence between them. *You know, Mike, I don't know what will become of us, but this is so perfect. I feel so completely happy, so close to you, that I really don't care what happens. We have known something I never thought was possible, and nothing really matters anymore. I know now that we are going to reach the golden bird. It's ours. It's waiting. Today, tomorrow, soon, we'll know. I feel certain now that the golden bird is the messenger of extraterrestrial life. It's coming. And it's coming to us!*

Mike put his arm round Katrina's shoulders, and they sat there silently for a long time, looking at the sea, before Katrina took Mike's hand and led him inside.

Whitehead looked at the map and pointed out of the window.

"There's Bergen. We should be in the circle in a couple of minutes. I'm going to start flying to pattern, so all of you keep your eyes open."

Once they were over the coast, Whitehead cut inland for ten miles then turned and made a run seaward about a mile further north. When they reached the coast again, Whitehead turned and made another run inland, another mile to the north. In this way, they hoped to cover the ground very thoroughly. It would take longer than a simple over-flight, but they thought it would save time in the end. They paid particular attention to wooded areas, and at one point they landed and searched a small copse on foot, much to the surprise of a farmer plowing a field a few hundred yards away.

An hour later, and twenty miles farther north, they reached the edge of the circle without having seen any trace of their quarry or the missing helicopter.

"I don't understand it," Lopukhin said angrily. "They've got to be there somewhere. We must have missed them!"

"Unless they've moved," Whitehead said.

"Yes, that's a possibility," Packham agreed.

"No, they couldn't have moved." Lopukhin objected. "Not without fuel. Of course they might have moved without the helicopter, but that helicopter has to be somewhere. We must have flown right over it."

"Let's make a few more runs north and south this time," Mambrino suggested. "If we don't see anything, we'll move farther inland. But I'm certain they're there. Okay, Whitehead, let's go, but take it more slowly this time."

"There's that wood we searched," Whitehead said after a few minutes, changing course, "but we didn't look behind that hill."

The helicopter turned, hovered, AD then set off again.

"Try that fjord again," Mambrino ordered.

They flew low over the water, scoured the beach, and then slowly flew up over the cliff.

"There's that burnt-out farmhouse again," Whitehead observed.

"Wait a minute," said Mambrino. "There's something odd about that farmhouse. We thought it was abandoned, but there's smoke coming out of the chimney. I think we should have a closer look. Whitehead, I want to land but not too close. Put us down behind that clump of trees over there."

Locked in each other's arms, Mike and Katrina willed the golden bird to come closer. *Please come. We await you. We wish you well!* they repeated. It seemed to them that the bird was no longer moving across their perception but toward them, no longer wheeling and circling as if searching but flying now with purpose and direction. As it came closer, it grew more luminous, and for the first time they heard it. They heard its wings beat, sweeping the surface of their senses like a giant heartbeat pulsing across the cosmos. Lost in themselves, they failed to hear another beat—the beat of a helicopter as it moved overhead and faded.

The afternoon wore on. Shadows lengthened. There was no movement in the house, but as night fell and darkness deepened, the windows reflected the dancing glow of firelight from within. When it was quite dark, two shadowy figures moved out of a nearby clump of trees, carrying between them what looked like a long tube. They did not walk very far but soon flattened to earth next to a hayrick.

Inside the house, Mike added more wood to the fire and turned to Katrina. She smiled and held out her hands.

This has been the fullest and the happiest day of my life, she said. *In it, we have lived out a whole existence, and now we are on the brink of another. The bird is here now. I can feel it. Hold me, Mike. It's time.*

Mike folded her in his arms, and the golden bird surged into their beings, triumphant now, joyous, and all-pervading. They could hear its wings sweeping through space, with each beat whispering a message they already knew: *Be patient. We are coming. Be patient. We are coming.* Suddenly, Mike froze and then raised his head, looking puzzled. Katrina looked Mike's face.

What's the matter, Mike?

I'm not sure. I'm getting a strange signal: a red triangle alternating with a blue circle. Where have I seen that before? He frowned and then exploded, *It's Packham. It's got to be Packham. And there's danger in there. Danger! Danger! I don't know if this is a warning or what, but I think we should get out of here. Now! Quick, grab all your things and let's go!*

They rapidly gathered up their belongings and hurried outside, climbing up the hill next to the fjord. At the top, they stopped and looked down at the farmhouse, which looked small from that height. There was a movement close to the hayrick, a glint of light, and a small thud. The farmhouse blew outward, and a sheet of flame shot high in the air, casting deep shadows against the trees.

Good God, said Mike, *someone's trying to destroy us.*

But who? Do you think it's the Americans or the Russians?

Maybe both. In any case, we must keep moving. Sooner or later they're going to search the farmhouse, and when they find out there are no bodies in there, they are going to redouble their efforts to track us down. We've got to move fast, because once they find out we're still alive, I bet they'll have people watching the airports, train stations, and ferries.

Chapter 21

Western Norway, August 1, 2007. 5:00 a.m.

Four hours later, the woods thinned out, and they found a small country road with no sign of traffic.

"*Where do you think this goes?*" Katrina asked.

"*Well, judging by the sun, which is just coming up, it looks like it runs north and south. That map that was in the survival kit showed a couple of small towns to the north. And south, if I recall, there's a bunch of small fjords, which would make walking difficult.*"

They set off north, with still no sign of traffic. But after a while, they heard the sound of a heavy vehicle coming from behind them.

Quick, behind that hedge, said Mike.

From their hiding place, they watched as a large tractor come round the bend, towing a trailer piled high with carrots.

Come on, said Mike, stepping out from behind the hedge. *That's not someone trying to track us down.*

The grizzled older man driving the tractor slowed down and smiled.

God dag, he said.

Mike raised his shoulders and arms to indicate he could not understand. The farmer smiled again and pointed up the road and then at the large bench seat on the tractor.

He's offering us a ride, said Katrina, smiling broadly, and she jumped up to sit beside the farmer. *Come on, Mike. We could use a rest.*

Mike climbed up beside her, and the farmer set off again. Katrina turned to the farmer and started talking to him. He shook his head several times but then smiled, nodded, and began talking back in what Mike thought sounded like German or Dutch. They chattered on for a while, with both nodding and smiling. Finally, Katrina turned back to Mike. *Our new friend is a farmer, as we might have guessed. He's called Edvard, and he's taking this load of carrots to the market in a place called Kristiansund, north of here. You were right.*

You're amazing. How did you find all this out? And what language were you speaking?

German. I tried a few others, but he was an army reserve in Frankfurt and learned a little German then. Anyway, we should be in Kristiansund in about an hour.

When they arrived, Edvard drove straight to a large street market very close to what looked like a busy fishing harbor. They climbed down and shook Edvard warmly by the hand. He smiled, waved, said, "Ha deh," and then turned to go about his business.

What now? said Katrina.

First, I want to get some local currency, and then I need to call a good friend of mine, Patrick O'Shaughnessy, in London. He's another helicopter pilot. We've worked together quite a lot, but more importantly he's Irish. On several occasions, hanging out in airports waiting for clients, he's told me how great Ireland is, how different the Irish are, and how remote parts of the country are. I think that's where we could hide out and establish contact with the extraterrestrials. And being a pilot, he could probably fly us over there without having to go through any formalities, which could be very valuable.

They found a bank on Wilhelm Dalsvei, a few hundred yards from the port. Mike bought some krone, and the teller told him where to find some public telephones.

The phone rang three times.

"Hello. Patrick O'Shaughnessy."

"Pat. It's Mike Marshall."

"Mike! Where have you been? I haven't seen you in weeks."

"Listen, Pat, I'm calling from Norway from a coin-operated phone, and I don't have a huge amount of coins. Could you call me back?"

"Sure. What the hell are you doing in Norway?"

"I'll tell you when you call back."

Pat called right back, and Mike told him as much as he needed to know then went on. "We think Ireland would be a great place to hide."

"We? Who's we?"

"This Russian girl and I."

"Jesus, Joseph, and Mary! What are you up to, boyo?"

"All in good time. Listen, if we can get back to England, is there any chance you could get us over to Ireland—discreetly?"

"There's nothing I wouldn't do for a fellow vet. And believe me, I have some very interesting connections in Ireland. I can open a lot of doors and, if needed, lock them up tight!"

"Great. Listen, I'm not sure how secure this line is. I'll call you when we're back—if we get back. Not sure how long it'll take."

"Got you, boyo. Mum's the word. Have a great swim!"

Mike and Katrina walked back to Fosnageeta, the long wharf on the south side of the harbor which was bustling with activity. This seemed like a good place to go unnoticed.

By three in the afternoon, they both needed to eat. They entered what looked like a tavern, which turned out to be very crowded, mainly with men, most of whom were weather tanned. Many of them had blond beards and wore thick sweaters. Sailors and fishermen, they guessed. Mike walked to the bar, picked up two plates of pickled herring and potato salad, and pointed at the beer pump and held up two fingers, placing a 50 krone note on the counter. The barman smiled, handed him two tall glasses of beer, picked up the bank note, and slid several coins toward Mike, who took the plates over to where Katrina had found a seat. He went back for the beer, sat down, and raised a glass. "So far, so good," he said. "Let's eat."

After bolting down the herring, Mike went to get two more beers. When he returned there was a tall good-looking man seated next to Katrina.

"This is my husband," said Katrina to the stranger.

"Oh," said the stranger, turning to Mike, "you have a very beautiful wife, my friend. You are new here. Welcome, or as we say in Norwegian, Velkommen!"

He held out a large fist to Mike and said, "My name is Roald Nansen."

"Mike. Nice to meet you."

"Hyggelig a treffe deg. Nice to meet you too."

"Roald," said Katrina, "how come you speak such good English?"

"Well, I own a fishing boat, and I go to England often, particularly at this time of the year when the herring are running. And I often stay a few nights in places like Hull and Grimsby and Great Yarmouth, which is perhaps the largest herring fishing harbor anywhere on the east coast of England, or anywhere in Norway for that matter."

Mike glanced over at Katrina and then back at the tall fisherman. "And when are you going next?"

"Tomorrow morning. I'm heading for Smith's Knoll, which is about thirty miles northeast of Yarmouth, but I have to stop in Hull first to have one of my generators repaired."

Mike paused. "Any chance we could go with you?"

"Yes," said Katrina, "it sounds like it would be more fun than the ferry."

"And we could pay you," Mike added. "I don't have a lot of krone, but I do have some English money."

"Well," Roald hesitated, "I don't know."

"Tell you what, how much is your generator going to cost?"

"They said about a one hundred and fifty pounds."

"I can do that," Mike said, pulling out a large wallet.

Roald's eyes lit up, and he grinned. "That's great. For that you can even spend the night on board. One of the crew's cabins is empty."

Mike quietly handed Roald some banknotes under the table. They shook hands, and Roald called over to the bar for three more beers.

The fishing boat turned out to be much larger than they expected, and they spent a comfortable but rather restless night before being awakened by the engine starting up.

"Hmm," said Mike, looking at his watch, "it's only three in the morning, but it's light already. Let's stay down here a little longer."

There was a rattle of feet over their heads and some shouted orders from Roald. By the time they climbed up on deck, the boat was well away from the wharf and heading for the harbor entrance.

"That's good," whispered Mike to Katrina. "No one will have seen us leave."

When they arrived in Hull, it was starting to get dark, and Roald dropped them off close to the center of the town before heading south to the fishing wharf to get his repairs completed. He waved good-bye, and they hurried away from the harbor in search of a telephone.

"Well, you old devil," said Patrick O'Shaughnessy when he answered the phone, "where are you now?"

Mike told him, and Pat went on, "Are you still interested in going to Ireland?"

"Yes."

"Let me think." There was a pause, and Mike heard a rustle of paper. "Yes." Pat came back on. "Listen, I have to fly some wealthy clients up to Liverpool the day after tomorrow to look at some property they're interested in. Do you think you could meet me there? I'm pretty sure you can get a train over without having to go through London. You remember the little general aviation compound and helicenter up there, right next to the main airport over by Hale Village?"

"Right," said Mike. "What time you going to be there?"
"About nine-thirty. These guys want to make an early start."
"Okay. See you there around nine-thirty day after tomorrow. And Paddy, my friend, many thanks."

The trip across England was uneventful although they had to change trains three times, and they found a quiet little bed and breakfast very close to the air compound. They were still too jangled to try to establish extraterrestrial contact, but they found themselves growing ever close to each other and impatient to find peace together.

At the airport Mike showed his pilot's license, and he and Katrina sat in a small lounge overlooking the tarmac and watching the arrival and departure of several small planes. Just before nine-thirty, Mike pointed toward the south and said, "That's Patrick coming in now. I recognize his chopper."

The helicopter set down not more than fifty yards from the lounge, and once the rotor had slowed, the door opened and out jumped a scrawny man in a leather blouson who pulled down some folding steps and motioned for the passengers to debark.

"That's Patrick," said Mike.

Next to the helicopter, Patrick conferred with three large men in suits carrying briefcases. They all looked at their watches as a Bentley pulled up alongside the helicopter. After a brief exchange, Patrick nodded and made a note on his clipboard, and the three men climbed into the Bentley and drove off. Patrick made another note on his clipboard and looked over to where Mike and Katrina were now walking through a sliding door from the lounge onto the tarmac.

"Mike," said Patrick, "so who's your friend, your beautiful friend, should I say?"

Mike made the introductions, and Patrick told them they ought to be on their way soon. He would just have enough time to fly them over to Ireland and get back for his clients.

"We'll have time to talk on the way over. Let's go."

The trip took a little over two hours, flying out over the Irish Sea, skirting south of Dublin, and heading even farther westward. As they flew, Patrick spoke at some length.

"Listen, Mike, there are a few things you don't know about me, and—" he paused to smile at Katrina "—there's obviously a lot I don't know about you. You said you needed a refuge, and I have taken the liberty of making a few arrangements for you. What you will learn is that I have a lot of influence here in Ireland."

"You're not a member of the IRA, are you?" said Mike. "I know that the Provisional IRA came into being a few years back. I can't see you as a terrorist!"

"You're right there, boyo. But—" and here he put his fingers to his lips "—I am active in Sinn Fein. What we're trying to do is find a peaceful solution to the issue and stop the violence."

Mike gave Patrick a somewhat condensed version of the last few months. "I can see why you need some cover! I can certainly get you and Katrina a new identity. That's not a problem, and where you're going, no one will know anything about you."

Mike held Katrina's hand and said, "Pat, you're probably going to save our lives, but I have a more practical problem: what to live on for however long."

"Ah," said Patrick, "that is a problem."

"But I do have a bank account in the United States, into which my military pension is deposited. And thanks to my father, I had an insurance policy that paid out quite a lot as a result of being shot down and injured. So that's all sitting in that account."

"Problem solved," said Patrick grinning. "I can arrange to have that account transferred to an Irish account in your new name. Thanks to my friends in County Kerry, I will always know where you are, how you're doing, and what you're up to. As you'll discover, Ireland is a very special place, and you'll have friends, my friends, and soon-to-be-your friends looking out for you."

True to his word, Patrick landed them in County Kerry, not far from Killarney, where they were met by someone sitting on a horse-drawn cart, looking like something out of a 1950s movie.

"Top of the morning to you," he said, true to his image, and he tipped the front of a battered hat with his index finger.

"Knock it off, Henry," said Patrick. "Stop trying to act like Michaleen in *The Quiet Man*. You're not on camera now. These are the two friends I told you about: Mike here and Katrina. I have to get back to Liverpool, but you know what to do, right?"

"Sure do," said Henry. "Hop on up."

They climbed up behind Henry, and the three of them watched as Patrick took off again and circled eastward.

Henry took them to the outskirts of a small village where he proudly showed them a brightly painted horse-drawn gypsy caravan.

"This is yours for two weeks. It's stocked with food, both for you and the horse, Bradley. Treat him well. He's very docile. Patrick said you needed a remote location for a project you're working on. He did not say what. Anyway, if you follow that road over there, it will take you to Dunloe Gap, which is one of the remotest and highest points in this part of the world. When you come back in two weeks, I'll let you know what other arrangements have been made for you."

With that, he tipped his hat again and said, "Go safely, my new friends."

Dunloe Gap was indeed remote, and Mike and Katrina felt not only secure but also capable of establishing contact with the extraterrestrials. As dawn came up the following day, they sat with their hands linked on a large stone slab at the highest point of a steep outcrop. Concentrating hard, they projected their thoughts into space. After only a few minutes, the golden bird appeared very close now, and for the first time, instead of "We are coming," they heard, *We are here. Greetings!*

Greetings, they responded. *We have a message for you.*

What is your message?

We need to warn you that our countries want to take advantage of your advanced scientific knowledge so as to rule the world.

We know that, but there is more to it than that.

Mike and Katrina looked at each other, and then Mike said, *What do you know?*

We have been observing your world for a long time, since before the Incas built landing sites for us in South America. We have seen many things. Your world has always been ruled by greed, and over the centuries greed has focused on land, on slaves, on spices, on gold, on women, and more recently on religious exploitation. Today, the new greed is something else entirely.

What?

Now, it's all about oil.

A week later, Frank Mambrino received a telephone call.

"Sir," a voice said, "I have to report that all UFO sightings over the North Sea have ceased."

Chapter 22

Crowne Plaza Resort, Hilton Head, SC. January 25, 2008. 6:30 p.m.

Jack Koehner poured himself a substantial dose of bourbon and slid a large decanter down the polished rosewood conference table around which sat the usual suspects: the oil moguls. The men had all arrived the night before, spent most of the day playing golf or lazing around the beachfront pool, and were now meeting before a private dinner was served.

"Well," said Koehner, "it's been a year now since the Dems took over Congress, and look what they have achieved, or not achieved."

The others nodded, pouring themselves drinks.

"And," said one of the men, "the situation in Iraq and Afghanistan hasn't gotten any better."

"Right," said Koehner, "but what concerns me the most is the situation in Northern Nigeria, particularly for my own company, which has thirteen hundred miles of oil and gas pipeline, ninety oilfields, and over seventy flow stations. If those damn MEND rebels have their way, we could be out of business altogether."

"Remind me what the MEND thing is."

"Hah!" retorted Koehner, "The Movement for the Emancipation of the Niger Delta! And they've been trying to wreck our facilities for two years now. You may recall that in January of 2006, they overran one of our facilities in the Niger Delta and kidnapped four Western oil workers. And it's been going on ever since."

"Wasn't that almost immediately after that Oil Shockwave exercise at which a number of former top US officials agreed to play government roles in response to an imaginary energy crisis?"

"That's right. And guess what? The scenario involved civil conflict in Northern Nigeria. In retrospect, it seems as though those MEND rebels took the scenario and played it out."

"Can't the Nigerian government do anything about them?"

"Well, they try, but these rebels, Ijaw militants, scare the living daylights out of the government soldiers. They live up in hidden creeks—there are thousands of them up in the Delta—and then they come out of nowhere and attack with powerful speedboats. I tell you, I've seen photographs, and they're scary as hell! And they have said that if they're attacked, they're going to do some real damage."

"Well, if the Nigerian government can't deal with them, who can?"

"My question precisely. Here we are now with the Dems running Congress and a strong likelihood that a democrat will win the presidential elections later this year. And I can't see either of the most likely democratic candidates having the balls to deal with the Niger Delta situation. Which is why we need to get the current administration involved as soon as possible. They've shown they have the guts to deal with this kind of situation, and they need to do it before they're out of office. If you all agree, I'll get with Henry when we get back and see what can be done. Anyone disagree?" He looked round the table. "Okay then, let's have a couple more drinks and see what they have for dinner for us."

Epilogue

Bantry Bay, Ireland, April 25, 2008. 4:30 p.m.

Three months later, Mitch and Kathy Murphy, as they are now known locally, are sitting in the garden of a small cottage overlooking the Bay of Bantry, holding hands and watching the sun go down slowly over the Atlantic. It was still a little chilly, but it felt like spring was not too far away.

"You know, Mike," said Katrina, "it'll soon be a year since we heard from the golden bird, but I can't help feeling that we will soon." She patted her stomach. "And Mikhail is telling me the same thing. We can already read each other's minds."

Mike leaned across and kissed her gently. "I miss the golden bird too, but not as much as I would miss you. But you know, there must be other people on this earth who want what we want, who want peace and tranquility and love. We should perhaps try that. Perhaps we can make a difference."

"Wait a minute," said Katrina, reaching out and grasping Mike's arm. "Is that the golden bird now?"

"Yes! Yes, you're right. And it's stronger than ever."

"*Beware! Beware! Beware! Beware! Beware!*"

"There's something wrong."

"What?"

Mike looked around. "Well, not here. Everything looks normal."

"Now what are they up to?"

"Who?"

"The Russians, the Americans, the North Koreans, the Chinese. Who knows?"

"Let's go and see if there's anything on the news."

They hastened inside and turned on the television set.

The message "Breaking News! Breaking News!" crawled across the screen in large letters, and a suave-looking political commentator in an impeccable suit and tie was saying, "As the Pentagon announced yesterday, three days ago, the United States parachuted four heavily armed combat units into parts of the Niger Delta in order to round up rebels who have been attacking and attempting to destroy Western oil facilities in this densely populated but extremely poor part of Nigeria, the largest oil producer in Africa, and America's fifth largest petroleum supplier. What we are now learning though is that in response, a group of rebels have attacked a major oil terminal on the coast. For the latest on this, we now go to our senior African reporter in Port Harcourt, Samuel Omogo. Samuel."

The camera shifted to a shot of a scrawny young man standing on the deck of what looked like a fishing boat, holding a microphone in one hand and pointing with the other hand to a huge conflagration behind him.

"What you see behind me is the Bonny Island Liquid Nitrogen Gas facility, which is the main terminal on the south coast of Nigeria, about twenty miles east of the Cawthorne Channel. I am told that several boatloads of Ijaw rebels sped down the river and fired multiple rocket-propelled explosives into the facility, which immediately began to burn. I am also told by the authorities that there is no way this fire can be contained and that it may burn for days if not weeks before pipelines can be shut off. This is likely to have a major effect on world oil supplies and oil prices."

Mike and Katrina stared at the television screen.

"The golden bird was right."